THE HOWLING TERROR

AND OTHER LOVECRAFTIAN HORROR STORIES

THE HOWLING TERROR

AND OTHER LOVECRAFTIAN HORROR STORIES

TONY RICHARDS

First trade paperback edition

Editor and Publisher, Joe Morey

Interior and cover design by Cyrusfiction Productions

ISBN: 978-1-957121-18-5

Weird House Press
Central Point, OR 97502
www.weirdhousepress.com

CONTENTS

ILLUSTRATIONS

THE HOWLING TERROR

I am writing this account from within a locked, cramped, brick-lined cell – one with a heavy metal door and with iron bars at the window – inside Dartmoor Prison for the Criminally Insane. And there are two salient facts which I need to point out before I start.

Firstly, I am not deranged. And in the second place, I have never committed any crime, and most certainly not the murder of a good close friend that I have been accused and then convicted of.

And those two statements being the truth, I have no doubt you are expecting me to rail against my sorry fate, to inveigh against this miscarriage of justice and demand I be set free.

Yet I make no such complaint, for I want nothing further than to remain in this cell.

It is the only place where I feel safe.

It was in the spring of this same year when my good close friend from school days, Harold Browning, finally returned to England from a ten year sojourn in America. Like myself, he was a practitioner of the legal trade, but whereas I had happily confined myself to the lesser and more basic aspects of that profession, Browning had provided both his services and his expertise to a large firm in Chicago which specialised in the purchase of quite sizable tracts of land, those to be developed for the purposes of industry, commerce and even housing. Such business had taken him all over the United States in the decade he had been away, and when we finally were reunited – in a little restaurant off Piccadilly – he had many tales to tell of his travels across that mighty nation.

He had come back to England to take up a partnership with one of the top law firms operating out of Lincoln's Inn, and his new job was keeping him so busy that he told me we should meet again in the same restaurant, but only every once a month.

It was an occasion that I very much looked forward to. Browning, since his school years, had grown up to be a quite sophisticated and an urbane man, a practised debater and a skilful raconteur, and our meetings were filled up to the brim with lively discussion and good-natured banter. Come the later weeks of August of that year, though, he seemed by far wearier than was normally the case, his humour muted, his speech slow.

"I honestly do need a proper break from work," the man confessed to me when I enquired what was wrong.

"So take one," was my immediate response. "Spend some restful days at home."

But his head shook. He tugged at his moustache.

"Staring at my ceiling is a way of wasting time I've never found too restful. Except that, back when I was in the States, I came across a pastime that was genuinely recuperative."

And he went on to explain that, while he had been in America, he had taken up the sport of fishing for big game, travelling down to Florida or even Baja Mexico, chartering a boat and going after marlin, sailfish, kingfish, tarpon.

"None of which I think we have around our coasts," I pointed out. "But give me awhile and I'll make some enquiries. I'll do my best to find out if there is any equivalent."

One month later, after much research, I was able to tell him the following:

"We have sharks, as it turns out. Most of them are blues and not too big, but there are other species further off the shore like mako, porbeagle and long-tailed thresher, and they grow to a greatly larger size."

I watched as Browning's eyes lit up, and thus encouraged I went on.

"If we hire a boat they will supply the bait and gear we need. But we'll have to drive to Cornwall."

That being the county at the south-western extremity of these isles, a narrow triangular peninsula that juts out sharply into the Atlantic. Browning, though, had gone far greater distances in the United States and he immediately agreed.

So it was, the following Monday morning, that he turned up early at my home's front door in the brand-new car he had acquired, a livery-green Austin 12. I loaded my valise aboard and we set off.

And our progress was a pleasant and untroubled one the first few hours. The day was typical of early September, the weather mild with little in the way of cloud, the countryside around us lit up gently in the manner of a pastel painting. There was not much in the way of other traffic, and we passed without hindrance through the outlying counties, Surrey, Hampshire and then Wiltshire, till we came at last to Dorset, that marking the start of the West Country.

As we approached the next border along, the one with the county of Devon, I could see the way the ground ahead of us was beginning to flatten out, as it does the further west you go, open proof that the weather coming in from the Atlantic had been scouring at this landscape and reshaping it.

A sign told us that we were getting nearer to the pleasant village of Burlescombe. We had been driving for hours by this time, and were growing weary of the ride and becoming much in need of respite and refreshment. Only that one small factor of the scenery around us was beginning to arouse in me a small slight feeling of unease.

Directly up ahead of us, on the horizon to the far southwest, the sky had started turning a decidedly peculiar hue, a colour I had only seen before on the leguminous flesh of certain types of flower. A purple that was like a bruise, the kind of injury that might turn septic. A diseased, unwholesome colour. It was very faint at first, but grew stronger with every single mile that we progressed toward it.

Accompanying this troubling sight, a wind had started up which had its origins in exactly the same direction, pushing up toward us as we drove along the road. It gave out a moaning which I could hear very clearly, even over the harsh rattle of the Austin's engine and the rumbling of its tyres. And bits of debris – brown dried leaves and filaments of straw – were being thrown up constantly against the windshield.

"This does not look very good," I opined after awhile. "Maybe we should reconsider and turn back?"

But Browning only shook his head and favoured me with a stiff smile.

"I've seen far worse weather than this while I was over in the States. Why, I could tell you stories that would freeze your blood."

None of which he had mentioned before, and I was left to wonder what he meant. But he was concentrating on the road, and so I did not wish to trouble him.

A couple of miles past Burlescombe, we came across a roadside inn which was called the *Edward's Arms*. We drew up on the gravel forecourt, and as we stepped out the wind increased quite suddenly, tugging fiercely at our frames and almost causing us to stumble. Browning, who was physically much sturdier than me, reached out and grabbed my arm to steady me, and thusly joined we went inside.

We were welcomed by a young waitress who led us to a table, though I could not help but notice that she kept on throwing anxious glances at a westward-facing window the whole time that she performed that task. Menus were set down before us, listing the simple but substantial fare that was normally the diet in establishments like this. I ordered sausage and mash and Browning chose the steak-and-kidney pie, and two small tankards of dark porter were set down before us.

"Cheers," Browning said. And then he stared across at the same window. Debris was still being blown against it by the rushing and increasingly-fast air. "I made mention of the weather in America, now didn't I? Let me explain."

And then he leant in toward me with the furtive air of some kind of conspirator, keeping his voice very low, since there were other diners seated nearby.

"A few years ago," he told me, "I was on a fishing trip in the Florida Keys when a hurricane struck. Not that I was out there on the open water, do not get me wrong on that. There'd been quite adequate advance warning – the harbour had been battened down, the stores closed and many windows boarded up. The local people had done everything they could to prepare for the storm, except it turned out that their efforts were of very little use. By the time the wind had dropped back down, whole houses had been blown away. Large trees had been torn up by their roots, and the harbour had been devastated. One boat – a sloop about some twenty feet – was found lying atop the broken roof of the only drugstore in the town. Such is the contempt that nature demonstrates to those of us who try to stand against its wrath."

"But," he continued, "I have seen with my own eyes conditions even more extreme than that. I was once in the Midwest when a tornado struck, though thankfully the thing was several miles away. By God, Jones, you've never seen the like – a dark and hugely churning vortex rising hundreds of feet in the air, Charybdis incarnate or perhaps the Viking's Maelstrom, stepped out of the ocean onto dry firm land, there to wreak quite utter devastation. Bolts of lightning flashed about its brow and the sky above was horribly tortured. As I watched, it ploughed into a little town and tore most of the place to bits. Yet that is not the most frightening part.

"As I watched, the thing destroyed a hundred homes and then began to move away. But then – I'm serious – it stopped and turned around again. It headed back and then attacked the section of the town that it had previously left undamaged. Almost like it had a conscious will, Jones. Almost like it had a brain and eyes. Like it were a living being, sentient and with a plan."

To my mind, that sounded quite absurd and I was ready to demur when I was interrupted. Our lunch had arrived, except that the plates being set down before us were now being handled rather clumsily, some peas and gravy getting spilled, because the young waitress who was carrying them simply could not pull her gaze away from that purple-tinged westward window.

"Careful, girl!" Browning complained.

"Oh, I'm ever so sorry, sir. But I have never seen a sky like this before, or heard a wind of this strange sort."

She found a napkin and she cleared the mess away, then hurriedly retreated to the kitchens at the back. The wind outside was moaning fiercely now, and not at an even pitch but with an undulant, reverberating sound, and broken small twigs were being thrown up against the glass. And a few of the patrons round us were beginning to grow nervous at that sight. A couple of them got up from their tables and went out.

Browning managed to ignore all that, exuding an air of utter calm and tucking heartily into his meal. I saw no choice but do the same and our plates were clean in ten more minutes. We called a different waitress over and then paid the bill. But by the time that we were heading off, the grim weather had not let up.

"Are you sure this is entirely wise?" I called to Browning as we struggled back across the forecourt to our car.

"This is England, not the States!" he yelled back almost cheerfully. "We rarely get extremes of climate here! No, this is just a squall, and more than likely will have blown itself out by the time we reach the Cornwall border!"

Climbing back inside the big square Austin, rubbing some grit from my eyes, I wished that I could share his optimism, since the sky above us looked no longer like a bruise but far more like a festering wound. Browning soon had the engine turning over and we pushed onto the road again and then moved off.

We were now fully into Devon, a place famous for its wild, expansive, open moors. But openness, in weather such as this, meant far greater exposure to the wind, and it refused to stop or even slow.

Occasionally we would catch sight of a little copse of trees; they were being bent right over sidewise by the sheer force of the moving air, entire branches being stripped from them. And several cottages we passed were missing parts of their thatched roofs.

Browning shook his head again and pushed the Austin confidently on. The windscreen wipers had now been switched on, despite the fact there was no rain, because a constant stream of debris and detritus was being carried up against the glass, the entire square-sided frame of the car shuddering quite ceaselessly.

As one mile overtook the next, our progress began to slow. Even a man as positive as Browning finally had to concede to reality. The air was buffeting our vehicle so fiercely it was hard to keep it moving in a dead-straight line. Yet that was not what troubled me the worst. Off in the far distance up ahead of us, great flurries of dust and grime had been scoured from the landscape by the gale and, by some vagary of the prevailing conditions, were not dispersing but were forming into shapes that lingered for a few seconds before they broke apart again.

Some were merely abstract constructs. Others, however, took on shapes my startled mind attempted to identify. A rounded one with tendrils flowing from it seemed to me like some kind of Medusa. And one like an oval but tipped over on its side appeared to close and then re-open like some blinking eye. And what was causing apparitions such as these?

But they were merely vague precursors to the most startling vision of them all.

The ground had flattened out completely by this time and the road was running absolutely straight for uncountable miles ahead. And – way off at its distant end – a quite enormous plume of darkened dust rose high up into the air, precisely like one of those huge tornados my old friend had told me of, and then took on a form that made my entire body clench with apprehension and then dread.

I tried to tell myself at first that I was merely imagining the sight, but I could not deny the evidence of my own eyes. The truth was utterly and terribly clear. It was a vast hominid shape that I was looking at! It had two arms and two stout legs! A torso, a neck, and atop that neck a massive head, featureless but with a jagged line across its jawbone where the mouth should be!

It was only there for a few seconds, then it came apart and vanished, except perspiration was now running down my face.

"Did you see *that*?" I asked Browning.

But it was clear that he had not, since his gaze was fixed robustly on the road surface in front of us.

The wind around us picked up even greater speed, the sound of it transforming from a hollow moaning to a deep and vicious howl. The car had started being slammed around and was no longer obeying my friend's efforts at the wheel.

"Maybe I was wrong!" he finally conceded, being forced to shout simply to make himself heard. "I think we're going to have to find somewhere to sit this out!"

But we were on wholly open ground, not a place of habitation anywhere in sight. And so we were forced to press on, the sky above becoming ever darker and the tyres of the Austin losing their grip constantly.

After something around half an hour of this, however, my gaze went abruptly to the south. I tapped Browning's shoulder and I pointed. About half a mile away, a little house had come in sight, only it was set completely off the road and seemed to have no pathway leading to it. Neither I nor Browning could see any choice – we drove as close to it alongside the road as we could and then he steered the Austin off onto the moor. The car had not been built for such terrain and it bounced furiously across the turf, its chassis creaking and protesting wildly. But we finally made it to the house and parked as best we could within its lea.

It was a small square cottage that we were now looking at, built from large blocks of grey stone, with little windows that were heavily recessed and with not a thatched roof but a solid one. No lights glimmered from within and we could not detect the slightest sign of life. But curiously, the front door of the place was hanging open, banging back and forth in the wind.

We made it to that doorway only with the greatest effort, having to lean forward just to move, the air pressing up so violently against our faces we could barely draw a breath. We finally got there though, straightening up and gasping with relief. And I was ready to slam the door shut when Browning reached out and stayed my hand.

"What's this?" he asked, his lungs still wheezing heavily.

And I looked where he was pointing. Right across the outward-facing surface of the door, there were three long deep gouges in the wood.

"What could have done that?" was my old friend's next question.

I had no slightest idea and so I shook my head. All I wanted by this juncture was to find some relief from the storm, and I pushed the door firmly shut.

Which action reduced the howling of the wind but did not block it out completely. The whole house was still full of it, and there seemed to be no other slightest noise. We called out warily but we heard nothing in the way of a response. And so we went carefully in, our tread slow and gentle now, since whoever owned this cottage might still be hiding in one of its small rooms, and more than likely convinced that we were of criminal intent.

It turned out, though, that the entire place was absolutely empty, and so we felt free to inspect it at far greater leisure. Downstairs we found a living room, a parlour and a little kitchen. Up above those were a simple bathroom and two bedchambers. A wardrobe door was slightly open and a grown man's clothes were hanging in plain view, and so perhaps whoever lived here was a bachelor. When we clicked a switch a light came on, and when we ran a tap over the bathroom washbasin the water flowed, so this cottage's amenities had never been cut off.

"This whole place has the look of being suddenly abandoned," Browning mused.

"Or else the owner is still living here but he has gone elsewhere today."

"And left his front door hanging open?"

I had no reply to that. The simple truth was, puzzlement had gripped us both. Heading back down the narrow flight of stairs, we went our separate ways awhile, myself into the living room to try and find some clue to where the resident had gone and Browning into the kitchen, presumably to look for food.

But then he let out another startled cry that brought me swiftly to his side.

"Holy Lord, Jones, look at *this*!"

When we had first stumbled into this place, the door to the kitchen had been pushed right back. But now Browning had swung it away from the wall. And on the painted plaster that had been revealed there were three more massive deep gouges, exactly corresponding to the ones on the front door.

We were doubly unnerved by that strange sight, but no explanation coming to our minds we were left with little option but to put the matter onto the back-burner of our thoughts. The plain truth was that we were trapped here for a while, and we had to live with our surroundings.

There were cutlery and steel cooking utensils in the kitchen drawers, but the only type of food we found was a small pack of biscuits in an overhanging cupboard, and they turned out to be completely stale, several weeks old at the very least.

"But we've both enjoyed a hearty lunch, and the tap water will keep us going for a while if needed, which I really doubt."

We went back through into the living room and settled down.

The sky beyond the small window was now almost a purplish black, though when I checked my watch I realised that there ought to still be daylight visible. And the howling of the wind continued on unstoppably, sometimes rising to a vicious piercing shriek, other times descending to a tuneless murmuring that seemed to my ears almost like some kind of angry voice.

"Sounds almost alive, now doesn't it?" Browning remarked.

Sitting upright in his chair, he had crossed his legs and had regained his far more usual air of utter confidence and perfect calm.

"This again?" I asked, and my own manner was one of slight frustration, recalling the conversation we had had back at the *Edward's Arms*. "The wind cannot *be* alive ... that's absolute nonsense, man. Weather such as this is merely the result of changes in barometric pressure, isobars and the suchlike. It's purely science and I will hear nothing else."

"Yet there are many cultures in this world where that opinion is not shared. Where I've lived the last ten years for instance, back in the United States. All the native tribes believed that there were living beings that moved with the wind ... they even gave them names like Okaga. And that applies across the globe and even back through time as well. Susanoo to the Japanese and Rudra in India. Vayu to the Persians, Zephyrus to the Romans, then the whole way back to Ancient Mesopotamia and Pazuzu."

"You're speaking of mythology, not anything that's real."

"But can you be quite sure of that?"

I was surprised for a moment, since I had always thought my old school friend to be a man of sturdy intellect combined with common sense. But then I caught sight of the twinkle in his eye and realised he was simply ribbing me a little, so to divert my attention from the dire and luckless circumstances we were in.

It was a clever tactic, but was doomed to fail eventually. The hours ticked by, our talk dried up, and the howling of the wind just did not stop. The very walls of this place kept on shaking with the brutal impact of its force, and the rooms reverberated with that noise the way a set of small drums might. And, as proper night began to fall, the same started becoming true of the tight space within my skull. The howling penetrated into it.

It was torture that there was no escape from ... that shrieking, that raging sound, echoing directly in my head now, almost tearing at my brain and reducing my thoughts to tangled mush. I thrust my head between my knees and clamped both hands over my ears and still I could not shut it out. Perhaps my old friend, in his jesting, had been right. Perhaps this *was* a living thing, and calling to me quite implacably, a horrible vile Siren's Song that I could find no method to avoid.

Browning – who seemed to be faring better than I was – had gone into the kitchen on a hunt for tea. I was alone here in the living room, a trembling shadow of the man I was, my knees now pressed up to my chest, my hands still clamped to both sides of my skull, the lids of my eyes pressing tightly shut, then opening with a swift start.

When suddenly, at the small window of the room, there was a brilliant white flash. The wind did not abate in the slightest, but it seemed there was a new change in the weather now. I managed to get up shakily and went across to find out what was going on.

Bolts of lightning were now flaring high up against the background of the darkened sky, bringing our surroundings into sharp relief the same way that some giant flashbulbs might. And there was nothing too much to be seen, since we were trapped out on an open moor. But then a shape came into view which had not been there previously. I believed at first it was a pair of trees, although I could not understand how that could be, since there had been no trees before.

Another even brighter flash revealed the truth. This was a massive pair of legs that I was looking at, solidly rendered in deep silhouette. And above them I could now see a torso and a pair of arms, and with a head like some great boulder topping that.

It was the same shape I had seen while we had still been in the car. A hominid shape, an almost human one, just as large as mighty Polyphemus but entirely featureless and dark.

I yelled with horror when I looked upon that massive form, and then heard Browning coming through to find out what had startled me. Only before my very eyes, the creature was dissolving, coming apart the way that smoke might come apart once it had arisen from a bonfire of damp wood. The whole thing appeared to be made of dust and nothing more substantial than that, given shape abruptly by the wind and – seconds later – broken up.

Browning was at my shoulder now, but staring at an empty landscape.

"What is it that you believed you saw?"

I thought about it and could easily predict his condescending manner if I came out with the truth.

"Nothing, man. The lightning merely startled me."

He stared at me carefully a long few seconds, but then simply shook his head.

"This whole business has left us shaken up, and we are both tired as well, and even getting hungry with it. It would be better if we tried to get some sleep. I noticed two beds in the rooms upstairs."

"And if the owner of this place returns?"

"He'll sympathise with our predicament, I'm sure."

And with those last words, Browning headed up. I made no move to follow him, however, since a suspicion had arisen in my mind that numbed me to the core and froze me to the spot.

Those triple gouges across the front door that we had seen when we had arrived here. And those same three marks up on the kitchen wall.

They could only have been made by something very large. And so I did not think the owner of this house was ever coming back.

The lightning flashes slowed down and grew much further apart after another while, except the howling of the wind continued quite unstoppably. But I was managing to partially ignore it by this hour, a slew of frantic thoughts now tumbling through my mind.

Had the thing that I had seen been fashioned only out of dust? How could the moving air do that, and do it not merely one time but twice? It simply was not possible, and so what other options were there?

That this wind really was a living creature? This howling sound its feral roar? Did it think and see and hunt? And was the shape that I had seen its truly-realised physical form?

The names Browning had spoken of went spilling wildly through my head. Okaga. Vayu. Zephyrus. Did this beast answer to such or did it have a different name?

I rubbed my brow in an attempt to ease the tension there, tried to tell myself that these were quite unfounded notions I was entertaining, merely the product of stress and being trapped in this small cottage for an age. Maybe I *should* try to get some sleep? But that idea held no appeal for me.

The screeching of the wind seemed to go up another notch, the glass panes of the window rattling furiously like they were being worried by an unseen hand. My gaze swung round toward that other sound ... and then abruptly stopped.

At first I thought that utter solid dark had closed around the cottage for some reason. Then I saw the awful truth,

That enormous head was there again, directly outside the window, so vast that it blotted out every last detail of the scene beyond. And it had no features I could make out, no eyes that I could see, no ears or nose, except there was that jagged line which counted as a mouth.

No eyes, as I have said, yet nonetheless I could feel its rapt attention on me. It was studying me hungrily, and I felt very small beneath its baleful gaze.

One of its hands lifted into view, almost as long as I was high, with just three bony spindly fingers and a slightly thicker curved inverted thumb, each tipped with a dagger-length cruel talon. Those claws scraped at the window, then rapped at it and I went lurching back.

Next second, though, both terrifying shapes lifted away and they were gone.

All the air had vanished from my lungs and there were no sounds left inside my throat. My legs were nerveless and buckled beneath me and I could not help it as I collapsed to the floor. There I lay with my chest wheezing, my whole body drenched in sweat. Had that thing been real or had I lost all sense?

But that was when I heard another sound, of glass breaking coming from upstairs. And then a scream from my old friend.

I struggled to pull myself together and react to his yells of distress. My limbs were still as limp as suet, but I managed to set my palms against a wall, lever myself up and make it to the doorway. My heart was pounding at a painful rate. Was it the case my friend was gone, the great dark creature bearing him away?

The next thing that I heard, though, were extremely rapid footsteps coming down the stairs. I leaned out into the hall, only to see Browning rushing down toward me.

He had obviously been sleeping when the beast had struck. His jacket and his tie were off, his shirt partly unbuttoned at the front, and I discerned he had no shoes on and was in his stockinged feet. It also became clear that he had barely escaped with his life.

The right sleeve of his shirt was ripped to shreds, blood flowing freely from the wounds beneath, and he was clutching his arm as he ran. He was heading directly for the front door of the house and did not even seem to notice I was there until I stepped out in his way.

His face was little but a ghostly image of the visage I had known before, drained of blood and turned a ghastly white, the eyes as wide as a large pair of coins, his bluish lips pressed tight and flat, all intelligence and nerve and sheer confidence gone.

He blinked at me sharply several times.

"How can this be?" were the four short words that managed to emerge, although I scarcely even recognised his voice.

There was more crashing from the room upstairs. The man looked back the way that he had come, a ferocious shuddering gripping his whole frame.

"We must get out!" was the next thing he said.

Which proved he was no longer thinking straight. Inside this cottage with its tiny rooms, we at least had a chance of evading such a massive beast. But out there on the open moor ... ?

I tried to take a hold of him but he responded angrily, pulling himself from my grip, his face now clenched up in a snarl. He pushed past me and went to the front door, and hauled it open as I watched.

That dreadful howling was washing over me next second, in my head again and tearing at my skull like claws. The force of the wind entering the cottage hallway slammed into me savagely and almost pushed me back. All that I could do was shield my eyes and then look on through slitted lids as Browning fought his way to where his car was parked.

I could not even hear the engine starting up, so furious was the racket all around me. But its yellow headlamps sprang up into view – the Austin 12 was moving off. It went bouncing across the rugged turf even more unsteadily than it had previously done, because the wind was now attacking it head-on.

As I watched, the lurching of the vehicle got even worse, more pronounced and more extreme. It was rocking like a rowboat out in a typhoon. The tyres on its left side lifted fully off the ground, then banged back down and then the right side followed suit, precisely as though some mighty hand were shaking it.

It skittered back and forth across the dark grass of the moor, not moving in an accurate straight line for any more than a brief second. Something in me wanted to cry out, but I knew how useless that would be. I raised my other hand but that was all.

The Austin skidded round in a full circle and its headlamps briefly blinded me. And by the time that revolution stopped, it could no longer move at all. Its rear wheels had become embedded in the mud.

The wind was still deafening me. I could not even hear the protest of its engine as the Austin tried to free itself. But a double-spray of wet earth sprang up from its rear, only to be dispersed by the raging air.

The car lurched sideways once again, and it should not be able to whilst trapped that way. No, it was as though something had purposefully struck it. It started tipping over on its left-hand side, its wheels rising several whole feet off the ground. And it teetered there a couple more seconds and then went the whole way down.

There must have been a loud thump but I could not hear that either. In the impact, had my friend been hurt? My eyes strained as I fought to catch a glimpse of Browning, but the windshield was reflective and it revealed naught.

I was gripping both sides of the open doorway now, the wind ripping at my hair and clothes, the very skin of my face being distended by its fury. Was my old friend even conscious? There was no way to find out. But a moment after that, the right-hand door of the Austin came pushing up. A definite human head appeared. Its face was still very pale, but there seemed to be a smudge of some far darker substance at its brow. A pair of shoulders and then arms came into view, and Browning started easing himself out.

He never managed to do that the entire way. There was an abrupt shifting in the air above him, a sudden coalescence built out of the darkness. Then it took on solid form, the same shape that I had already witnessed twice. A vast figure more than thirty feet in height, its limbs like the spindly trunks of pine trees and its hands gangling with brutal claws.

I watched as Browning's gaze came up. I could see it as his mouth flew open in another scream.

But then, in one swift vicious action, the gigantic creature snatched at him, pulling my friend from the car and lifting him high off the ground. The beast's jagged lips came open and it made the self-same howling as the wind. It held Browning in its palm, studying him for a brief while, then turned away, the man still in its tightened grasp. It was retreating from the cottage now, its stride a lurching, loping one as though it were some vast simian ape. But then the wind began to break it up.

It dissolved in seconds and was gone without a trace.

And the same proved to be true of my old friend.

I was still standing rigid as a statue in that open doorway, the vile wind continuing to claw at my body but my mind gone to another place where it was scarcely capable of taking in what had occurred. But finally, I realised how exposed I was, how vulnerable to the same kind of attack. I think my primal instincts kicked in at that point. I went staggering backward, still facing the open door. And my gaze remained fixed on the dark space beyond it till I reached the kitchen, where I finally found the strength to swivel round.

I rummaged in the kitchen drawers until I found a butcher's knife. And with that weapon clutched in both my hands, I pressed myself into a corner, sitting sharply and then curling up into a ball, my head pressed down. And I remained that way for many hours.

"Sir?" enquired an unfamiliar voice.

I had not slept a wink all night, but neither had I moved an inch or even raised my head. But when I finally lifted it, I could see that at last clear morning had come, pale light streaming through the kitchen window. And there was no longer any howling noise. The wind itself had dropped away completely, as if it had never been.

"Sir?" enquired the voice again. "If you would care to put that knife down?"

My gaze rose towards it source. There was a uniformed constable in the kitchen doorway with another standing in the hall.

It turned out their attention had been drawn here by the overturned Austin halfway to the road. And once I had set aside the knife, they helped me carefully to my feet.

"And where has your friend gone to, sir?" the second fellow asked of me.

It proved to be the case they had already taken note that there was luggage in the car for two.

More constables were drafted in during the course of the next couple of hours. And then a detective showed up, listened to the facts on offer and then started up a search for Browning. All that I could do was stand and watch as shapes in uniform progressed across the moor. Several of them even had large dogs accompanying them.

And one such party finally came back holding the remains of Browning's shirt. It was torn not only at the sleeve by now but had three large gashes down the front and it was liberally soaked in blood. That, with the knife, was evidence enough.

They never did find my friend's body, but the prosecution had no need of it. More blood was discovered on the bed where he had slept, and there were further drops of it where he had hurried down the stairs. The smashed window gave them proof of a fierce struggle. There was no trace of red fluid on the actual knife, except the lawyers argued that I could have washed it off. Before pronouncing his sentence, the judge directed me to a psychiatrist. And so I finally wound up here.

On summer nights of pleasant clime, I sleep peacefully in my cell. Only the same cannot be said of the far colder months.

In the deep winter especially, when a harsh wind blows, moaning, sometimes howling as it passes by my window, which is very small and too high up to reach and constructed of thickened glass with solid iron bars across it. And that sound alone racks at my brain and brings back memories which torture me. But occasionally, when a storm is truly blowing, there is even worse than that.

My window abruptly becomes even darker, all light blotted out by some giant obstruction. A vast round shape, a massive head, and with a jagged line where the mouth ought to be.

Sometimes bony fingers begin tapping up against the glass. Perhaps the beast regrets the fact that it only took Browning and not me as well.

And so I have no wish to ever be let out.

THE DEATH OF VANESSA FELL

I

The heavy deep grey gloom of dusk was falling by the time my taxicab drew up outside the high brick walls surrounding the grand home of my old friend David Cossett-Byrne.

And those walls stretched for quite a way, and so I instructed the driver to continue on until we reached the massive wrought iron gates which marked the entrance to the vast estate. They were closed and had a chain around them and a padlock, but I had been here numerous times before and knew there was a smaller wooden door a few yards further on by which I might gain ingress to the property. And so I told the cab driver he should wait, then went along and checked, and it was indeed open. So I paid the fare, retrieved my valise, then completed my urgent quest on foot, twilight's murk still thickening around me.

The gravel crunched tiresomely beneath my tread as I made my way along the huge driveway that led from the public street to the porch of Chesley House. On either side of me there was a row of statues, each of them a reproduction of a classic rendering from Ancient Greece. There were some rose bushes too, though fairly naked at this time of year. The moon was already coming up, except a new one and extremely thin so it cast barely any light. My surroundings were growing ever dimmer.

And ... this was extremely odd. As well as the statues, there were tall lampposts to either side of me and they were usually lighted up just as soon as darkness started falling, but that was definitely not the case on this particular night. In addition to which, I could now see the house itself, a large and sprawling place built in the neo-Georgian style. Every time that I had visited here previously, it had been lit up as well, most of its windows gleaming warmly and a sense of homeliness and comfort radiating from the entire place. But looking at its outline now, the place was wholly dark and cold.

I felt sorely discomfited by that sight but continued on, since I had it on the very best authority that my good friend of many years had found himself in serious straits. Information of that kind had brought me here from London in a mighty rush. And so I did not let the unfamiliar darkness of my new surroundings make me falter in the slightest way; rather, I tightened my hand's grip round my valise's handle and increased my pace. And I was stepping up beneath the big rounded front portico of Chesley House within another minute.

There I stopped, going still and listening. Contingent with the lack of lighting, there was not a single sound emerging from my old dear friend's abode, and that did not match either with the circumstances I had previously known. A staff of round about a dozen tended to this place, so there were usually some general noises of activity. And David himself was a lover of the great baroque composers, so a record of some sort was almost always playing on his gramophone.

Was he even present here? And if not, where had he gone? The only solution was to yank hard on the brass bell-pull, and I did that thing several times.

The ringing faded off and was replaced with silence and a puzzled frown creased up my brow. It was usually the case that David's butler – Noakes – would answer such a summons. The man had a pronounced limp and you could hear as he approached the door, except there were no such sounds right now.

I waited for another minute, evening turning quickly into proper night around me at this time of year. And then – losing my patience and a sullen kind of fury taking hold of me – I set down my valise and began banging at the doors with both my fists.

That too got me nothing in the way of a result at first. But finally, I heard a small metallic clack.

One of the two large doors came swinging open. And, against the depthless murk contained within, I could make out the faint outline of David's face suspended in that horrid gloom, and I almost reeled back with shock.

It had been a rounded face the entire time that I had known him, but by this juncture it had shrunken inward and had become noticeably gaunt and narrow. His mouth had lost all of its shape, seemingly as pliant as the body of a jellyfish. His blond hair – usually well-groomed and immaculate – was long and loose and stood up in wild strands around his head. But the most alarming sights of all were David's eyes themselves.

They appeared huge and round and were almost glowing, standing out against the murk like a pair of pallid headlamps. Flecks of brightness seemed to almost dance in them and their colour, a deep green, had faded to a watery blandness.

And their gaze did not fasten upon me at first. It went across into the air above me, as though David might be seeing ghosts.

Finally, however, his attention settled on my face, except that there was not the slightest touch of recognition when he managed that. And we had known each other and been firm decided friends for nigh on fifteen years.

He gawped at me like he was wondering who I was, and swayed a little as though he were in a trance. But finally he blinked, then repeated that simple reflex several times, and a vague touch of sanity came back into those hollow eyes.

He tried to move his lips but could not form whole words at first. Then:

"Charles?" he murmured, just the tiniest of whispers.

"What on earth is going on?"

And on hearing that quite straightforward inquisition, his face seemed to collapse into a pasty formless mess, his eyes tightening up and leaking tears, his cheeks sucking further in, his chin and mouth both crumpling up.

"It's really you," was the next thing he mumbled. "Thank the Good Lord that you're here."

"Because?"

"I've *seen* her, Charles, and several times!"

I stepped forward very carefully and laid a hand on his shoulder.

"But who exactly is it that you've seen?"

"Her, Charles, her! In the gardens! In the woods! She's waved to me! She's smiled at me! Only from a distance, but it's definitely her! My beautiful beloved Vanessa is still here!"

And those words hit me like a solid blow, since if he was referring as he seemed to be to his fiancée Miss Vanessa Fell, then there was one slight issue with such claims.

We had both attended her funeral almost two months back.

David and myself both met each other on our very first day at Balliol College. We nodded to each other politely in the lecture hall, and when the noon break came along we bumped into each other once again whilst walking in the spacious grounds and started up a casual conversation which rapidly transmuted into something more.

Heaven only knew why we became close friends so quickly, since we were two entirely different men. He was of a medium height and fairly soft around the edges, whereas I was tall and had a sportsmanlike physique. He was an eternal optimist where my view of the world around us was a greatly sterner and a bleaker one. He was a devout High Anglican whereas my take on such matters was agnostic at the very least. He was a romantic; I was not.

Oil and water, then. Or chalk and cheese. But it is often said that opposites attract.

The truth is, though, that there were two parts of our histories where we were linked. Each of us was an only child. And – even at the age of eighteen – both sets of our parents were already gone. Mine had been taken by the Spanish Influenza when I had still been very young indeed … I had been brought up by a wealthy uncle past that point. And David's had yielded far more recently, first to cancer and then to tuberculosis. So the pair of us were cast adrift in this world and with no parental hand to chivvy us, which circumstance could be – we both agreed – a kind of freedom, but an imposition too.

Different in nature though we were, our ideas seemed to complement each other so that one of us would make the other think or one of us would make the other laugh. And we remained largely in each other's company the next three years, till finally came graduation day and we were forced to leave Oxford and go our separate paths, David back to the West Midlands to take up the running of his family's steel business and myself to a large bachelor flat in Mayfair, from the living room of which I started up a string of newsstand magazines. We stayed in constant touch, however, and we visited each other when we could.

The next decade and a half seemed to simply fly past though, both of us keeping very busy. The impending prospect of another War was doing the steel industry no slightest harm, whereas I had moved on from the weekly magazines to a full-blown and respectable new publishing house with a suite of offices in Bloomsbury.

As for our personal lives, they were just as different as our physical build or our beliefs. I had no intention of starting up a family till I reached the age of forty, which ought not mean – not in this Modern Age – that I had to live like a monk, and so I entertained young women constantly in my spacious Mayfair home. David though, romantic that he was, was constantly falling in love. He would call me on the phone or else arrive at my front door and start babbling about some gorgeous young thing that he had come across socially and had instantly fallen for. The problem was that he was far too smitten – and thusly enthusiastic – far too early on and he invariably scared the new lady in question off. (I even tried to counsel him on that whole subject, but it proved to be of no use).

But then, about six months ago, one of the Cupid's Arrows he had constantly been shooting finally managed to hit its mark. And in the May of this same year, I rode up to the Midlands to attend an engagement party thrown for David Cossett-Byrne Esquire and Miss Vanessa Fell. The wedding date was set for the middle of September; I congratulated my good friend with genuine and heartfelt vigour.

Which made the news of two months back – well -- practically unbearable to hear. Vanessa was suddenly deceased. The apparent facts of the matter were that she had gone up to a high tower protruding from her large ancestral home, at night and for no sensible reason that could be discerned ... and had somehow fallen from it to her death.

I went rushing up to the Midlands again and stayed with David – who was almost inconsolable – for the next two weeks. I stood right beside him at her funeral, and I even sat there with him in the Coroner's Court. And when I finally had no choice but come home, he was still withdrawn and very quiet for sure, but he seemed to be managing to live with his enormous loss. A mutual friend of ours from Balliol, Miss Sophie Griggs of Worcester, lived not too far from his home and I tasked her with keeping a close eye on him and informing me of his progress.

And I heard little more about the matter till the lunchtime of this very day, when Sophie called me in my Bloomsbury office.

"Charles!" Her voice was frantic on the line. "I've just come away from Chesley House! No, correction – no, I have just been ejected out of there! I was confronted by a David who was raving most bizarrely, yes! He's lost his mind, Charles, suddenly and out of nowhere! You must either do something about it or I'll have no choice except to go to the authorities!"

I did not have to think about it twice. A cab took me to my apartment, where I hurriedly packed a valise, and then there was the frantic dash to King's Cross station, where I boarded the first train to Dudley.

The day was a gloomy one, the view beyond my carriage window thoroughly familiar and uninspiring. And this train was not an express; no, it stopped at every station on the way. But an earlier passenger had left a folded copy of the *Times* on the seat opposite me when he had departed and so – rather than spend this whole journey caught up in nervous anticipation – I picked it up and did my best to read it.

Over in America, a man had been arrested in the Lindbergh baby case. Closer to home, Great Britain, Italy and France had re-affirmed their support for a free and independent Austria. And Winston Churchill MP – a politician I was starting to admire, despite the earlier mistakes in his career – had been warning Parliament yet again of the perils he believed were being posed us by Herr Hitler in Berlin. Except that I had my own problems now – what perils would I face when I was reunited with David?

At Dudley, I took another cab – black and with a running board, precisely like a London taxi but older and slightly dirtier than you would find in Mayfair – directly to Chesley House.

Surrounding me as we rode out to the edge of town were forests of high smoke-stacks belching noxious fumes. Further out toward the edge were large mountains of dug-up slag and I could make out the huge wheels at the tops of coal mines, the cables of which lowered scores of workers into their abysmal depths. I was now in the part of England commonly known as the Black Country, and called that because of its vast prevalence of dirty and befouling heavy industry. As well as the mines there were iron foundries, factories for making glass and coking plants and brickworks, each of them releasing a miasma of filth on the air that I could smell strongly even in the cab. The surfaces of every house around me had been darkened by this constant effluence, and the sidewalks all had layers of grime that were age-old and looked diseased.

This horrid and unwholesome scene gradually began to ease, however. The street that we were on grew narrower and began to wind, and we were at last out of that industrial hell into the countryside of Staffordshire. There was still the odour of pollutants for a while and traces of dark sediment on everything we passed. Finally, though, we were completely clear.

Occasionally, I could still catch a glimpse of the pit-face of some small coal mine. Otherwise, this was pure, pristine, bucolic land with open fields and cloistered little woods and dotted about with pleasant-looking farmhouses. This county was the location as well of grand residences such as David's home and the resplendent Himley Hall, where the newlywed Duke and Duchess of Kent had spent their honeymoon quite recently.

The light was already bleeding from the sky, the scene around me losing all its colour, the green of the woods turning darker than the deepest jade and the thin pale moon already up. There was, of course, no street lighting way out here.

And it was in this profound dimness that I found myself approaching my friend's house and banging on his door and then hearing his uttered claim.

"Vanessa is still here!"

Except that could not be.

II

He stared at me through the dusk, those washed-out eyes blinking several more times. And I could not help but notice that his clothing – which seemed rumpled and unkempt – was far looser on him than was usually the case, so he had obviously and recently lost quite a lot of weight.

The other thing I noticed was that there was not a single light on in the house behind him, and I had presumed there might well be a couple that could not be seen from out here on the porch.

"You don't ..." were his next words, a dull and feeble murmur from his shapeless lips. "You don't *believe* me, do you? *No one* does."

And I was frozen for a moment by a most awkward uncertainty. How should I respond to that? In all the time that I had known David, he had always been a sane and cheerful man and had managed to retain those qualities even when life's fortunes had turned partially against him. He had even seemed to be coping fairly well when I had left him on his own here a couple of weeks back. But now he appeared to have descended into fantasy ... or was it something worse than that?

I recalled our years of solid, sturdy friendship though, and knew I had no choice except to deal with this and put it right.

"Have I ever once," I asked, "called you a liar? Really, David, just calm down."

And I stepped forward, wrapping both my arms about him.

The subconscious reactions of his living frame appeared to take that as some kind of signal, because the next moment all the strength departed from his limbs, his whole body sagged formlessly and he collapsed into my grasp. I could feel him trembling uncontrollably; his face was pressed against my neck and there was – I was sure of it – the saline warmth of tears. But I ignored all that and held him for a while, then tried to help him stand up on his own two feet, a venture that was only half-successful so I had to let him prop himself against my shoulder with one hand.

"Do you believe me, then?" he asked me tremulously.

"First, I need to know what has been going on."

I left the front door open, my valise beyond it on the porch, and together we went slowly into the great depths of Chesley House. As well as being very dark, the mansion was freezing cold and had the beginnings of a musty smell, and there was not a single small noise issuing from its numerous large rooms nor the slightest hint that there was anybody else about, which puzzled me enormously.

"Where's Noakes?" I inquired. "And all the rest? They cannot all have the day off?"

But that slight attempt at a joke went right over his head, which he shook angrily.

"They tried to force a doctor on me, several times. And so I fired the whole lot of them."

Good God, so he *was* entirely alone in here? A deep apprehension started taking a firm hold of me. As I have already stated, I had been a visitor at Chesley House a good number of times, and it had always been a comfortable and an inviting place, with the staff all bustling about, delicious smells emerging from the kitchens, fireplaces lit during the cooler seasons of the year and more usually than not a melody by Vivaldi or Purcell emerging from the gramophone in David's reading room.

But now the place had the abandoned aspect of a chill and sunless mausoleum. It was practically as though the house had died and all that remained was its lifeless corpse. Blackened corridors stretched out around me. There were gaping holes that must be open doorways. When I glanced upward I could barely make the ceiling out and the oppressiveness was such as men must experience in those narrow coal mines I had passed.

In spite of the feebleness with which my old friend was progressing, I received the distinct sense that he was trying to lead me somewhere. We were heading for a broad and curving flight of stairs.

"But where are you trying to take me, David?"

"To the ballroom, Charles."

Which I knew was up on the next storey of this house.

"Yes? And why to there?"

"So that you might see her yourself. And then you'll know I'm right."

I felt my jaw drop open slightly. Was he actually seeing ghosts? Did his fiancée appear to him finely attired in a silk ball gown, and did he even dance with her, twirling her across the polished floor? Such images plagued my mind as we went up, except I held my tongue.

The moon had risen slightly further by the time that we had reached the ballroom, gleaming in extremely weakly through the huge French windows so that I could make out faint outlines but nothing more. Out beyond this empty space there was a large semi-circular terrace exposed to the open air, and David took me slowly out there, only stopping when we reached the balustrade. A wind had sprung up and was tugging at my clothes and ruffling my hair.

Sprawling out before me now were the enormous grounds of Chesley House. A huge expanse of lawn that I had walked across before, and it had taken me several minutes simply to transverse it. Then off past that, a gentle wooded slope that stretched off almost as far as the eye could see.

David had by this juncture let go of me and he was standing with both hands on the stone balustrade and leaning out, his gaze so tightly focussed it seemed utterly transfixed. And he remained that way, completely immobile, for around three minutes, during which I felt despair close over me since I felt certain that his mind was gone.

When suddenly, a spasm ran through his entire frame. His right hand came up and his index finger pointed.

"There!" he cried. "My darling Vanessa! Can you see her, Charles?"

I stared in the direction he was indicating, to the point precisely where the lawn left off and the heavy darkened cluster of the woods began. And I could not make out anything at first.

But then there was a flash of paleness in between the trees. And that flash of paleness moved.

I only ever met Vanessa Fell one time, and it was at that very same engagement party I have previously mentioned, right out here on the same lawn below me in a pleasant evening in late May. A grand marquee had been set up, a string quartet had been hired and the event was catered splendidly, the entire garden so lit up that it might almost be the middle of the day.

Two impressions struck my mind about her practically immediately.

The first was that she was as very lovely as had been described to me by David on the telephone. But the second was that her great beauty was of an extremely dark type. Standing at about the same height as her beau, she was shapely, slender, and her bearing was dignified. Except that her skin was so very pale it seemed sunlight had never touched it. And her hair, which was thick and long, was the densest shade of black, that matched by her arching eyebrows. And her eyes were practically black too, with just the faintest inner hint of purple.

She had applied no rouge but her lips were painted a bright red. The ball gown she had on was as black as her hair, with just a few tiny diamante studs across it. A symphony in monochrome then except for her mouth. But she smiled frequently, was charming and polite, and whenever she was close to David she constantly touched his arm. They had met, she told me, at a civic function held in nearby Stourbridge's town hall.

I have left out one other fact which I shall relate now. Around her neck there was the most curious necklace I have ever seen. At first glance it appeared to be gold, only it had a most peculiar sheen to it, a lustre that was peculiarly reminiscent of weak sunlight on the surface of the sea. And it was fashioned into patterns that seemed, simultaneously, fascinating and somehow repulsive ... weird designs of a marine nature, depicting scenes that never were and could not be.

"Do you like it?" she asked brightly when she noticed my attention on it. "It's been in my family for generations. I believe a great-uncle of mine found it whilst travelling the South Seas."

The crowd was mostly our own age, and mostly David's set of friends. But she moved among them confidently, chattering and even making a few jokes. And David – I could not help but notice – seemed utterly besotted with her, constantly attending to her needs and almost fawning on her like a puppy dog (but I knew his nature and expected little else, so I was not much bothered by all that).

What *did* bother me was the one guest at this party who was wholly different from the rest. Standing at the edges of this happy crowd was a far older man in a grey pinstriped suit and a stiff-collared shirt, both items of clothing cut in such unfashionable style they looked like they belonged to the Edwardian age. In spite of the jovial air around him he had a black

Homburg planted firmly on his head, with no apparent plans to take it off. Gloves of thin black leather covered up his hands. His face stayed lowered the entire time and he did not try to talk to anyone. Perhaps this was some elderly relative that Vanessa Fell had brought along out of a sense of duty or of simple kindness? I studied him for an extended moment but then looked away, since I did not want to be caught staring.

But a while later, when we sat down for the evening's meal – and to my stark surprise and shock – this dour and unappealing figure took a seat directly to the left of Miss Vanessa.

I was sat across from him, and up close he was even more unsettling. His nose was hooked. His mouth was small and grimly tight. And his skin was not just heavily lined with wrinkles, it was practically grey and it looked almost scabrous in some places.

Most confounding of all were his eyes, which bulged slightly and never seemed to blink. I could not tell what colour they were because his head was still bowed low.

Once again, Vanessa noticed my interest.

"This is Mr Innes," she told me. "He has been my family's lawyer for many years and he has always been a close and trusted friend."

Which left me with little choice but try and make some kind of gracious response. I rose slightly from my chair, reached across and offered my hand.

The fellow did not respond to that in any way, not moving and not even looking up. But as I leant in closer I believed I could detect a curious and quite repugnant odour coming off of him, a mouldering and rather fishy smell that made me wonder at his state of health, or even of the hygiene he observed.

I sat back down, my hand untouched. The uncomfortable moment passed and very soon lively chatter was in progress all around me. I joined in. After the dessert there was dancing and I even waltzed with our good friend Sophie Griggs. The evening finished up just after twelve and everyone who was not staying started going to their cars.

My last image of Vanessa Fell was of her climbing into an enormous chauffeured Bentley, with that strange odious lawyer of hers shambling along in her wake.

That moving strip of paleness ... it was only there the briefest instant before vanishing again. And that being the case, I was then struggling to understand my old friend's urgent and insistent claim. It could have been anything that we had seen – a shaft of weak moonlight being reflected off the leaves or else the silvery trunk of a larch being revealed momentarily by the action of the breeze.

But then, a few yards further along, that pale apparition showed itself again. And it seemed to be a vaguely human shape this time, but much too far away to be entirely sure. If it were such then it might quite suggestibly be clad in black, since only a pale tiny blotch that by chance might be a face and a white crest that could be shoulders were perceptible. There *might* be someone down there but I could not tell. Might this be, again, only an illusion conjured up by the wan unhelpful gleaming of the moon?

"She's *smiling* at me!" David cried.

Which was an impossibility at such a distance ... I could make out neither mouth nor eyes.

"She's *beckoning* to me again!"

I could detect no such motion and glanced over at my friend with real concern.

And when I looked back at the darkened stretch of woods, that brief pale shadow was completely gone.

Next moment I was turned around, and entirely against my will, because David had reached across and seized me very firmly by the shoulder, pulling me toward him with real force and near inhuman strength. His gaunt colourless face was gathered up into a mad, demented rictus of a smile and his eyes were glowing so fiercely an eerie heat almost seemed to issue from them and then touch against my cheeks.

"She's back, she's back, Charles! She is here! The Good Lord has returned her to me!"

I was still thinking how to reason with him, by what methods I should calm him down, when suddenly events took a violent and startling turn, since David followed up this wildest of proclamations with a lengthy, strangled choking noise. Before my very gaze, his eyeballs rolled up in his skull. A spasm ran through the entire length of his frame. His body suddenly went limp, so that he would have collapsed heavily onto the hard stone tiles had I not grabbed a hold of him.

Realising he had fallen into some manner of stupor, I lowered him gently down. His eyelids were now closed and he would not wake up. Trying to hold my desperate concern in check, I made sure he was still breathing and then tested his pulse, which was fast but which seemed to be slowing down.

He had fainted, that was all. I patted gently at his cheeks but he did not revive. So, a firm resolve taking a hold of me, I stripped my jacket off, draped it across the balustrade, then bent down and worked my arms beneath him and then picked his whole motionless body up, which proved to be an easier task than I had thought because he seemed a good deal lighter than he ought to be.

I knew where his bedchamber was and carried him there slowly, setting him down on his four-poster bed. His mouth was hanging open now, his breathing slow and fairly smooth. I wiped a trace of dribble off his chin, removed his shoes, then set off to retrieve my jacket, switching on some lights in the corridors I passed through as I went. I had been here so often I did not have to hunt too hard to find a telephone.

Dialling for the operator, I asked her to connect me with a competent physician who lived close to here. I wound up speaking with a Doctor Howard Pearce, who when he heard who his potential patient was assured me that he would arrive in no longer than twenty minutes. I warned him of the locked main gates and told him where the side door was, and then I went to gather my valise, which was still sitting on the porch.

Doctor Pearce, when he showed up, turned out to be a rather short man, bald-pated and bearded and sporting a pince-nez, but with an air of placid confidence that radiated from him like a source of energy. He wasted little time with social pleasantries, immediately asking to be shown to his prospective client.

"None of this surprises me," he told me as we headed up the stairs.

"You already know of Mr Cossett-Byrne's condition?"

"Many of the household staff who he dismissed were from the little villages round here and told their families and friends how he had been behaving. His fantasies about his lost amour have been on people's tongues for practically a week."

But when we reached the open door to David's room, the good doctor went quiet and would say no more. I stood back and watched him as he set his black bag down upon the bedside cabinet then removed his own coat – he handed it to me without a word. And with an air of utter gravity, he began to examine his new charge.

He checked David's pulse more thoroughly than I had done. He laid a palm smoothly on the somnolent figure's brow. He leant in and sniffed at David's breath, then unbuttoned David's shirt and pulled out a stethoscope from his old medical bag. He even produced a little penlight torch and carefully prised open one of my friend's eyelids – David did not even stir when he did that.

Finally, the doctor stood up straight, reached across and drew some bedsheets over the prone form of my unconscious friend. He indicated I should go outside, then followed me into the hallway, clicking off the bedroom lights and pulling the big oaken door nearly the whole way shut.

"He's not suffered a stroke or even had a fit," I was informed in a low, hushed voice. "This is surely pure nervous exhaustion we are looking at. It might be days till he wakes up. And since you are the only person here, do you think you can live with that?"

I told him that I definitely could.

"It might be the case that when he recovers from this, those demented illusions he's been having will have faded from his tortured mind. We can only hope that it will heal. Meanwhile, you have my number and should call me the first instant his condition changes in the least."

I thanked him, handed back his coat and paid his fee and then accompanied him down to the front porch.

With the door shut behind the man, I stared around at my surroundings. There was not a sound that I could hear, not even the ticking of a clock – there had been, obviously, no servants to wind them for a while. So I was virtually alone inside this massive empty house, and I had never found myself in such an eerie situation in my life.

I could hear my footsteps clacking dully as I made my way across the great expanse of parquet floors, every slightest sound I made producing an echo that was oppressive and loathsome to my ears. I knew full well where I was headed off to, though. In a small study at the back there was a cabinet where David kept a few bottles of strong liquors – being a religious man he hardly ever drank, but kept such refreshments for his visiting guests. I rummaged through and ignored the sherry and the cognac, settling instead on a fine Normandy *calvados* – apple brandy to the likes of you. I grasped the bottle by the neck and selected a crystal glass.

But when I stood up straight again, I realised I was near a leaded window overlooking the back lawn. So I stepped over and could see a portion of the trees again, though from a lower angle than before.

Nothing moved there save when the wind stirred it. Nothing could be seen except a muddled mess of gloom and shadow. There were no pale figures, no beckoning arms. Those were tricks of moonlight and confounding darkness. That was all.

I knew where the guest rooms were and yet I did not feel like sleep right now. And so I quietly went back up to David's room, pushing the door partway open so a narrow shaft of light was playing across his covered form. His mouth was hanging open slightly wider than before but that apart he had not moved. And so I pulled a chair up closer to his bed, lowered myself into it and poured myself a glass of flowing amber. This was going to be a tedious wait for sure, but I was certain, if our circumstances were reversed, that he would do no less for me.

Despite my reluctance of before, I finally fell asleep in that same chair, an empty glass on the carpet by my side. And I dreamed dreams in which the dark woods came alive and pallid eyeless dead women danced madly in between the swaying, grasping branches.

III

"Tell me what you know about the Fells?" I had once asked Sophie Griggs.

That had been back in the June of this same year, a bare few weeks after the engagement party. She was down in London for the opera, since the new sensation Mario Lanza was performing at Covent Garden.

Miss Griggs smiled at me ironically across our little table in the Tea Room of the Ritz.

"Ever since you were at college, you have always been just like a fussing mother hen when it comes to our dear mutual friend."

I did not much care for the allusion to poultry, but I was used to Sophie's biting wit and took the comment with good grace.

"He is a fine, capable man in his own way," I attempted to explain, "but not worldly like you and me. I simply like to make sure – to stretch your analogy – that there are no foxes prowling near his coop. And so ... the family Fell?"

The grin dropped from Sophie's face since she could see I was entirely serious. Her delicate eyebrows and her mouth both tightened and she leaned back in her chair and lit a cigarette.

"They've never had the best of reputations ... rather grim, if you ask me. Before industrialism came they were one of the largest farming landowners in Staffordshire, and by all accounts they did not treat their workers well. Then there was the whole seafaring side of things."

"In the West Midlands?" I blurted out, since the counties around that part of the country were entirely landlocked.

"Of *course* not, you silly ape! But the Fells were once a big extended clan and a branch of the family lived in a coastal town some way north of Liverpool. They were reputed to have travelled far and wide, to the Orient and even the Antipodes."

Which caused me to recall what Vanessa had told me when my eyes had fixed upon that curious necklace that she wore. *"It's been in my family for generations. I believe a great-uncle of mine found it whilst travelling the South Seas."*

"Again," Sophie was going on, "there was darkness in the telling of that section of the family's history. Allegations of smuggling and even piracy. Maybe David's getting married to a Pirate Queen?"

She smirked broadly at the thought of that, pecked at her cigarette and then drank some tea.

I waited for her to go on, since I was certain she had more to tell. Sophie was unwed thus far, and she hailed from a family so extremely wealthy that she genuinely was that rarest of beasts, a lady of complete and utter leisure.

Each second of the day was her own time to do with as she would, and inquisitive of nature as she was she made it her constant quest to find out everything she could about the upper echelon families around her, both in her environs and in her broader social circle, which I understood was pretty huge. She ached to find out what their backgrounds were, how it was they had become so rich, whether they comported themselves properly or not and how each member co-existed with the others. Sophie Griggs of Worcester was, in truth, a veritable living catalogue of second-hand facts, dubious half-truths and rumours and dark gossip.

"Once the heavy industry started up," she told me, picking up the thread again, "I believe the Fells delved a little into mining, and again not treating their workers too well. But their main business was – still is – the trade in currencies and also bonds. And that has made them hugely rich."

I must admit I felt a little discomfited by this news. Call me snobbish if you will, but the type of commerce Sophie was describing produced nothing and contributed to the welfare of the nation in not the tiniest discernible way. Highly lucrative it might be, but I saw it as practically a form of scavenging.

"That's all you know about them?"

"They've always kept themselves in large part to themselves. I've never heard of any Fell attending a civic gala."

Which sounded odd, suspicious too. I thought about it for a while.

"How about that awful Innes, that horrid lawyer she was dragging round with her?"

"Gruesome, wasn't he?" And Sophie actually shuddered. "I know very little on that subject, except for a story I picked up on once, and not about any lawyers either."

She took a deep draw on her cigarette, her expression becoming far more serious.

"It seems that as regards the family's seaward branch, numerous fellows of a similar type used to be seen hanging around the docks owned by the Fells from early evening until late at night. This was not recently, you understand, but not long after the Great War. Apparently their presence so disturbed the local people the police were called. The ugly men dispersed of their own will. Perhaps some of them came inland?"

"I have to say," was my next comment, "I am horribly perplexed by what I've heard. The thought of David marrying into a family with such a past ... ?"

Sophie stiffened. "Don't you know?"

She studied my face closely and could see that I did not.

"She's just like you, Charles, and like David too. She is an only child and all her kind are gone, her parents both deceased. She lives alone, although with servants, in the family estate not far from Bobbington. Fell Manor it is called, and a dismal pile from what I've heard, though I have never seen it for myself. So David isn't marrying into any clan, you see. He's simply marrying her, since there is nobody else left."

I awoke in the chair with a sudden violent jerk, then squinted fiercely. I had forgotten to shut the bedroom's curtains the previous night and bright sunshine was streaming in, the gloom and drizzle of the previous day having been swept away by the prevailing wind. This was one of those respites from the foul autumnal weather that we occasionally are treated to in England while winter is setting in.

I rubbed at my eyes and then at my poor back, which was aching quite ferociously. But then I studied my immediate surroundings.

David was in the exact same supine position I had seen him before sleep had claimed me, his head tilted the same way and his mouth even open precisely as wide. And his face looked so blanched in the pale harsh sunlight I became afraid at first that something terrible had happened. But his chest still rose and fell beneath the sheets. A very faint grunting sound came issuing from his throat. I reminded myself what the doctor had suggested and left my friend to his recuperative doze.

What I needed right now was some fresh air and to stretch my limbs. It had always been my habit, even back at college, to take a constitutional in the early morning, so to set me up for the vicissitudes of the ensuing day. And so I went downstairs and headed for the back and another French window let me out onto a broad flagstoned veranda chequered pink and grey.

The sunlight washed across me again but there was a stronger wind and little in the way of warmth. I did not let that bother me too much. Out ahead of me was the precise same vista that I had surveyed last night, the massive lawn and then the upward-sloping woods, but looking rather different in the morning's lustre.

I struck out, already knowing it was a lengthy walk, and the first thing that I noticed was the grass was looking slightly shabby. Normally it was so neatly mown that you could see the straight parallel lines that had been left by the passage of the machine, but it now was apparent that David had sacked his garden staff as well. I went past a gazebo and an arbour of rose bushes, then was on completely open ground.

And striding across that bare space, my mind turned to the facts of Miss Vanessa Fell's demise, which I had listened to carefully at the coroner's hearing. The cause of her death was quite clear, and yet the facts surrounding it were not.

There was, or so I heard, a high tower attached to her property. And she had, for some entirely unknown reason, climbed up to its summit in the middle of the night. Past that point, the Staffordshire police had investigated this matter quite thoroughly – the floor up there was dry and so she had not slipped; the walls surrounding her were not particularly low and so it seemed unlikely she had simply lost her balance. And there were no signs of any struggle.

'Suicide' was the thought on many minds (including, I have to admit, my own) although we dared not breathe a word of that to poor, beleaguered David. Only that ... why would a young woman, splendidly endowed with wealth and apparently healthy take her own life within a mere few weeks of marrying a kind man she was obviously fond of? I could think of no answer to that question. And the coroner, doubtless out of respect for my friend, finished up the proceedings by recording an open verdict.

I was almost at the trees by now. And there before me – it had been difficult to make out in the earlier darkness – was the most curious feature in this entire garden. The Cossett-Byrne's had never put it there. No, but it had been there for a good long time before men had even given themselves names.

A massive boulder, half again the height that I was and twice that in width, a dull mid-grey in colour and more pitted by the elements than any rock that I had ever seen. If you looked very closely at some portions of its surface, you could make out a few unnaturally-straight paler lines that might even be fossil bones, and so this mighty stone was vastly old.

"People have suggested that we blow it up," David told me once, "but my father liked it and refused to do that. Said it gave our family's home a strong connection to the past."

I stopped before it, brushed a palm against it, then moved on.

I had turned to the right and was moving purposefully toward the spot where David had believed he had seen his fiancée last night. The trees were being stirred up by the wind and made a solemn hissing sound as I approached. Being forced to avoid some low branches that lashed at me, I made my way along with my gaze fixed upon the bases of the foremost trunks.

There was not a single footprint, neither had any of the dead brown leaves that carpeted the forest floor been in any way disturbed. Maybe this was not precisely the right spot, so I went slowly further on then doubled back, and I could still find nothing.

I was perfectly sure that no one had been here, then. David's fantasy, as I had believed, was utterly unfounded and it had no basis. I was just about to turn away when something caught my eye.

A sudden glint amongst the sepia-tinted mulch. Something in among the brown leaves that was brighter than them although very small. I ducked under another branch and stooped right down and picked it up, holding it between my fingertips.

It was a tiny little diamante stud, exactly like the sort that had adorned Vanessa's ball gown on the night of the engagement party. And I had not once seen her venture out this far. But then – I reproached myself – I had not been watching her the entire evening.

I stepped back into the sunlight with the tiny jewel still held up and it gleamed strangely in the brightness of the day, flashing in a curious, quite repellent way that made me feel for a brief moment as though I had lost my sense of balance. But I had spent the whole night in a chair and did not trust my perceptions completely, so I popped the gem into my trouser pocket and then headed back.

Only to see, as I drew near to Chesley House again, the movement of a blond familiar head at David's bedroom window.

He was standing in his stockinged feet beside the chair I had been sleeping on, the glass I had been drinking from held aloft in one hand. And he was peering at it in a sleepy, bleary although curious way, like he was trying to fathom some great mystery contained within the empty crystal. His head came round slowly as I hurried in and a weak and slightly distressed smile flitted across his numb lips.

"You were here all night, Charles?"

His voice was faint and croaky, his throat obviously extremely dry. And his eyes still had a slightly bleached-out look, except there was more life in them then there had previously been. He was still thin; he was still pallid; he was swaying very slightly as he tried to hold himself in place. But the consuming mania of the previous evening seemed to be completely gone – he was getting slowly back to his more usual self.

"All night?" he repeated.

And I must admit I flushed a little.

"Well, a part of it. You were seriously, badly ill."

He nodded then looked down along himself, and then across at my trousers and my shirt. They were badly rumpled from a night of sleeping in them, and his own were in the same sorry condition.

"Just look at the state of us. We have turned ourselves into a pair of ragamuffins."

Despite the circumstances we were in, I smirked, and David did so too. Ever since we had first known each other we had always enjoyed sharing a good joke, even at our own expense.

"Would you like to return to your bed?" I asked.

"No," he mumbled vaguely, his gaze drifting off a moment. "No, I'm not honestly inclined to go that course."

"Then … how exactly are you feeling?"

David thought about that with his eyes half-closed.

"Hungry," was his final judgement.

So I went down to the kitchens and I made us breakfast. By the time it was ready he had showered and changed into some casual clothes, a pair of cream slacks and a tennis shirt topped by a loose fawn sweater. His movements were still tottery, his demeanour feeble, but I felt certain that he was on the mend because he went at the eggs I had poached with a genuine gusto.

We ate in silence for a while, then finally he decided to speak up.

"I remember how I acted, yet recall it only as a dream. Not real at all. Not credible, you see, and so not like a proper memory."

His gaze was still fixed on his plate, but I could feel a strong air of embarrassment arising off him.

"I never thought I was the kind of man whose sanity could fall apart so absolutely, and yet ..."

"You've been through a terrible ordeal. An awful loss."

"But did that ever once entitle me to treat others so miserably? My loyal staff? And Noakes, who's been with me for countless years?"

"Such matters can be fixed. I'm sure they'll understand."

He nodded but did not look sure. His brow still refused to come up.

"I really did believe that I was seeing her. It's quite appalling what the mind can do when placed under extremities of stress."

And he did finally move his head. He shook it, very slowly.

After we had done eating, I decided he would benefit from a dose of good fresh air. I made sure he put on a warm coat, then led him gently to the garden furniture outside on the broad veranda. We sat there talking generally for a while, supping from a pot of coffee I had brewed us, and I was glad to see the sunlight and the wind were now returning colour to his cheeks. By noon, his whole manner was almost back to normal, and he followed me quite steadily as I returned to the kitchens and watched with genuine interest while I fixed us lunch.

"I see you've become a dab hand with a frying pan."

"I enjoy it," I grinned. "I don't employ a cook."

The truth was that in the past I had impressed many a young lady with my culinary skills.

By two we were listening to a broadcast on the radio, an interview with the novelist E.M. Forster, who was trenchantly demolishing the Nazis' theories regarding racial purity.

"The man is quite right," my friend nodded.

By four o' clock we had retired to the games room and were playing the second of two frames of billiards. And David had recovered so well by that hour that he almost won.

He paused and stared at me across the baize.

"How long do you imagine that you have to stay?"

"As long as it takes, and there's no 'have to' to it."

"But to what effect?" he asked. "I'm clearly on the mend. The fantasies have vanished and I do not think it likely that I will relapse."

"I'd still prefer to be entirely sure."

"Oh nonsense, man. You have a home to go to and a whole business to run. You're making me feel guilty keeping you like this."

And so I made him promise me one thing – that he would get in touch with his old staff and re-hire Noakes and all the rest before the ending of this very day, since I did not like the idea of David spending much more time alone in this enormous house. We spent another hour in his reading room, chatting generally again while a Vivaldi concerto murmured in the background. Dusk was falling for a second time when David picked up a phone and called for a cab to take me back.

I was in the front hallway and clutching my valise when my old friend suddenly grasped my sleeve, a deeply earnest expression on his face.

"Charles, before you go, friend, would you care to pray with me?"

I was immediately concerned his mind was drifting off again, but there was none of the last evening's madness in his eyes. Awkwardly, I shook my head.

"I could do that, but it would be desperately insincere. You know my opinions on that whole subject."

That got an understanding nod from him.

"Then would you at least stand beside me as I pray?"

"I would be happy to," I told him, and then watched as he went right down on his knees in the style of the High Anglicans. His hands were clasped before his chin. His eyes were firmly closed again and there was a look of quite intense solemnity written across his taut features.

"Dear Lord who art in Heaven, watch this day over the blessed soul of my departed but still beloved Vanessa. Clutch her to your bosom, Lord, and lead her gently into the sweet gardens of the afterlife and Paradise. Keep her safe there so that I, your servant, might rejoin her one day and we shall spend Eternity in bliss together. This I pray most fervently. Amen."

He let out a slow breath and climbed back to his feet, and I could make out that his gaze was damp.

"You see," he breathed, "I acknowledge that she's gone. This entire business is now over with. And thank you so much, my dear friend, for all the good things that you've done for me."

I set down my valise and we embraced each other firmly, and then I was setting off along the drive towards that little door in the high wall, the shadows gathering closely around me.

It was almost fully dark by the time that I had reached the street. The road was empty; there was not a moving soul or even a lit window in my line of sight. But finally I heard the distinct sound of a motor and a pair of rounded headlamps drifted into view. The cab approached me and pulled up. I clambered in the back.

But I could never have once guessed at what would happen next. No, it came as that much of a shock.

It began with merely a few simple spoken words, which took me on a path into a brand-new kind of Hades. This whole tale was not yet done.

IV

The cab wheeled around and started heading back to Dudley. I could see in the rearview mirror that this driver was not the same one who had brought me here but a scrawny and rather rat-faced little man with a pronounced squint and a thick layer of stubble on his chin. He kept on glancing back at me himself, and for some reason seemed to be amused about the situation we were in.

"Stopping with is nibs, was you?" he asked after a while. "I do ear tell e's recently gun off is nut."

I felt myself stiffening at this uncalled-for, unwarranted intrusion.

"Mr Cossett-Byrne was incapacitated, yes. But he is now recovering and very well, not that it's any of your business."

And I had hoped that that reproach would shut the fellow up, but it appeared he had far more to impart.

"That fiancée uv is, that dark-haired lass. I ad er in this taxi many times."

I went even stiffer, but from puzzlement this time.

"No. That cannot be the case."

"An ow's that, matey? Does yer think that I's imagining stuff?"

In a rather chilly manner, I explained that Miss Vanessa Fell had had her own large chauffeured car.

"That big ol Bentley? Yeah, I's seed it roun these parts, an several times. But you dun take a car like that where Miss Vanessa wanted ter be taken."

What on earth was this unpleasant wastrel babbling about?

I listened uncomfortably but with nonetheless a strong sense of absorption as he described his history with Vanessa Fell. Many were the times, he claimed, that he had picked her up from her ancestral home and delivered her to Chesley House, most normally in the early afternoon. He would wait outside on the driveway for several hours, but a good while before the light was close to failing Miss Vanessa would come out again. Part of this made sense, of course. David – ever the devout Christian – would not for a moment dream of entertaining an unaccompanied and single woman, not even his own fiancée, in his home beyond the hours of darkness, he being resolved to keep back such behaviour for his wedding night.

"And where did she go after that?"

"Dannerswhyche," was the scrawny man's reply, a single word, except he spoke it with such gravity it seemed to mean something quite oppressive to him.

We were still headed for Dudley, but I asked him to pull over to the ditch.

"Dannerswhat? I've never heard of it!"

"Oh, it's an orrid little town, awthough it didn't used ter be. It ad a coalmine and a factory once, eggcept the factory closed down an the mine collapsed, burying many a poor soul alive. Beyon that, the place fell first inta disrepair an then inta disrepute. Most decent families departed, leavin behind juss the feckless an the indolent an wicked types."

"And what would a lady of the station of Miss Fell want there?"

"I's not the slightest clue, old son. I never took er right inta the place, since I'd prefer to keep the ubcaps on me cab, thank you. I'd park out on the edge an wait for er, an in a couple uv hours she would come back out, an as appy as a lark she seemed. I never knew exackly where she went or what she did."

Burdened with this brand-new and alarming information, my head was whirling furiously now. Why in all the heavens would a woman with great wealth and high social standing venture into such a place, constantly and past dusk as well? I kept on trying to think of a solution but my mind came up with nothing that made any sense at all.

An impenetrable mystery then … but was its answer one that might explain that other confounding puzzle, the circumstances of her fall from that high tower at her home? I had already come to a decision.

"Take me to this place," I said.

The driver twitched.

"It'll be a bigger fare."

So I paid him on the spot. He turned the cab around again and we were heading through the night for Dannerswyche.

Along winding and ever more tortuous country lanes we drove, up inclines and down into hollows and finally we plunged into a stretch of woodland the branches of which sprawled across the road so that even the firmament above was shuttered out.

We finally emerged onto the crest of a low hill, and stretching out before us was the town the driver had described.

The moon was up again and it was slightly fuller now, and in its pearlescent luminescence I could make out the place fairly clearly. No traffic was moving on its streets, all of which appeared to be cobblestoned. There were a few lights apparent in windows, but not nearly so many as one might have expected at this relatively early hour of the night. Some homes looked abandoned, with their rooftops sagging pendulously, and there was an unhealthy and rather mouldy lustre to the entire place, like it had been neglected for a good long while and it was slowly going soft with rot.

Over to the north there was a larger building, dead as stone, the derelict factory that had been mentioned. And slightly further out there was another of those mighty iron wheels that by its cables drew up miners from the shafts below. It was silent too, its use expired, and was even leaning slightly to the side.

We paused a short while at that vantage point, then the rat-faced man hauled on the wheel again and took me to the edge of town.

"An at's us far as I'll be goin," he announced to me. "I'll wait un hour. If yer've not come back by then, I fancy that yer never will, a fine and prosperous-lookin gent like you."

And I could see what he was driving at. In a place like this, a well-dressed man such as myself would likely stand out like the proverbial sore thumb. Except that Miss Vanessa Fell had been here many times and still come out in one whole piece. And so I steeled my nerves, got out and started walking.

There was very little in the way of street lighting. Many of the cobbles underneath my tread were broken, making progress hard. And up close, this place turned out to be a lot more dismal and decayed than it had appeared from a distance. Far more homes were empty and abandoned than I had previously thought; some of their doorways were boarded up and the glass at a good number of windows had been smashed.

Of the houses that were still occupied, filthy ragged curtains hung across the panes of grimy, lit-up glass, and from behind those dismal veils I could make out a variety of sounds. A man and a woman arguing furiously, anger raising their tones to an insane pitch. A baby wailing miserably, and ever louder since it was being ignored. And there was another deep voice raised in drunken song, each bar of the lyric laced with foul profanities.

There was a sudden bestial growling to my right. And surging out from the gloom came a large and pale triangular face, that of a truly huge bull terrier, its lips curled back with spittle flying from them and its sharp teeth bared. I froze completely still at that point, knowing that it was the best way to respond to an attack by an angry dog. Except the beast kept coming, almost reaching me before its whole thick body came to a halt with a savage thump. It was – thank heavens – fettered by a chain about its neck which allowed it to get within a yard of me but not a single inch more.

Its eyes turned almost red and it howled its frustration through the dingy air. I stepped around it and moved on.

Ahead of me now there was a crossroads to the street, and sitting on one corner of it I could see the biggest source of light so far. The long frosted-glass windows of what seemed to be a tavern – one of them was broken too, and covered up with masking tape. A dull yellow illumination was oozing from within and there were voices raised in murmurous conversation too. Closer up, the place looked just as unkempt as its neighbours, with the glass greasy and fly-speckled, the paintwork peeling from the rotten wood surrounding it. That even applied to the door.

But where else could Vanessa have gone? Carefully, I stepped inside. And the moment I was in across the threshold, every trace of conversation faltered and then halted.

Each head had turned and every beady eye was on me. I had found myself in the middle of a tableau worthy of Hogarth himself.

The whole place stank of mildew and stale beer, and the air was blue with a miasma of smoke from dark-wood pipes and little black cheroots. And it was about three-quarters filled with customers, except exclusively the male of the species.

Grouped around the bare stained wooden tables was a collection of the lowliest figures I had ever come across, very burly men for the most part, in suspenders and scuffed boots, largely wearing striped shirts with the sleeves rolled up, and the majority of them wore flat cloth caps. Tattoos could be seen on almost every stretch of exposed flesh, most chins were unshaven and the general pallor of this crew was unhealthy and often downright grimy.

But there turned out to be worse to come. Once that silent hiatus was over with, two of the ruffians nearest me started rising to their feet in a threatening manner. I drew myself up, going stiff again, but they were halted the next second by a stern exclamation from the rear of the establishment.

"That's enough a that lark, lads!"

Stood behind the long bar counter was a literal giant of a man, easily eight inches over six feet tall, with ginger whiskers and sideburns and with shoulders just as broad as any ox. Beneath his stern unflinching gaze, the fellows who had been menacing me immediately subsided.

"Any man," he announced next, "who steps in through that door is mine own guest an under my protection. That's the way it's allus been an that's the way it stays right now."

And it seemed the case that his word in this tavern was the undisputed law, since all the men around me remained in their seats as though they had been riveted to them. Their gazes, however, remained fastened on me and did not divert, and there was genuine distrust and balefulness in them.

I was not fully sure what I was even hoping to achieve, but I was in here now – I had made my move and ought to see it through. So, stiffly and uncomfortably, I went over to the bar and ordered a half pint of porter. The giant poured it silently and took my cash without a word. I turned to face the mob again, who were still watching me as intently and as cruelly as a flock of crows.

At the centre of the sprawling, poorly decorated room there was a table that was round and larger than the rest. Seated around its broad arc were five more of these ne'er-do-wells, but that still left three empty chairs. I went slowly across and pulled one out, then sat down on it with the air of a convicted man facing his judge.

Silence ensued for another while, but their attention on my face felt harsh and hot. Then the largest of them at the centre of the crew – a shapelessly fat fellow with a battered bowler hat perched upon his crown – leant forward on his thick elbows and blinked at me. One of his eyes was colourless and milky but the other was a warmthless brown.

"What's yer business ere then, mucker mine?"

I cleared my throat.

"I was simply wondering if a woman around my own age has ever been in here?"

The entire clientele of this unpleasant tavern had edged their bodies slightly forward so that they could listen to my words, and when I finished up my question, why, a stir went through the room.

And the very next moment they were all roaring with laughter, nudging each other fiercely with their elbows and slapping each other's shoulders, such was the extent of their amusement and their mirth.

"Gawd, e's lookin fer a doxie fer the night!" "Come ta the wrong place, e as!" "Muss be trooly despirate if that is what e's after!"

"Maybe I shud put on a blonde wig!" a wag at one table yelled. "Does yer fink e'll treat me nice?"

I could feel my face go almost rigid, but I remained where I was and waited for the cacophony to subside a little.

"That really is not what I meant," I tried to explain carefully. "It's a specific woman I am asking after, and I'm simply trying to find out why she might have come in here."

And I went on to describe in full detail the physical appearance of Vanessa Fell.

To my absolute astonishment, the laughter started up again, but with greater force this time. Many of the ruffians were now shaking their heads with unbridled hilarity and disbelief.

"We know er, and know er very well!" was the cry that was now going up. "It's Crazy Nessa what e's on about!"

What was even *going on* here? The whole room seemed to shrink away as though I had somehow floated from it and was now regarding it from high up in the air. They were all very *familiar* with her? She had come here *often* then? And as for that unwholesome sounding moniker ...

Crazy Nessa? Crazy how?

The fellow in the battered bowler hat was rubbing tears of laughter from his eyes. But finally, his head came up and he stared at me sarcastically.

"Want ta try yer luck as well? But she ain't bin ere fer the last couple uv months."

This was a largely isolated town and they had obviously not heard the news, except that seemed to be beside the point.

"How often did she come in here?"

"Allmuss every week," was the reply I got.

"And what exactly did she want here?"

More low chuckling started up around me and there was an ugly gleaming in the man's good eye.

"Obviously, mucker mine, she wanted what that Holy Joe she wus promised to would not give er until they wus wed."

In a place like *this*, with gutter dwellers such as *these*?

"She was seeing someone here?"

"But no, pal, she took er pick, a different one uv us each time."

My head was reeling badly by this juncture, I could feel sweat on my cheeks and I was struggling to even think of the next question I could ask,

"But ... why call her 'Crazy Nessa?'"

"Every single time, once she wus done, she'd fix er gaze on the ground below er feet, stretch er arms toward it an cry out the self-same words. 'See? You see? I worship your darkness with every fibre of my being and my mortal form!'"

"And she was last in here ... some eight weeks back?"

Which meant she had been betraying David the whole while that they had been bethrothed.

I went staggering out into the open air, my legs stumbling as though I might be drunk and my confused, tortured thoughts whirling viciously inside my skull. Almost blinded by the chaos in my head, I somehow made my way back to the edge of Dannerswyche and saw the small dark shape of the waiting taxi up ahead of me. A sudden clacking noise from back behind me on the cobbled street brought me to my senses just a touch – had some patrons from the bar followed me out? And so I made the final hundred yards considerably more briskly, jumped inside the taxicab and clicked the lock.

"Found out what yer wanted, then?"

But I could not find it in me to respond.

A group of dark shapes could now be seen moving on the same street that I had traversed and my driver noticed them too. He hurriedly kicked the ignition into life and then moved his car swiftly off, heading back the way that we had come.

"Goin ta the rail station at last, are we?" he asked as we powered through the formless blackness.

But after another while, I asked him to stop again, and he did that thing though very grudgingly.

"You say you know the way to Fell Manor? I think I'd like to take a look at it."

"At's back the other way, chum, allmus the ole way ta Bobbington, an I'm not goin there at this time uv the night – I ave a life all of me own, yer know."

"So ... how far are we from your home?"

"Bout two mile," was his puzzled answer.

I made him turn round in his seat then took my wallet from my pocket, and I made him watch while I counted out its entire contents, five large white new five-pound notes. His eyes, even the squinted one, opened as wide as saucers, so I felt sure that he had never seen a sum like that in one place in his entire life.

"If you tell me how to get there, I will drive myself."

"You ... want ta buy my cab?" he stuttered.

"Merely rent it for the night. All things being equal, you should find it come tomorrow's dawn parked either outside Chesley House or near to Dudley train station."

He snatched the banknotes from my grasp and then described the route that I should take, and my last view was his retreating back as he hurried off until the gloom swallowed him up.

The section of the lane where we had stopped was narrow and I was forced to make a five-point turn. But finally I was heading toward the home of the Fells and whatever revelations waited for me there.

V

My mind seemed clearer by the time that I was close, though dozens of questions still reverberated through my head. I drew the taxi to another halt, its engine still idling, on a steep slope just before I reached the place.

The moon was fully up by this stage and was slightly larger than the slim crescent that I had seen the other night and cast a slightly better glow. And silhouetted against that iridescent sheen was a façade so monstrously imposing that I felt a slight sense of revulsion even gazing upon it.

This was no pleasant sprawling pile like Chesley House. Its walls were high, as sheer as cliffs, and it looked so solid that it stood there like a rock, impervious to passing time. No ordinary home this but almost a castle, practically a fortress, with no battlements for sure but with the same oppressive look. Its windows were small upright rectangles, and there was not a single light on show beyond them. I had assumed the place would still be somehow occupied, by a residual staff at least, except it now seemed possible that I was wrong.

The roof was a sharply-inclined one ... and were those gargoyles at the gutters? At the left-hand side of the manor and overlooking a low group of trees of the genus salix was the same high tower I had heard of several times at the coroner's court. My gaze went to the very top of it: I imagined Vanessa standing there during the final moments of her life. Had she indeed pitched herself right off, consumed with guilt perhaps at how she had betrayed my friend? Or had plain insanity driven her off the edge? Crazy Nessa, once with us, now gone.

I pushed the cab forward to the outskirts of the place. Set around the property was another brick wall, but far higher than the one round Chesley House and with both iron spikes and great loops of barbed wire at the top. There, by rights, I ought to have been forced to abandon the cab, except that the huge gates were hanging wide.

The driveway was potholed and awash damp, despite the fact it had not rained while I had been around these parts. The gardens about me were bare save for a couple of small, stunted trees. I continued on to the forecourt and got out.

Only to see the lower windows of this place had bars on them, every single one, giving the entire house the grim look of some prison or some mental institution. That sight added to my growing sense of repulsion.

A great stout wooden board had been firmly nailed across the house's massive double doors. And above those, a crest was carved into the near-black stonework – a lion's face, but not the calm and noble type you most usually see in English heraldry; no, this one had its muzzle furrowed up, its jaws spread wide, its awful fangs on view. It seemed almost like a stern physical warning not to step inside the place, and my unease began transforming into something worse.

Nonetheless, I returned to the taxicab and rummaged in its glove compartment, finally coming up with a small flashlight. And then I hunted through the rear until a tyre iron came in view, and thusly equipped I headed up the manor's broad flight of stone steps.

It took me several minutes to work the wooden board free, but it finally came crashing down. The doors seemed loose when I pushed at them, so they were most probably not locked.

I grasped a big iron handle, turned it and then pulled.

Beyond which point I was assaulted with impressions, visual ones and audial ones too. First, the creaking of the door as it came gradually open, as if I were opening up a tomb. Then the clacking of my slow and cautious footfalls as they alighted on bare stone floors. There were no carpets and no rugs.

I wandered down the main hallway and then through room after vast and gaping room. In some, there were weapons hung up on the walls, massive swords, halberds eight feet long, shields with strange symbols emblazoned upon them and even savage implements like heavily-spiked maces. In other rooms there were the mounted heads of stags in row upon row, their antlers fracturing my flashlight's beam into a thousand shards.

The curtains at the small windows were all of the same dark red velvet, so aged they were almost black. The only furniture that I could find consisted of a couple of sofas in the Chesterfield style, low-backed and of stiff looking leather, full of metal studs, those and a huge dining table with some straight-backed very solid wooden chairs. I did not come across a single corner where the family who had lived here could relax in comfort. Everything was hard and rigid and there was not the slightest relief from that.

I finally came to a high-ceilinged chamber whose tall walls were lined with massive portraits in dull frames of tarnished ormolu. These had to be Vanessa's ancestors and they went back for several hundred years. There were Fells in opera hats and Fells in frock-coats, and there were even a couple wearing powdered wigs. And as my flashlight swept across them, my hand shook and my apprehension grew.

The menfolk all stood proudly tall but they had angry brutish faces and a vicious look. And the women were mostly painfully thin, their visages unsmiling and haughty.

Many of them had the same very dark eyes, with just a hint of purple, I had seen on the one night I had met Vanessa.

In the fractured gloom, the huge shapes of these rendered figures seemed to loom around me like some race of Titans. And I knew that they were merely oil on canvas, but I still moved on.

Only to reach a little downward flight of steps that ended at a smaller door.

Opening it, I shone the white beam of my flashlight through, played it around swiftly and then gasped with shock.

And stepping very nervously inside, I felt a sickening light-headedness sweep over me, an awful sense of nausea permeated with a quite profound feeling of loathing.

The plain fact was, I did not feel like I was in possession of my own mind any more. No, it was far more like – when I had walked in through that door – I had stepped into someone else's horrid and repugnant dream.

This was some kind of chapel I was in, windowless and lightless and with a high curving ceiling. But it was not like any place of worship I had ever previously seen.

It was a long and narrow space that I was looking at, an aisle down the middle, pews along the sides, though not too many of those since this room was reserved for the rituals of a single family. Yet when I played my beam across that austere seating, it came back reflected black. Either it was some peculiar optical illusion or they had been constructed from some very dark wood like ebony.

Fastened to the wall at the far end was a large crucifix, bare and plain and apparently constructed of the same black wood. It was inverted though, and I understood what that meant. My anxiety grew even worse, since I now knew that I was in the presence of deep evil and perversity.

Once my head had cleared a touch, I made out that there was another symbol back there too, a weird confounding spiral like a serpent eating its own tail, and I could not fathom what that signified but I felt certain it was nothing good.

Further in toward me – in between the crucifix and the dark pews – there was a large stone block that seemed to be an altar, maybe six feet long and a yard wide and rising four feet off the floor. It had been hewn out of a type of mineral I struggled to identify, pale grey in colour and yet very smooth and with a curious faint reflective sheen, as if it had recently been immersed in water, although I could clearly see that was not true. To each side of it, against the walls, were two tall cabinets, their upper shelves containing scattered books.

But it was none of these details that startled me the most.

On those same walls, starting some five feet up, vivid murals had been painted. And of such a bizarre, appalling and confounding nature that they seemed to be trying to distort my mind and warp it out of shape the moment my gaze fell on them. Scenes were being described of strange unworldly realms that never were, inhabited by beings that could never be. Subterranean caverns were filled up with snapping jaws that had no faces behind to support them. Fathomless green ocean trenches had whole cities in their depths, in which slept giant things with myriad tentacles and other kinds of limbs. There were beasts halfway in between fish and frogs, and some of those were standing upright. There were massive, shapeless and unspeakable monstrosities with savage beaks and grasping claws.

On the far wall – above the upturned crucifix – nothing but a single eye had been depicted, almost as large as the altar and set in relief so it appeared to jut toward me and regard me with real threatening menace. Its huge iris was colourless and limpid, but the sclera around it was tinged with red and the pupil was a long upended slit which seemed to follow me each time I moved.

Quaking now and sick of heart, I went along that wretched narrow aisle, only to have fresher horrors suddenly revealed to me.

The altar had dark shapeless stains upon its surface, and I had a good idea what that might be. And at each of the four corners of the block, an iron ring had been half-sunk into the stone. To fasten chains or ropes to? What had happened here?

The books on the shelves to my left side were large and looked professionally-bound, so I crossed over to them first. And when I picked up one and opened it, Latin script was revealed in my flashlight's beam. And there were names in there like Lucifurge, and Beelzebub as well and even Ba'al and Moloch, so I snapped it quickly shut.

The next couple of books were filled with symbols I had never seen before. I knew that they were neither Chinese nor Arabic, but rather bizarre geometric shapes, great strings of them that made no sense under my baffled gaze.

Another large tome caught my interest. It was bound not in leather but in some manner of reptilian hide that glowed a faintly luminous green when my flashlight struck it. It felt unnaturally cold beneath my fingers when I picked it up. And working my way through its pages, I could see that they had not been printed on but written on, in copper-plate script enlivened by curlicues.

Reading just a little of it took my mind to new dimensions of repulsion and sheer horror. There were references to the same ghastly places that had been depicted on the walls around me. There was mention of 'the Dark Ones' and 'the Great Old Ones.' Of races such as the Chthonians and of cities with impossible titles, R'lyeh being one of them.

And there were singular entities referred to as well, with names so utterly bizarre they might have arrived here from alien worlds. Cthulhu and Gol-goroth, Yog-sothoth and Garga-heth and Dagon and the Shoggoth. My hands were sweating as I set that volume down.

The books on the case to my right were slimmer and had thinner covers lined with fabric; they looked in fact like diaries, which is what they proved to be. I selected one of the oldest looking ones and scanned its entries carefully.

By some of the dates at the top, this was from the middle of the previous century, from the early years of the Victorian Age. And the jagged handwriting was bold and impressed firmly on the paper, and so I supposed it had been Vanessa's grandfather who had been setting down his history here.

At first all I could find in these reports was utter nonsense. Phrases that made no real sense like: *If they keep digging deeper with these mines, then they shall come across some denizens they never looked for nor yet dreamed.* That or: *They make the air dark with their smoke, and if they keep on doing that Eternal Night shall fall upon us.*

Which remarks led me to suppose that her grandfather had been a quite fanciful fellow, filled with superstition to the brim and badly unsettled by the sudden uprush of industrialism round him. Had he yearned for more bucolic days? But then a later entry cut that supposition short.

I understood this was nothing but a business meeting, but the arrogance and impudence of the man so enraged me that – before we were even done – I took hold of a nearby bottle and smashed it against the desk and attacked his face with the jagged remains.

My God, what was this? But I forced myself to read on.

He complained to the constabulary, of course. But I put Mr Innes on the case, and using that persuasive manner and the powerful contacts he has he suppressed the matter and we heard little more of it.

Mr Innes ... the same gruesome lawyer I had met at the engagement party? But that could not be, so perhaps his was a long-standing family firm and the man being mentioned was an older relative. I flipped along several pages.

He thought that he had bested me and cheated me out of a lucrative deal. But I knew that he habitually worked late, and so I waited in the darkness outside of his offices till all his staff had retired to their homes, then I crept in and attacked him with a cudgel. He wound up lying on the floor, unconscious and with gore flowing from his brow and my original plan had been to leave matters at that. But the sight of his prone and helpless form so tempted and allured me that I took a folding knife from my pocket and stooping down I put it to his throat and swiftly

I started violently back at that point. This was the diary of a maniac that I was reading. And it turned out that once he had done the murderous deed, he had acquired a quite insatiable taste for many times repeating it.

Walking across the wild heath, I came across a nicely-dressed young couple who did naught but smile and nod politely, wish me a good evening then move on. But the moment that their backs were turned to me, I pulled out the dagger I had hidden 'neath my coat.

And later:

"Durst you contradict me?" I cried. We were alone in the alley. When he tried to walk away, I realised I had no edged weapon with me, but I pulled my belt from around my waist and used that to

Finally, toward the end and most shocking of all:

I finally grew quite abysmally weary of the constant braying of my feeble wife. And so I waited until she took a bath, and stealing up behind her I put both hands firmly on her shoulders and I

Trembling so badly I could scarcely hold the thing, I set the wretched journal to one side.

So Vanessa's grandpapa had been a psychopath. But it was generally accepted in this modern day and age that sickness of the mind was an individual thing and not passed on by birth. So what of the man's descendants?

The next diary was newer and had a name written inside the cover, Victor Gerard Fell. And the dates were mostly from the Edwardian Age, so this must be Vanessa's father.

He had performed acts of violence too, but there was something else and even more obscene. It had been his pleasure – he recorded this in a luxuriant gloating tone – to tempt young attractive although low-bred women from the villages hereabout into this house with the promise of domestic work. But once they were inside here, he would bring them to this chapel and then forcibly chain them to that altar, after which he would subject them to a series of quite vile and profane acts worthy of the deranged Marquis de Sade. Reading about this, bile gripped my stomach and my throat.

All my modern theories had been cast aside by this juncture. I had never once believed evil could be inherited, and yet here was the proof. Was it the way they had been brought up, or was it ingrained deeply in their genes?

The next journal belonged to Victor's wife. She had not joined in with his filthy deeds. No, she had simply sat right here and watched. Enjoyed. But surely she was not of the same debauched bloodline? I flicked back through until I found a record of their wedding day and discovered the truth … Victor Fell had married his own cousin.

What purpose did these journals have, though? I struggled to understand it, finally arriving at a dawning truth. And that truth had its basis in those words Vanessa had cried out, as repeated to me in that horrid inn at Dannerswyche.

"See? You see? I worship your darkness with every fibre of my being and my mortal form!"

And so were these appalling deeds I had been reading of a ghastly form of worship, each act of violence and obscenity an homage and obeisance to the Dark Ones in those other books? Did bloody murder please them? Did the helpless screams of abused women make their ancient lips curve upward in a smile? If that was the case, then setting down in script each loathsome detail had to be a ritual in its own right.

The last journal was slim and newer than the rest, and had a pale lilac cover, and I reached for it with a shivering hand.

VI

I love the Old Ones with a passion so profound that I could never feel such love for anybody else.

This had been written in a delicate and girlish hand, and it was dated more than twenty years ago.

Their wisdom is so deep. Their power is so vast. How could I feel any adoration for an ordinary mortal man while I feel Their Presence near me?

And a couple of years later on:

By means of certain drugs and potions I have caught glimpses into Their World, and it is beautiful beyond belief, ancient and yet uncorrupted by time's passing, immune to the entropy that grips the normal world, a place of subterranean caves and plumb-less oceanic chasms that are filled not with the sun's light but a glorious eerie brightness of their own. How dull and ugly is the world of men when compared with such Eternal Majesty.

And it went on like this for page after demented page, the author singing praises to these dark lords and their realm whilst at the same time bemoaning her sad fate at being trapped in this far more mundane world amongst the common, boring human race. I went through these ramblings ever quicker till an entry from a year back caught my eye.

I have decided to depart this place and join Them in Their Everlasting High Grandiloquence. By this time I have learned how to freely and openly communicate with Them, and so I have begun a Respectful Series of Negotiations. It will take a while, since They are always slow in Their Solemn Deliberations, but Mr Innes – with his intricate experience and expertise in such matters – shall assist me in this task.

And later:

I cannot go there in this mortal frame. No, I must pass through Death's chill Door. But once on the Other Side, I do not wish for Them to view me as a sort of servant or a slave. No, I would be almost the equal of Them, sitting on a throne of black obsidian beside Their Glorious Forms.

Later still than that, my hands flicking furiously through the scribbled leaves?

They have agreed, but have demanded a great price from me. There must be a Sacrificial Lamb.

And back in the April of this very year?

I have found him! Firstly, a devout and pious man! But more than that, a paragon of decency who is absorbed with me and treats me like I were a queen! This gullible fool, this David

Which was where my reading of Vanessa's diary stopped, because the moment that my startled gaze descended on that written name I was running for the flight of stairs, the front door of the mansion and the taxicab.

Back down on the lanes again and back once more amongst the woods, I lost sight almost wholly of the crescent moon, catching only brief selenic glimpses of it. I was plunged into an utter blackness then, only my weak headlamps guiding me, the partial-blindness that I was subjected to increasing my frantic dread to ever greater heights.

Sudden hairpin bends rushed up at me – I almost missed them several times and came close to taking the whole taxi off the road. A lane would rise but then dip alarmingly and the chassis would swing under me, wildly creaking so I almost lost control. But none of this served to slow me down. So desperate was I to get to my old friend I kept my foot down firmly on the pedals and I cranked the gearshift like a lunatic. Had there been any walkers on the lanes that night, I surely might have failed to see them and then mowed them down.

I finally arrived at a series of low hills I did not even recognise. This entire district was new to me, since I had only ever been to David's house. And so I finally drew to a halt at the top of a rise, my head going around frantically and my eyes almost starting from their sockets. Not only did

I have no idea where I had wound up, I was not even sure I had been travelling in the right direction!

My fraught gaze hunted urgently for a landmark I might recognise, except nothing of that sort came in view. I could make out not the edge of any village nor so much as a single lonely house – not one speck of yellow light broke up the gloom.

Which made what happened next even more perplexing from my point of view.

Over to my left, to the west I presumed from the position of fair Luna, a different and very strange glow suddenly appeared, though very low and weak at first against the dark horizon. It had no colour I had ever seen before, a weird and sickening melange of sea-like green and diseased-looking blue. What was causing it I could not tell, but as I watched it spread out slightly wider, grew up taller and became considerably more intense, its ghastly phosphorescence smearing the low clouds that had gathered in the last couple of hours and were looming overhead. I was frozen with shock a moment. Then I wrenched on the taxi's steering wheel again and turned the cab in that direction.

And before much longer I was on a better, straighter road, one that I felt sure I was familiar with. The walls of David's home were now resolving into view ahead, and the glow was emerging from behind them, so I worked the throttle furiously.

When I finally braked, the cab came skidding off the asphalt onto the grass verge and almost hit the brickwork. But I paid that not the slightest mind, throwing myself out and running for the side door.

Once through it, I was confronted by a sight that brought me to an appalled halt. The whole of Chesley House was now in silhouette, backlit by that horrible cyanic radiance, which was emanating from the gardens at the rear.

It was so strong it made my eyeballs sting and seemed to carry a strange chill with it that worked its way into my limbs. Something in me wanted to go still, but I reminded myself of the genuine peril my old friend was in and pushed myself on once more.

Inside the main hallway, I made for the curving flight of stairs, taking them three at a time in my efforts to reach the ballroom. I rushed out onto the open terrace there, leaning across the low balustrade.

The source of the foul, bilious glow was now apparent. That huge ancient boulder by the trees that I had commented upon before? It had by now split fully open vertically along its front, releasing that awful brightness.

Staring directly into it a moment, I felt almost hypnotised. Shapes seemed to be on the move in the far depths of that weird incandescence, ones my brain could not decipher and which fluctuated constantly. Was that some kind of pliant limb that I was looking at? Was that some manner of distorted mouth? Were those enormous eyes now staring back at me? And if they were, their gaze was ageless, utterly profound.

But I broke myself out of that trance and then looked down upon the lawn. Two figures were apparent on it, both distant and seeming small, except I recognised them both. One was David, dressed the same way he had been when I had left, but with his back to me and moving off.

The other was Vanessa Fell.

She was standing right before the opening in the boulder, a broad smile etched across her pale discoloured face, her right arm lifted, reaching out, and the fingers of her right hand beckoning.

It was horrible to see the dead come back to life, yet there was an even greater horror. She was done up in a wedding dress, all flowing white lace with a long train.

David, I could see, was walking toward her with the compliant stiffness of a man who had somehow been turned into a mannequin.

I yelled his name as loudly as I could, but his head did not turn and he did not even seem to hear me. And when I tried again I was met with the same lack of effect. So I went hurtling down those stairs, throwing myself toward the doorways at the back.

By the time that I was out into the gardens, David had reached his dead love. He was stretching his own arm toward her, and her lifted hand came down and closed around his palm.

And then she turned her back on me as well and joined together in that way they moved toward the blue-green light.

I was running faster than I ever had in my whole life, the muscles in my thighs burning, my breath heated and heavy in my throat, my footfalls almost merging as I sped across that great broad lawn. David and Vanessa were both past the opening by this juncture, their outlines fractured and diminished by the glow, flickering like two dark candle flames. I called again, but uselessly. They were getting fainter, and the split in the huge boulder was beginning to close.

And had done so fully by the time I hit its surface. The glow had winked completely out and darkness was around me once again.

I scrabbled furiously at the rock, trying to find a way through. And I kept on doing that until the facts of the matter eased their way into my fuddled brain. By some alien and unholy sorcery, this boulder had become a doorway for a while, but then had returned to its more natural state. There was *no longer* any opening, since this was just a massive lump of stone again.

Exhausted and bereft, I let my whole body go slack against it, pressing a damp cheek to its pitted coolness. And at first I could hear no noises other than the wheezing of my lungs.

But finally I heard another sound, this one coming from beyond the boulder.

It was a human voice. David's voice, and screaming. First in utter terror, then in ghastly agony as he was sacrificed not swiftly but at leisure and at length.

Several times – between those strident and tormented wails – I heard him babble out her name. "Vanessa, please?" "Vanessa, *no*!"

And so I had no slightest doubt who his grim executioner might be.

I have returned to Mayfair by this stage, but I am no longer the man I was. I cannot sleep or eat or think clearly. The merest movement of the tiniest shadow makes me jump and my mind almost fractures. When night falls I sit down on the floor and curl up in a trembling ball and remain that way for hours.

It is I who am now haunted by Vanessa Fell!

THE DARKNESS IN THE HARBOUR

I

I yearn to leave this humid, crowded, seething island and yet I cannot. And that is a fact which tortures me, since almost every time I shut my eyelids – whilst awake at least – images spring up before me of the place where I originated from, the rolling green hills and the open fields of calm and temperate England, the charming little town in Surrey where I once used to abide and the laughing smiling faces of my friends and family.

It has been many years since I have looked on any of those pleasant things. But am I locked up in a prison here? Do iron bars confine me? No, to all outward appearances I would seem to be a wholly free and unencumbered man, no wardens standing over me, no manacles about my wrists. And yet there is another truth beyond those facts which can be studied openly, a different type of gaol that exists, but only in the captive's mind.

For every time that my eyes fall shut not in waking but in sleep, visions appear that make me shriek and flail wildly and madly howl until my nearest neighbours hammer at my door to make me stop.

Yes, it is utter terror that imprisons me in this strange place … a deep, abiding and immovable dread that I might once again come face-to-face with That Which Lies Beneath.

The year was 1923, a full half decade past the end of the Great War, which conflict I had very much participated in. I was returning from a lengthy visit to some old friends in Australia, and since that sojourn had depleted my reserve of funds I had been left with little option but to settle for the cheapest form of passage back, that being as the sole passenger on a tramp steamer called the *Saigon Breeze*.

It was promising to be a long and weary voyage, since the steamer's route was not direct. It had to first go to the Philippines, there to unload a big shipment of coal, and then on to Taiwan to pick up some new goods (at least these stops gave me the opportunity to briefly explore the cities of Manila and Taipei).

Finally, however, those transactions were complete and we were fully on our way, though many more weeks on the open oceans yawned before us. We would need to re-cross the South China Sea, go past British Malaya via the Malacca Strait, skirt Ceylon and then attain the Gulf of Aden, thence to reach the Suez Canal, the blue Mediterranean and so to home.

I was fully prepared for this long impasse though, since of the two trunks I had had carried aboard, one of them was a quarter full of books. I had always been a devout and prolific reader, although not one single word that I had ever perused was of the made-up or imaginary sort. Not for me the familial sagas of Charles Dickens, the futuristic outpourings of H.G. Wells or the arcane musings of dire Edgar Allan Poe. No, I preferred my pages to be full of facts and on a wide variety of subjects. Science, yes, and natural history and even astronomy, but mostly human history, geography and foreign culture, so that I was familiar with the pasts of other places, with their beliefs and their customs, and even with brief snatches of their languages.

It was past mid-afternoon when I began to notice there was something wrong. We had only left Taipei this morning and our passage so far had been very much the same as it had proved to be the past couple of weeks, the South China Sea fairly calm, the *Saigon Breeze* chugging along not exactly swiftly but yet evenly.

When suddenly the engine faltered, then began to stutter. Ensconced in my cabin, I looked up sharply from the book I had been browsing through.

Shortly afterwards I could hear voices raised in both alarm and anger in the depths of the old ship, and I presumed that these were crewmen shouting in the engine room. Not long after that I felt the steamer veer around and – going to my porthole – I could see that we were changing course, the white foam of our wake and the grey smoke from the ship's one stack forming a pair of lengthy arcs behind us.

Ought I go down and enquire what was wrong? But the *Saigon Breeze* had nothing but the scantiest of crews, and if there might be some kind of emergency then I supposed their hands were full and they would not enjoy my interference. Captain Rodrigo – the master of this ship – had proved himself so far to be a straightforward and honest man, and I felt sure that he would keep me abreast of our situation as soon as the time was right. Except I could not find the will in me to return to my book, and I remained at that porthole for what seemed like hours.

The stuttering from the engine room grew worse and worse and the ship's progress became ever slower. But finally, the outline of a high-peaked island rose up into sight.

There was the sharp rap of knuckles at my door and I went hurrying across to open it. And – precisely as I had expected – Captain Rodrigo was standing there, his face thoughtfully lowered and his white cap in his hands.

His name implied that he was Spanish or else Portuguese, but there was much about his features that spoke of an Oriental flavour to his blood. A half-breed then, and being that way, many of my countrymen would have distrusted him immediately or even instantly despised him. But – as I have already stated – I had found him from the start to be an un-capricious and a decent man, and one whose word I was prepared to take.

"We've run across a problem, Mr Howard," were his first words to me.

And when I indicated with a nod that I was already cognisant of that, the man went on.

"The *Saigon Breeze*, she is a good old lass, but very heavily with the emphasis on 'old.' And she has not seen much repair these past few years.

And now, I'm much afraid, the steam boiler that powers her is close to coming apart violently."

"Can it not be patched up?" I asked.

But the captain shook his head.

"I cannot risk the lives of my crew, some of whom have families back home, not to mention your good self. No, sir, we have no choice to put in and replace the thing, which task shall take several days."

"But put in where? I need to know."

"Hong Kong, sir. And not even the best part of that island realm."

At which he apologised again, and then excused himself and went quickly away, leaving me with little else to do but return to my window and my gloomy thoughts.

My head was clouded with dismay. For how long would we be becalmed in this place? I had already read much about the island of Hong Kong, and I believed it to be in greater part a dismal setting, filled with shanty towns and slums, with dreadful poverty and rampant crime, not least from those pigtailed gangs which went by the name of Triads.

But I finally decided I should look on this delay from a Stoic, philosophical perspective. I had already known my journey would be long. And that being the case, what real difference did a few more extra days make? Surely I could find out various types of ways to keep myself diverted here?

Except I did not realize at the time that some diversions which a man can take can lead him ever downward into mayhem and then madness.

That Which Lies Beneath was yet to come.

II

The forward momentum of the *Saigon Breeze* gradually dropped away till it was barely limping across the low waves. And so it was that evening was already falling by the time we made it to the coast, the dusky hues of twilight veiling everything I looked upon.

We had drawn up to a rickety old quay, so badly neglected that it looked as if a sudden breeze might cause it to collapse. Set back from this structure there were double-storeyed shanties of the same dark-coloured wood and equally unsteady in construction, a whole great row of them along the waterfront so that the town beyond could not be seen. Moored around us there were wooden Chinese boats called 'junks' in a variety of sizes, but none of them looked seaworthy and so I could not help but wonder what their purpose was. Could this be a 'marine graveyard' of some kind?

Our gangplank was set down gently. And less than a minute later I could see the captain stepping off, accompanied by his first mate and his bo'sun -- the three of them went heading away through a small gap between the shanties, presumably in search of those engineers who could effect the necessary repairs. Some five minutes after that, the remainder of the crew appeared, sturdy ruffians for the most part who were laughing and chortling as they sauntered off, doubtlessly planning to find an establishment where they could drink (or else satisfy some different, baser appetites).

I was alone now on the old tramp steamer and the scene around me was completely dark, not a light showing anywhere I looked. I had not left my cabin all this time.

Wearily, I threw myself out full-length on my bed. The ship rocked gently underneath me and a curious foul smell had started assailing my senses, part stagnant sea water but also something rather worse than that. What curious turn of fate had brought me to this place? My mind cast back.

During the Great War, I had been a captain with the King's Royal Regiment. And I had found myself – in that position – seconded to the offices of High Command and tasked as a liaison with our ANZAC allies in our quest against the Ottomans and Hun. I had performed that duty for well over a year before being moved on to the front, and in the course of it I had made several very good Australian friends. And finally, after long years of waiting, I had kept my promise and had gone to visit them. They had welcomed me just like a long-lost brother and had hosted me as though I were some visiting prince. It had been the most enjoyable and thoroughly memorable of trips ... and so for it to finish up like this?

There was a sudden hollow thud as something bumped against the *Saigon Breeze's* hull. I could not tell what it might be, except the sound was soft and flaccid rather than a sharp hard bang. With my eyes wide open, I waited for the sound to come again, but it did not.

Maybe I should try to get some sleep? Except my mind refused to turn in that direction and before much longer my stomach, which was empty, started to complain. I lay still for as long as I was able, but finally I could take no more.

Adjusting my clothes, I headed for the galley, which I had always been allowed free access to. Hunting through its cupboards, though, I could find nothing that appealed to my tastes at this late hour. And that was the point at which I began growing angry with myself.

'Days,' the good captain had told me. We were going to be here in Hong Kong for considerably more than a few hours. And did I plan to spend the whole entirety of that wait holed up on this rusting ship and largely confined to my cabin? Rodrigo and his henchmen had strode out, and so had the others in the crew. And I might be only one man on my own, but there were ways to remedy that.

Returning swiftly to my cabin, I pulled on a short dark overcoat and then withdrew two objects from out of my luggage. The first was my service revolver, which I checked was fully loaded and then tucked into my belt. The second was a walking cane, made of solid ebony and with a good heavy brass pommel at the top.

And thusly prepared, I went ashore.

The moon had started lifting by the time that I was standing on the quay, a gibbous moon that cast plenty of light, although some strands of fog were drifting in from off the sea. But a stench had risen up around me too, the same one I had detected in my cabin but far stronger in the open air. I knew we had to be in Victoria Harbour, but I also knew the words 'Hong Kong' were Cantonese for 'fragrant harbour.' And what a horrid irony that was proving to be!

Because the waters down below my feet were of such an oily nature they reflected the moonlight as a sickly, shifting, indistinct miasma and were full of chunks and fragments of debris. They were polluted to the very hilt and let off vapours as if from a dung heap.

And when I pulled my gaze away and looked toward the shore, a sense of genuine astonishment overtook me. This was no longer the evening's gloom but fully into night and yet, in the long row of shanties facing me, not one single light had managed to appear. Studying them carefully, I came to the only conclusion that was even possible ... that these small humble dwellings were utterly deserted and had been so for a good long while. A few of the doors were leaning off their hinges in fact, and every single small rectangular window gaped out at me like a staring vacant eye. Yet I knew for a certainty that Hong Kong was a very crowded place, its people making homes for themselves anywhere they could. So why were all these shanties lying vacant? How on earth did *that* make any sense?

That was when I realised I was not quite as alone as I had first believed. I saw a subtle movement in the corner of my eye and, turning swiftly, caught the briefest glimpse of a small narrow head in a conical straw hat as it poked for a moment up above the bow of one of the adjacent junks. It vanished again as rapidly as it had shown itself and it did not reappear, but memories from my years of reading all came flooding back.

What I had caught a very brief impression of was a man or woman of the Hakka people, they being a tribe among the general Chinese who were remarkably old-fashioned in their manner, extremely traditional in their way of dress, and hugely superstitious too and thusly very shy of strangers. They were notoriously poor as well, and so they lived aboard these rotting aged hulks because the sole alternative was to subsist in the gutter. They lived here, in other words, since they could not afford to leave.

Casting my gaze about, I could see that there were chinks of weak light shining through the gaps in the decaying hulls of some of the other junks around me. So the shanties might well be deserted, but these Oriental ships were not.

Then – nearby me, from the *Saigon Breeze* – there came another underwater thump of the same kind I had earlier heard. But it was much louder than the first report, making the whole ship resound, and the old steamer rocked at its moorings as if something heavy had impacted it. What *that* might be I could not tell, but the abrupt disturbance alarmed me, making me aware I was exposed out here, and so I turned away and then moved quickly on.

A short and very dirty alley in between some of the shanties led me to an open street, and the sight of it astonished me anew since it was instantly apparent there were huge numbers of people living here. Behind me at the waterfront? Sheer silence and largely utter emptiness. And yet ahead of me to either side there were hundreds of lit windows, several storeys high and all apparently the openings to very small apartments which were packed together as tightly as eggs might be inside a crate.

Faint noises drifted to me from behind some of the little panes, babies crying and children bickering and adults calling to each other. I even thought I could make out a Chinese melody emanating from some gramophone. Due to the height of these new buildings round me, far less moonlight reached down here. There was, however, the occasional working streetlamp and the windows themselves cast some additional illumination. At street level there were little storefronts, each and every one of those shuttered and then padlocked for the night (which reminded me again of the reputed high crime levels in this place and I gripped my cane far more tightly). But further down the street, some quarter of a mile away, I could see a lit glass storefront underneath a big unfolded awning. An establishment that was still open at this hour might well turn out to be a place to eat and so I headed off in that direction, although with my anxious gaze probing the shadows round me swiftly and expectantly.

But as I progressed, my mood began to turn from nervousness and apprehension to practically a sense of shame. This place was a colony of ours, a part of the British Empire. And I had, and from a very early age, been brought up to believe that institution would bring civilised and modern values to each last corner of the world it ruled. Yet we had managed to do nothing to improve this place – there were flaking paint and rusted metal everywhere you looked, mildew in the halls of the apartment blocks, heaps of rubbish piled in the abutting alleys, rats darting everywhere and sewage flowing freely by the kerbs. So much for modern values, *pah*! We had done nothing but exploit this island and its poor inhabitants!

I finally reached my destination and, peering through the smeared and steamed-up glass, I could indeed discern it was a small café. A tiny silver bell rang overhead when I pushed open the door and stepped inside.

The place looked to be nine-tenths full, mostly with young Chinese fellows, dressed in pyjamas that were light grey or ecru. They looked to me to be a sorry bunch, thin and gaunt, their complexions sallow and their every movement hurried and furtive. They were seated on the floor, upon square cushions around tables that were no more than nine inches off the ground. And they were working hurriedly with chopsticks at the bowls of victuals clasped in their pale, narrow hands.

But the moment I walked in, they stopped. Every single face swung round toward me, every single dark eye widening for a second.

Time hung frozen for a single moment. Then, as one, the diners looked away from me again, returning their attention to their bowls of nourishment, although they did this with their heads tucked down even lower than before. It was as if they were all trying to pretend I was not there.

Two gazes remained on me, however. Down at the far end of the narrow room – beside where the kitchen ought to be – a man and woman, both of middle-age, were stood upright and staring at me fixedly, a look of genuine concern and even fear tightening their narrow faces. The man had on a well-stained apron and the woman had a notepad clasped between her fingers, so they were obviously the owners of this place. Perhaps it was the case that they had never had a European step in here before, and might it be they were afraid I was some taxman or some government inspector?

There was one free table to my left. So – to allay their fears – I sat down at it, going cross-legged like the customers around me and taking great care to ensure that my revolver was not showing.

The husband and wife, which was what they had to be, conversed in low whispers for almost a minute, with a lot of brisk head-shaking going on. Then finally, the woman drew in a slow breath and moved toward my table, taking very tiny steps, her eyes still unhappy in her pallid face.

When she stopped in front of me – and I could see that she was shaking very slightly – it dawned on me that I had not the faintest idea what kind of food to ask for or else how. But the young men dining to the right of me were working at small bowls filled up with noodles that were immersed in some sort of beige broth. So I pointed to those, then nodded heavily.

The woman uttered just a single word in Cantonese and then retreated to the back again. Her husband disappeared through a small door and less than a minute later a fresh bowl was being brought to me. Fortunately, this being a Crown Colony, the English coins in my back pocket were sufficient payment of the tariff for this food. The wife, in fact, looked very slightly pleased and I had the impression I had paid too much. But then she turned quite rapidly away from me.

The fact was I *had* pleased her, though. So I had the advantage now, and making hasty use of it I came out with one of the extremely few words in her language that I knew.

"M'goi?"

It meant 'please?'

The wife stopped rigidly, pausing as though to rebuild her courage, and then gradually turned to face me.

She was waiting tremulously for my next request. What precisely might I want? But that was when I recognised the awkward fact that I had no way in the slightest of communicating with her sensibly, not by verbal means at least. And so – and I had done this several times already at the *Saigon Breeze's* earlier stops – I let my arms and fingers do most of the talking.

I started pointing, one after another, to the diners seated round me.

"People," I was saying. "People, people, people, people. Many people, yes?"

At first she looked completely puzzled by my frantic pantomime. But after a while with her brow furrowed up, she seemed to comprehend and pursed her lips.

"But there," and I then pointed off in the direction of the waterfront and shook my head emphatically, "no people, none. And why is that?"

Her expression went entirely blank. It seemed to me a darkness had come over her, evidenced by a depthless glimmer that had appeared in her eyes. Had I offended her in some strange way I was oblivious of?

She did not even try to answer me this time. And when she turned away again it was extremely swiftly.

But I heard her mutter, underneath her breath, another single word. And I felt certain that one word was *mogwai.* Beyond which point she was retreating quickly. She went through the same door through which the man had disappeared and she did not come back.

I felt rather stunned, both by her reaction and the term she had employed, since I had read enough of Chinese religion that I understood the word *mogwai* meant none other than 'demon.'

Was she calling me a 'foreign devil' ... yes, could that be what her meaning was? I could not fathom why she would do that, and was dull of mood and very pensive as I finished up my meal.

The quay was still empty when I came back to it, the moon still shining down except the fog a little thicker than it previously had been. It was immediately obvious that neither the captain nor his crew had yet returned – the *Saigon Breeze*, still lit up like a beacon against these dark waters, looked as hollow as some floating mausoleum.

The windows of the deserted shanties stared at me blindly once more, and even in the rotting junks any hint of light had by this hour been extinguished. Out there on the surface of the harbour, something unseen swirled a moment and then ceased.

My footsteps ringing tediously on the steamer's metal floors, I made my way back to my lonely cabin. I did not undress but simply removed my coat and shoes and set aside my cane and then lay down on my hard narrow bed. My revolver came out from underneath my belt and, for safety's sake, I put it beneath the corner of my pillow.

Sleep came to me only gradually, but once that I had reached its depths I found myself assailed by dreams of a familiar but horrid sort. It had been fully five years since the Armistice had come and I had departed the Western Front, yet even after all that time my nightmares were still filled up with the inhuman barbarities that I had witnessed. Men hung suspended and half-dead from massive loops of cruel barbed wire, moaning piteously and weeping. Others had been struck down by artillery fire and were lying round in mangled bits, their blood mingling with the cloying mud which surrounded their loathsome trenches. Still more had breathed in mustard gas – they all were drowning from the fluid in their lungs, gouts of foam erupting from their throats, and they were clutching at their chests and making awful choking noises, helpless terror flaring in their eyes.

I woke up drenched in sweat.

It was still quite dark and deep into the night. But then I heard a sound from the open deck above my head and my heart leapt with sudden exultation, since I believed at first the crewmen had come back. I was about to sit up joyfully, but stopped myself. In fact, I went completely motionless.

These were not footfalls I was hearing. No, rather they were a slow rasping sound, like something large and heavy being dragged across the floor up there. And that was followed by a sinuous damp slithering, and then some kind of bubbling hiss.

And these noises continued ponderously, on and on, till it struck me that whatever might be up there could be heading for a hatch, just past which were the stairs that led down to my level. My gaze went darting to my cabin's open door. My hand closed round my pistol's grip. I set my teeth, my frame painfully stiff, although I was shaking too.

The rasping sound had almost reached the entranceway. So should I hurry myself to my feet and go out and so confront its source?

When suddenly a thin low voice – a woman's voice – sounded out across the harbour, and it seemed to be coming from somewhere along this quay. There were only a few murmured words, yet I felt certain that they were not Cantonese. They sounded European ... some Teutonic tongue, perhaps?

But instantly, the rasping halted and then changed direction. And a moment after that I heard a splash as something hit the water and was gone.

Still shivering badly, I rose up – the gun still in my tightened grasp – and went over to the porthole and stared out. Aside from the shallow motion of the waves, the scene before me was as moveless as a mural, with the moonlight framing everything in stark clear tones of black and white.

Could I have really listened to those curious and frightening sounds, or heard a European woman calling out? The latter seemed unlikely in a setting such as this, and the former made no tiniest bit of sense that I could even see. So maybe they had merely been products of my subconscious mind imagining things whilst I had still been half-asleep, a nasty adjunct to my vile War-dreams.

I could discern no threats to me now, so breathing heavily I returned to my bunk again. But it was a good couple more hours before Lethe reclaimed me, and during that time nobody returned. It seemed as though the whole world had forgotten about me.

These days I wish it had, since there are terrible things hidden 'neath the surface of this world, dark appalling secrets that a human being ought not to know.

III

I was awoken by the steady and insistent hammering of metal against metal far below me, presumably coming from the engine room. And that sound of activity made me sigh with genuine relief. Bright sunlight was flooding through my porthole, with the fog and shadows of the last night swept away like they had never been.

My neck sore from sleeping in a quite uncomfortable position, I got up and changed into some fresher clothes, my manner more relaxed now I was certain I had company. Then I sought the galley once again, where I found some salted crackers with which to break my fast. The heavy banging was continuing below ... and as for that other noise which I believed that I had heard, that shuffling and shifting and that slithering sound? I was by this time utterly convinced that it had been no more than a semi-waking dream.

I began wandering through the ship and it became quickly obvious that – other than the thumping coming from below – I was still alone up here, and so I sought out the engine room. I had never been down there before, but found it easily by going down another set of steps and then a near-vertical ladder.

The racket down here was deafening. In a scene lit only by a single lamp, three Chinese workmen – not dissimilar to the diners I had seen in the café last night – were busily engaged in dismantling the ship's old boiler, hammering apart the riveted sections, carrying them off and laying them in an untidy pile. Overseeing them – and wearing just a pair of dungarees, his thick and hirsute arms and shoulders on display – was the burly, sullen bo'sun of this vessel, an individual who I knew hailed from Constantinople and who could speak very little of my native tongue.

I tried to communicate with the man nonetheless, shouting out to make myself heard over and above the calamitous din.

"The captain? Where exactly has he gone?"

The bo'sun glanced across at me with piercing, knavish eyes, but did not seem to understand what I was asking him.

"Your Captain Rodrigo?" I tried again. "For heaven's sake, where is he?"

And at last, the penny dropped.

"Wit fren!" the Turk barked back.

"And where might this friend be?"

The man's response, however, was to simply shrug then look away and pretend that I was not there. So it was pretty clear that I would get no more from him.

I returned to the higher decks, except the racket from beneath was so intense that – in my newly-woken frame of mind – it soon became unbearable to me. And so I found myself stepping out onto the rickety boardwalk of the quay again.

The sun was bright and hot this day, and if it had not been for the foul stench from the harbour then I might have pronounced this a pleasant and agreeable morn. Further out across the water, craft of many different shapes and sizes were all plying the low waves, from small sampans to great freight vessels. And beyond those moving shapes more dry land could be seen, presumably the Peninsula of Kowloon, equally a part of this Crown Territory. Clusters of low buildings could he made out there, but so far off they looked like nothing more than a great shapeless and homogeneous brown mass.

I was still drinking in this fascinating scene when footsteps coming up behind me made me start then swivel about. And I found myself facing not a local man but the same Captain Rodrigo who I had enquired after.

He looked tired, his face quite drawn and the dull fever of stressfulness glimmering in his dark eyes. But his expression as he stopped before me became rather rueful too.

"Mr Howard, I must sincerely apologise. You are my passenger, and yet I have abandoned you. And for a considerable while as well – it's unforgivable, but I've been having just a devil of a time."

He repeated those last five words, took in a weary breath and then went on.

"The engineer who I've commissioned to repair the *Saigon Breeze* has come to realise the predicament I'm in, the absolute advantage he has over me, and in that light he has been trying to double the agreed price that I ought to pay to install a new boiler. The fellow is as ruthless as a Tartar Lord, and I have spent most of last night and a few hours of this morning trying to resettle a fair deal with him."

He pulled his cap from off his head and mopped at his flat brow with it.

"I'm getting there, but it is very hard. It is no excuse, nonetheless, for abandoning you so utterly. I'm glad to see that you are well and safe. Were you all right here on your own last night?"

For an answer, I gave him only a sardonic smile. I was – after all – a full-grown man, and one used to the stark horrors of war as well, and so I ought not be the least afraid of things like loneliness and darkness.

"I'm staying with a man I know," the good captain was going on, "a Dutchman who trades in rare metals. But he only has room in his apartment for myself. And my first mate and my bo'sun are both similarly installed."

I noticed that he did not make the slightest mention of his other crew. So I presumed that they were holed up in some drunken, squalid house of ill-repute, such as can be found all over the Far East.

"I could help you check into a hotel here," the captain was suggesting, "except the only ones you'll find around these parts are utter flea-pits, crawling with cockroaches and infested with lice, and open to thievery as well."

"And so it might be better if I remained in my cabin?" I completed the man's thoughts with a tight nod.

"If you don't mind? You can help yourself to whatever's in the galley."

"I already have."

Which got from him the first smile I had seen today so far. His whole manner lightened up a little.

"Listen to me, Lord Almighty. Babbling with concern as though you were a little child. It's obvious you're perfectly okay remaining here. And it should only be a wait of two or three more days before we're able to set sail again."

And then the man glanced at his watch.

"I now need to get going, I'm afraid. My negotiations, they are not quite over and the grasping Lord High Tartar still awaits."

Once he had departed – and once I found myself alone again upon the quay – a curious but very placid state of perception began to overcome me. Time seemed to have slowed down nearly to a crawl around me and I felt so light that I could almost float. What peculiar circumstances I had found myself engaged in, marooned in this alien port, trapped in solitude aboard an empty ship, and destined to stay that way for several dozen more hours at least. But my previous impatience and uncertainty were both dropping away from my chest, acceptance and a calm passivity replacing them, since there was nothing in the slightest I could do to change this oddest of all situations. (Maybe such passivity and calm is felt by lonely lighthouse keepers too?)

In this submissive frame of mind, close indeed to a narcotic trance, I began to study all the rotting junks that had been moored against this quay.

They were the most curious of vessels, so massively rounded and pot-bellied it seemed barely credible that they had once been able to put out to sea. They were certainly not capable of such a voyage anymore; as well as the gaps along their hulls, their masts were broken and had little in the way of sails save for a few strips of ragged canvas.

Their decaying bows were very tall though, with their outer decks a good way off the ground so that you could not catch a glimpse of whoever might be back there lest they came up to the very edge. Perfect private hiding places, then, for people like the Hakka who were shy of other people. As I wandered slowly down along the quay, a small dog started barking at me from behind the walls of one decrepit craft, but otherwise I could detect no signs of life.

But slightly further on, I came across a curious feature which – due to the darkness and the intervening junks – I had not noticed until now. Set perpendicularly to the quay there was a very narrow jetty, built of the same darkened wood and even more rickety-looking than the main body of the structure, that ran out some fifty yards into the fetid waters of the harbour. And moored right at the end of it – leaning partly on its side – was the most damaged Oriental vessel of them all. Its masts were broken down to stubs and there were large rents down its sides, which had been bleached almost to colourlessness by the tropic sun. How the thing was even remaining afloat was an enduring mystery.

I tried to move toward it, but the thin boards of the jetty creaked and groaned so perilously under my weight I rapidly gave up on that idea and confined myself to regarding the vessel from a distance.

Situated further out to sea than all the rest the way it was, the tides of Victoria Harbour – in truth no more than a broad channel between this isle and the Kowloon Peninsula – kept plucking at it continuously. And the bow waves from larger moving vessels worried at it too, so that it shook and trembled all the time and let out constant moaning sounds. Its wooden sides looked rotted to their very core, so how did the whole thing avoid falling apart?

It was a mystery I finally gave up on. I went ambling back in the direction of the *Saigon Breeze*, stopping just before the hammering of the engineers could do more injury to my strained senses. And I wound up sitting down on the edge of the quay, letting my feet wave above the filthy water like some child up in a tree and trying my best to enjoy the sunshine and the folding warmth. And I do not even remember for quite how long I stayed there. The lit-up strip of ocean danced before my soporific eyes. There was another swirl beneath the surface, though I was not able to make out the cause of it.

Finally, however, I was broken out of this slumberous stupor by the unexpected sound of yet another voice. A woman's voice, it seemed to me, and it was calling out across the harbour plaintively.

"*Mid-barr?*" was what it sounded like, although it seemed to be distorted by the lapping of the waves and the noise of the ships' engines in the distance.

This was not Cantonese that I was hearing, yet it was not English either. And it struck me in that moment that it might be the same voice which I believed I had heard only in a dream last night. I looked swiftly around but could not see where it was coming from.

"*Mid-barr?*" it sounded out again.

And that second utterance gave me the chance to fix upon its source.

Apparent now above the prow of that same decrepit vessel I had earlier focussed my attention on, a face and head had abruptly appeared where there had been no signs of life before. A woman's face, it seemed to me, though it was too far away to be truly sure.

And … I was not quite certain if I was really seeing this … not the type of face of the locals round here. A narrow visage and a pale-skinned one, like you might see borne by a European like myself. But it was topped off with the self-same type of conical straw hat the Hakka wore, and was too far distant to be verifiable.

I was staring fixedly at her, and yet she could not even seem to see me. I believed her eyes to be so very pale that they might almost be blind, and she was staring out across the surface of the harbour as though she had lost something extremely precious that she wanted back.

Her image lingered for a moment, then she disappeared. But in the moment that she turned away, I thought I caught the briefest flash of coppery red hair.

Had I been dreaming again whilst wide awake, my forced solitude so affecting me that I had conjured up in fantasy another European face? I felt shaken and unsure of my surroundings now, and so I tried to force my mind back along more practical routes.

Staring at my pocket watch, I took in the fact that it was by this juncture almost noon. And what could be more prosaic and practical than a decent, healthy lunch?

The small bell rang above my head again as I stepped into the café for a second time. There were far fewer patrons than there had been the previous evening but otherwise the place looked much the same, since the surrounding apartment blocks cut off a great deal of this day's brilliant sunshine.

The middle-aged owners were both standing at the far end once again, and when their gazes fixed upon me it was with a good deal less suspicion than the first time we had met, but also with a touch of genuine surprise. I nodded to them cordially and then set myself down at the same low table I had occupied the last night.

And I expected the woman to come trotting over with her notepad, but that did not happen. Instead, she and her husband both turned to the kitchen door and began putting out low hurried whispers, making urgent motions with their narrow hands. And at such summoning, a little girl emerged.

She could have been no more than eight years old, round-faced and delicate and fairly pretty, done up in a very neat pink frock and with a bow of the same-coloured ribbon in her hair. She stared across unabashedly at me, then favoured me with a broad smile. And at the urging of her elders, she came steadily toward my table, stopping just before she reached it.

"Hello, sir. Are you an Englishman?" she piped up in a clear high voice. "My Auntie thought you were from the way you were talking."

And when I answered with a gentle nod, her smile went up another watt. She looked very pleased, and partly with herself.

"My name is Min, sir, and I speak English because my schoolteacher is a Canadian priest. But please tell me, what are you even doing here?"

She listened carefully while I explained the strange predicament I had found myself in. And once that I had finished up, she went hurrying back to tell my story to her uncle and her aunt. There was a considerable deal of consultation and head shaking, and then Min came back.

"My Auntie seems to think that, when you were in here last night, you were trying to ask her why there are no people down there by the waterfront. Is she correct?"

"She is," I responded. "And I still don't have an answer."

At which, Min's smile dropped away more than a touch. It was still there but looked uncomfortable and taut.

"The people who dwell around these parts, they are mostly highly superstitious. And they genuinely believe there is a devil living underneath the water here, and so they do not like to make their homes beside its edge."

I could tell from the extent of her vocabulary this was a very clever little lady I was dealing with. But *this* was the meaning of that *'mogwai'* I had heard. This small girl's aunt had not been offering me an insult in the least, but had merely been speaking of a local legend.

"Except the Hakka are still there," I pointed out.

"Yes, sir. They have nowhere else to go, since they were living there for many years before the devil came."

So it was not an ancient myth that I was hearing of.

At which point, another thought occurred to me. Could this be my opportunity to test out the veracity of what I thought that I had seen less than an hour ago?

"Min?" I asked the girl slowly. "Might there be somebody else living on those ancient boats except the Hakka?"

And I paused.

"A woman of my type, perhaps?"

The young girl's smile had faded badly by this late stage of our conversation. As I watched, her body became tense, her shoulders lifted stiffly up, her small head tilted slightly to the side and her fingers twisted round each other.

"Did you see her?" she enquired.

"Yes, Min, I believe I did."

"Her story is very sad. She belonged once to a noble, wealthy family, and she came here from ... Dane-land?"

"Denmark?"

"Yes. She arrived here to learn her family's shipping trade, and all was well at first. But then she met a sailor of my kind, a young strong man, and fell in love with him. And a few months later her belly was swelling with a child."

I was faintly shocked to hear so blunt a way of describing such matters coming from a girl of such a tender age. But I reminded myself she had grown up in this area, with little homes piled one atop each other and with families living crowded up in tiny abodes, so that the basic raw details of life and death and even childbirth had to be a mystery to no one here, however young.

"There was a great scandal after that," she was already going on. "Her family disowned her and they cast her out, leaving her so penniless she could not even return home. And my people shunned her too, since she was not one of their own."

"And the sailor ... ?" I prompted her, wondering where this tale was really leading.

Min became still more uncomfortable than she had seemed before, her smile vanishing completely, her teeth clenching and the bridge of her nose wrinkling noticeably up.

"To answer that, sir, you need to understand one thing."

"Go on."

"It turned out the sailor was a member of a cult that worship a sea-god."

And I had come across numerous mentions of such deities in my books.

"Mazu?" I enquired earnestly.

Except Min shook her head.

"Mazu is a benevolent goddess and is widely worshipped round these parts. But there are other kinds of sea-gods, and the worst of them we call Shor-gorth."

In all my reading, I had never come across a single word regarding such a being and my bewilderment must have been palpable, because the young girl picked upon it instantly.

"He is sometimes called The Indescribable when he is mentioned at all, which is very rarely. No one can say any more about him. But his followers, sir … they show a normal, pleasant nature to the world around them, but they secretly delight in heartless behaviour and in outright cruelty. It is the way that they pay veneration to their dismal lord. And so it is quite possible the sailor man did not really love the Denmark woman in the slightest, but was simply using her."

And relishing in her fall from nobility and wealth, perhaps?

"And that being the case … ?"

"He moved her onto that same junk where she still dwells, installing her with a very aged great-aunt who is by now surely dead. And then he abandoned her."

"And the child she bore?"

"Has never been seen."

Beyond which point my lunch was brought and Min was ushered away again, disappearing back into the kitchen at the rear. I ate my noodles but I barely tasted them, and wound up leaving half the bowl untouched. And then I went carefully out.

The day was still warm and clear, and by this hour the street was fairly full of people, most of them in those same plain pyjamas I had seen the previous evening. A few small children ceased their play and gawked at me quite openly, but the adults simply shot me a quick glance, then averted their gazes and walked quickly around me. No one had tried to waylay me or rob me yet, not even in the night, and I could see no hint of any gangsterism here. So maybe the reports that I had read had been exaggerated in the main? And thusly I decided to explore the place.

I wandered along narrow streets and down thin twisting alleyways for more than several hours, and no one so much as tried to lay a hand on me. And this might be a poor area indeed, except it was a very busy one. Every little shop was open by this hour with a huge variety of goods on view. There were lacquered Chinese wicker screens and fans. There were ornaments in metalwork shaped cleverly and deftly, often with the craftsman sitting working in the store. There were food stalls too, letting out a rich aroma of mixed spices. And there was even one small shop devoted to the sale of tiny, brilliantly-hued singing birds, each such creature housed up in a little cage, cleverly constructed from fine pieces of bamboo.

And as I progressed on and on, a new kind of conjecturing occurred to me. These humble but industrious folk who were displaying such skill and ingenuity? Left to their own devices and set free from the colonial yoke, might they one day turn this wretched home into some great centre of commerce and of trade, a shining new metropolis which gleamed against the waters even in the depths of night?

The light had started failing by the time I made my way back to the quay.

I stopped on its loose boards again a while, peering through the gathering twilight at the outline of that bereft junk out at the end of the thin jetty. Nothing seemed to be moving aboard there now and I could hear no further sounds. But, recalling the story Min had told, I felt my head reel slightly with the visions it incurred.

That unhappy and doom-stricken Danish woman ... how long had she lived like this? (I quietly cursed myself I had not thought to ask). What did she subsist on? Fish and crabs and other slimy objects from the fetid waters, I supposed. Did she speak to no one? Did she ever come ashore? And the child that she had borne? Not once had I heard it wail.

My mood somewhat gloomy now, I tore my gaze away and returned to my ship. The workmen were just leaving and the bo'sun was now in the cabin, bent over some kind of big panel of instruments. I nodded to him as I stepped on board, then headed down toward my cabin. And I was just about to sit down on my bed when …

All the lights around me stuttered out.

Angrily, I floundered blindly up the stairs, and when I saw the Turk again in the half-light above he was twirling a large key on a ring around his index finger. He had obviously switched something off.

"What d'you think you're doing?" I protested.

"No light," was his terse response.

"But I'm living here! I cannot go round like some blind mole in the utter dark!"

All he did was shake his head with a firm air of stubbornness.

"Wit enchin no boom-boom, battaree wiz kaput."

What he was trying to convey, I thought, was that without their renewal through forward locomotion then my constant usage of the lights would deplete and finally exhaust the charge of this ship's batteries, so that even when the boiler was replaced, why, we would still be trapped here in this port.

Grudgingly, I recognised his point, which was not to say I was too happy about seeing it. He took me to a drawer where some flashlights had been stored, and then showed me the mechanism that pulled up the gangplank.

After which he left me on my own without a single other word.

IV

Night closed fully on the *Saigon Breeze*. The moon had come out and was as bright as before, but a good deal more fog had drifted in.

The ship rocked dully underneath my feet. A bell rang in the distance and a horn sounded from one of the more distant ships, a low bellow that rang out like a dismal and tormented moan across the surface of Victoria Harbour.

It faded off, but I had now become aware of every tiny sound – the tinkling splash of wavelets as they lapped against my vessel's hull, the creak of the boat's moorings as they were strained and then released. My own footsteps seemed horribly loud and my isolation felt as though it might be infinite.

I had taken two flashlights from the drawer, stuffing one into my pocket as a spare and finding my way with the other. Large and shapeless shadows danced all about me, unsettling me and unbalancing me slightly so that I had to resort to feeling my way through the ship's corridors in the manner of a man whose sight had partially gone, the heel of my free hand banging and resounding on the metalwork surrounding me.

I was starting to grow hungry again but felt too disheartened to head out. And so I returned to the galley, found a tin of powdered milk and another one of powdered egg and with those unwholesome ingredients I managed to construct a queasy sloppy kind of omelette which I consumed with no slightest pleasure. Just as I was finishing it up, a new sound drifted to my ears. I could not fathom what it was at first, and went curiously to the galley's porthole.

From one of the nearby junks, music was emerging. Not recorded music either but some type of Oriental fiddle being played, some stringed instrument that let out a reedy, warbling kind of tune, one that was not at all rhythmic and exceedingly strange to Western ears.

It lasted for some half a minute and then stopped.

Wearily – my mind exhausted rather than my frame – I made my way back to my cabin, my free hand still groping out ahead of me.

And once home – if you could call it that – I decided, since I was not actually sleepy yet, the only thing that there was left for me to do was read. My room had one little chair. I moved it near the porthole so it caught a shaft of moonlight, then selected a new book on history, sat down and began studying it by my flashlight's beam. It was a bad strain on my eyes though, and I could only read slowly. And I found myself chewing my lower lip from repressed anger at the circumstances I had been forced to exist in.

Finally, I tossed the volume aside with an annoyed grunt. Except that how else could I occupy myself? Another walk, just along the quayside this time?

And I was rising slowly to my feet with that expedition half in mind when a sudden very loud commotion from outside the steamer changed all that and made me stand up with a violent jolt. A man was yelling furiously, though his voice was high in pitch and sounded deeply scared. A woman was shrieking with stark terror. And some small children were wailing too.

I turned to my round window, except I could not make out what was going on. So, running now, I hurtled up the stairs until I reached the outer deck. Just as I attained that level, there came to my ears a heavy splash.

At the bow of the old junk nearest me – half-shrouded by fog but still apparent in the clear moonlight – an entire Hakka family was standing in plain view, the very first time I had witnessed such a thing. The wife, a haggard, deeply-wrinkled woman, had both claw-like hands raised to her chin and she was shivering and still screeching.

Two infants were clinging to her skirts, their heads fully buried in the cloth. And right in front of them, directly by the edge, stood a bare-chested man just as haggard as his spouse. His eyes were wide, his mouth was gasping, and he was holding across one shoulder what appeared to be a broken section off an oar, wielding it as though it were a weapon.

Below him in the water, great ripples were still spreading out and slopping heavily against the junk. The man leant over and stared down at them and did not notice me at first.

What had disturbed these people so? I *had* to find out what was going on.

So I called out to this ragged, distressed family.

"Hello? What's happening? Do you need any help?"

Every single head – even the children's – came darting abruptly up. They stared at me with genuine alarm, like I might be some monster from another world. And the next moment they had turned away and vanished silently into their mouldering home.

So they were even shyer and more secretive than I had first imagined. Thoroughly bewildered, I peered down myself at the still-disturbed and churning water.

Was this finally an instance of the crime that I had read about, with some thief trying to climb aboard? But to steal what, from people so intensely poor? Perhaps the children, it occurred to me. I knew that there was still some kind of slave trade in these parts.

And said kidnapper, once found out, had dived into the harbour and then swum below its filthy surface? I went around the whole length of the deck, trying to spot where the man had come out, some trail of water somewhere or some footprints on the quay, but the fog was much too thick for that.

Going back down inside the *Saigon Breeze*, and feeling quite unnerved by now, I made sure that the door that housed the gangplank was securely shut. And on regaining my cabin, the first thing that I did was check my firearm was still under my pillow.

I sat down on my bed then, out of sheer mental fatigue, let my body loll across it. This was promising to be a very lengthy night.

Only that just *how* lengthy I was not to know till later on.

I thought at first that I was dreaming once again about that heavy, ponderous rasping noise across the deck above my cabin.

But then I realised I had fallen into a light doze, but had fully woken up from such and I was genuinely hearing that precise, alarming thing.

I drew in an involuntary startled breath, a sharp hiss through my nostrils and my teeth. At which, the sound above me stopped and gave a fairly lengthy pause, but then commenced to reach my ears again, moving slightly faster than it had before.

It was pitch dark in my cabin save for a thin solitary shaft of pale moonlight that barely reached into that space at all – Luna must have swung a considerable way across the sky whilst I had been asleep and the angle of her glow was far less fortunate than it had been. And out beyond the front door of my little room, the ship's corridor was as black as coal.

I had gone so absolutely rigid I could barely blink. Except that horrible vibrations took hold of my taut, cold flesh, making my skin quiver so fiercely that it was almost painful.

With an unfeeling hand at the end of a numb arm, I reached for my revolver.

And then I took in the fact that the noises were approaching me now even faster than before. They had come inside the ship and were proceeding down the stairs. And not just scraping, rasping, either. I could hear that dreadful slithering again. And then there came another loathsome bubbling hiss.

This could not be any thief, although I could not fathom what else it might be. And I will not try to tell you I reacted bravely – it was simply that I had no choice, because there was just no other way out of this cabin; it would be my tomb if I remained completely still.

And so I pushed myself into a seated position and then arose – tottering very slightly – to my feet. The spare flashlight was still inside my pocket. I grasped it in my left hand. And with my pistol held out from a straightened arm, I swung myself out into the dark corridor. And switched the flashlight on.

My mind, my perceptions and my logical stability all tried to leave me at that point. Because the sight that the electric beam revealed defied everything that I had ever thought of in this world as sensible and real.

It was no human figure coming down the stairs at me. And it was not like any creature I had ever seen.

Mostly a vague white it was, but with the very slightest touch of an awful and repellent fleshy pink. It was largely cylindrical in shape, some two feet in diameter, though it tapered at the far end and there were some blunt appendages like stunted fins back there. Its body was slimy but had random patches of rough scabrous scales as well, and there were twin rows of thin uneven openings – narrow flapping gills, perhaps? – along most of its length.

Except it was the front end of the beast, and the creature was maybe two yards long, that appalled me the worst.

It was ringed with greasy lengthy tentacles that writhed and thrashed with that same sinuous wet slithering that I had previously heard. Some of them were narrow and looked fairly weak, but others seemed much heavier and had flattened oval pads at their extremities which were covered up with rows of curving, cruel barbs.

All of which was bad enough ... and yet at the centre of that circle of tendrils, I could make out quite clearly a face.

And it was halfway to being a human one.

Two eyes, yes. A definable nose, and something in the same position where a mouth should be.

Except the eyes were colourless and had no lids; there was nothing but two black slits for the pupils. The nose was little but a flattened shapeless stub not unlike the remnants of a burnt-out candle.

For the mouth there was a snapping beak, a stunted hard one such as you might find on a macaw or on a squid.

The sight of this unholy apparition wrenched my senses to their core, leaving me so wholly shocked that I seemed frozen in eternity. And I was only dragged out of that mesmerism when the obscene thing slid down the last few steps and one of its thicker tendrils reached for me.

A quake ripped through my body at that juncture and I think that I did yell out loud. But practicality – or perhaps it was simply my old training from the war – still had a strong influence on me, so that I did not try to turn away but held my ground and employed my revolver. That same practical state of mind told me not to fire at the reaching limb but shoot a round into the main body instead.

A narrow jet of fluid slopped out from the wound, as black as oil in my flashlight's beam. And the creature made a high, vibrating screeching sound. But it continued to thrash and move and three more heavy tentacles came lashing out.

Reeling back, I fired twice more. Considerably more fluid came spurting out, so maybe I had struck some vital organ. The whole beast seemed to concertina in upon itself, then shift itself around till it was facing *up* the stairs. Those same heavy tentacles reached up for the top step. And a second later, it was sliding quickly off. I heard it reach the outer deck, and then there was a splash.

As to how I behaved next … I could have sat down in a swoon or else leant against a bulkhead, breathing heavily. I could have left the whole matter at that, in other words, but I did not. Perhaps my training in the soldierly arts still held a degree of sway over my most basic instincts. And so I went racing up the stairs.

I had expected the thick fog to still be surrounding the ship, except a slow and humid breeze had sprung up from the west, driving most of the murk off. A few dull strands remained, but I could make out my surroundings clearly.

Down below me in the dark and filthy tide, a large bow-wave was moving rapidly away. And it was headed for the lone desolate junk on which I knew the Danish woman lived.

I knew that I would not be safe until this entire business was over and done with. So I dashed to the landward side, climbed up onto the ship's railing and then flung myself down to the quay. I feared it might collapse under the impact of my weight, and yet it shuddered badly but remained intact. And a moment later I was pushing on.

The jetty was of an even flimsier construction – as I had discerned earlier that day – and it clattered and swayed madly as I ran along it. I even got the sense some sections had collapsed once I was past, except I did not linger or look back. In front of my startled gaze, the bow-wave had already reached the junk. The pale tentacled thing came surging out, reached a large hole in the rotted hull and slithered through it sinuously.

I reached the decaying boat myself. Its walls were just as high as all the rest and I could see no ladder, no way up. And so I thrust my pistol in my belt, gripped the flashlight in between my teeth and then began to climb, using the many holes and rents in the junk's side for purchase.

When I was halfway to the top, something reached out from within and tried to wrap itself around my ankle. But it was fortunately not one of the tentacles with barbs, and so I shook it off. I reached the upper deck, replaced the flashlight in my hand and drew my gun again.

My electric beam revealed an upright human shape barely three yards ahead of me.

A woman's form.

Filthy rags hung off her grime-smeared limbs and she looked to be starved right down the whole way to the skeleton. Her frizzled hair had shades of coppery red in it, but a lot of grey as well. Her face was so tortured about with wrinkles and deep creases that she might have been a hundred years of age, although she could not possibly be anything like that. And her eyes – just like the creature's – were intensely pale and gleamed like opals in the wan moonlight.

But I could tell from her tiny dark pupils she was staring fixedly at me. I watched in horror as her fist came up. It was holding a long pointed shard of glass, clutching it the same way one might hold a dagger. And I could see there was blood dripping freely down her wrist. She was clutching the glass shard so tightly that its sharp edges were cutting deep into her palm, but she seemed to feel no pain and did not appear to even notice what was happening.

Her mouth dropped open soundlessly – there was spittle round its edge – and a few remaining rotted stubs of teeth could be made out. She tipped her chin up slightly, her neck very stiff, and drew in a lengthy breath.

And then she commenced to rave at me in what I presumed was the Danish tongue, and spread her arms to block my way.

Knowing of her sorry tale, I understood she had already suffered more than any person should, and therefore I had no wish to hurt this luckless wretch. So I tried speaking to her in a low quiet voice in an attempt to calm her down. And when she heard my British tones, she went very still. Her eyes came open slightly larger and a touch of their original blue returned to them.

Perhaps it was the case that I had sparked off an old memory from her earlier life of privilege and grace, of fine fee-paying schools and private tutors in her luxurious home. All educated Scandinavians, you see, learn to speak plain English and they speak it well.

But then she shook her head and leaned right forward, her gaze going colourless again.

"You cannot *do* this!" she yelled right into my face. "No, sir, you've already hurt him quite enough! How much more harm would you do him? No, my son! My son, my son! My child! *Mit barn!*"

Which was the exact moment when the most dramatic of all realisations took a hold of me. The horrid infant that this poor woman had birthed – it could not possibly be the product of any normal union between man and woman. The Chinese sailor that this sorry girl had bedded with had not been the proper father, but had merely acted as a vessel for the Dark Lord who he served. No man was the proper father!

Shor-gorth was!

The woman seemed to see that I had understood the truth, and that brought her up short again. She mouthed something silently. She wobbled on the spot and her gaze went down to the deck.

Next moment, her face became contorted far more strenuously than it had even been before. Her dim eyes went completely glazed. The shard of glass dropped from her grip. A gurgling noise came surging from her throat, foam appearing round her mouth, and she collapsed onto the mildewed boards and started to writhe and kick, in the grip of some stark violent fit. Her fall from grace and the resultant destitution must have driven her half-mad a while ago, and the horror of the thing that she had brought into this world had driven her the rest of the way down, so that she was firmly gripped in the sucking tar pit of insanity. I wanted to help her, only there was nothing I could do. Her mind was too far gone and the spastic fit was raging through her body like a hurricane. And so I stepped around her and pressed on into the decomposing innards of the ship.

My beam revealed nothing but empty rooms at first, some of them with barely any flooring left. Planks had rotted and then dropped away toward the bottom of the hull. And I could find no steps, merely ladders which creaked horribly as I descended. My flashlight wobbled and I almost lost my gun, since it began to slide out through my sweaty grasp. But finally I made it into the junk's bowels, a single space but filled with debris.

This was where the collapsed floors from up above had ended up, great piles of mangled and misshapen wood. But from behind one of them, I heard a scrape.

The creature was bleeding very badly now, great pulses of fluid oozing from its flesh. But when I moved up into view, its ghastly stare pinned itself on me and *four* strong tentacles came rearing up.

I fired twice more and then the hammer of my gun clicked down on an empty chamber. So I flung the weapon aside and then swivelled round. And from the nearest pile of wood, I pulled out a shaft some five feet long, mildewed, but sharpened at its broken tip. And – ignoring the rasp of those thorned tentacles across my face and throat – I went pushing in and drove that makeshift spear into the vile abomination's body, setting my whole weight behind it, pushing even with my chest, so that it went in very deeply before drawing to a halt.

The tentacles flailed in a palsied fashion and a liquid from deeper inside the beast came churning out, a thick and stinking yellow goo. And in that ghastly parody of a face, the eyes turned up in their sockets so I could not see the pupils anymore.

The creature's beak came open very wide and released a sound so ferociously loud I went stumbling backward with my hands clamped to my ears. A tremendous high-pitched cry which seemed to last for practically a minute till the whole beast slackened and went still.

And I honestly believed that was the end of it till – out beyond the harbour, from the heaving green depths of the great ocean beyond – that call was answered.

But this responding voice was lower-pitched, far louder and infinitely stronger, like some blast on an enormous curling ram's horn that might usher in the finish of this world.

V

Shall I describe to you the mad and the engulfing horror that ensued? When I turn my mind toward it, even these days … why, I almost fall into a faint and everything that happened next is reproduced before my eyes.

My responding to that dreadful noise by going to a hole in the junk's side that pointed out to sea. And what I saw out there caused my jaw to lock stiff – a bow-wave vast as a tsunami in the moonlight, and rushing toward me with unearthly speed.

I turned back to the ladder and tried to regain the upper deck. But the approaching bow-wave was too fast – before I was so much as halfway up, it crashed into the vessel. Or rather, the thing below it that was causing the wave did.

The junk exploded inward with a mighty crumbling noise. Then all around me there was crashing water, surging foam, shattered bits of wood that struck at me, multitudinous shades of darkness and deep extremities of lunacy. I was below the surface many times, and panted like a terrified dog every time that I broke back into the air. I saw the Danish woman being dragged down by a snaking limb and she did not come up again. The sea round me was like artillery rounds were dropping down on it, the oxygen above the surface filled up with a million confounding tiny droplets so that when I tried to breathe it, it was partly brine and I choked horribly and retched.

But most of all I remember huge staring round eyes with slitted pupils, hundreds of the things, and they appeared in one place and then sank away and reappeared in yet another. I recall myriad tentacles that did

not act normally but whirled in savage circles like elongated teeth on some mechanical saw. I recall beaks and other types of mouths that snapped at and devoured everything within their reach, organic or not.

And I remember an oily black skin which seemed to fill my entire vision and which gleamed with its own dark phosphorescence. Lord Shorgorth, arisen from the deepness to avenge his son.

I could see the jetty was completely gone, so I began striking for the quay. Something grasped hold of my foot – I screamed and kicked my shoe away.

And once that I had dragged myself out I did not stop, no, even for a second. No, I simply went hurtling on, pushing inland as far as I could go and not once looking back the way that I had come.

I kept going till I could run no more, then collapsed to the dirty pavement and there I lay completely still.

That was all a good number of years back, although precisely how many I am not entirely sure. The *Saigon Breeze*? She must have sailed away a considerable while ago, though I have no doubt that good Captain Rodrigo searched assiduously for me before giving up the hunt.

I live now in one tiny, bare and miserable room – its wallpaper peeling off, its little window smeared with grime, its single light bulb stuttering constantly – above a gambling den at the centre of a district even poorer than the one I first encountered. I chose this place because it is the furthest from the edges of Hong Kong.

Several times a week, I take myself to places like the Man Mo Temple in the Sheung Wan area. And there outside its walls I sit down beside the beggar-women, cross-legged with my head bowed and with my own alms-bowl extended in my hands. And the better-heeled locals, they take pity on this mad shivering scarecrow of a European who has somehow wound up in their midst and favour me with a few coins, thus stretching out my drab existence for another sorry week.

I yearn with all my heart to regain England and my previous life. But that would involve stepping on a ship … and I?

I cannot bring myself to do so much as even go down to the waterside. Every time I catch the briefest glimpse of the depthless oceans that surround this little isle, my head rears up with my eyes wild, my heartbeat thumps almost in my throat and I go staggering backward like a man partially paralyzed.

I see those mouths again. I see those eyes.

I am consumed with an utter mindless terror, remembering the Thing which I know Lies Beneath, and I am quite convinced it is a terror that will only vanish on the day death takes me in its grasp.

Hopefully, that day is coming soon. Meanwhile, I bid you a farewell.

THE ORPHANAGE AT TRELLAREE

I

Only one aspect of the scene before me jarred at my senses and left me with a distinct and rather chilly feeling of unease. It was the low dark building in the middle distance directly ahead of me, apparently two storeys tall but practically as wide as a whole city block. What was such a massive building doing abutted to a little town like Trellaree?

The rest of the view was just as picturesque and pleasant as I had been envisioning in my mind's eye – the rustic little coastal town with its quaint small houses and its winding cobbled streets; the hills rising around it, some decked with open fields and some with shady woods, all of them in those resplendent shades of green the Irish countryside is famous for; the spires of two churches rising above Trellaree's low roofs, a bell ringing from one of them; black-and-white cows, Holstein Friesians, grazing in the leas; the open ocean glittering beyond all that. It was as charming and as welcoming a scene as you could ever hope to find on any picture postcard, but that dark low building marred the view, disfiguring it the same way that a livid ugly scar might do.

At which point, I must explain my circumstances. I had arrived in Ireland just today. Stepping off the ferry which had moored at Dublin's docks – two porters coming up behind me with the trunks containing my worldly belongings – I had secured a taxicab and asked to be taken to the same town that I was now looking at. It had proved to be a drive of well over an hour, but finally, at the crest of the final hill, the cab had slowed down to a halt.

"I simply thought you'd like to take a proper look at the place you'll be livin in," the driver informed me.

During the ride, I had already told him why exactly I was coming here, explaining what my business was.

"That's very kind of you," I nodded. But then my gaze went back to that broad enormous shape, which seemed to be so dark it almost soaked in daylight like a sponge. "But what on earth is that place over there?"

"Ah, that would be the orphanage, sor. Menningdale, I do believe it's called."

"But it's so very big. How many orphans can there be? And it looks like a prison too."

"Twasn't always what it is right now. Back in olden times it was some kind of fort, not during the Great War, see, but right back in them distant days of auld short-britches Bonaparte."

And I recalled the history of those times. It was commonly reckoned to be Napoleon's plan to attack England from the flank, coming in from Ireland rather than across the Channel, and with that in mind additional bulwarks had been built to guard against that kind of threat.

The whole place sat there in my field of vision for another few brief seconds, then I looked away.

"Drive on, please," I told my erstwhile guide. "After such a trip as this, you have a good tip waiting for you at the end."

The fellow grinned and put the cab back into gear, and before much longer we were heading down the slope and entering Trellaree.

It proved to be the kind of place that I had dreamed of living in for well over a year. The high street was lined with little stores, their window displays heaped with goods. The houses in the side streets all looked neat and clean, with brightly-painted doors and even floral baskets hanging in their porches. There was a small green where children played and people walked their dogs. We passed one of the churches I had seen and past its open doors there was the gentle glow of candlelight and organ music coming out. There was even a horse-drawn cart rolling down the road ahead of me.

And as for the people out there walking, they were obviously not rich but were not shabbily-attired either and, more importantly, they were going about their business at an almost sedate pace, quite unlike the inhabitants of Liverpool, that being the city which I had arrived from.

Near the top end of the high street we turned right, which route took us closer to the sea. This was Sinclair Avenue, my destination, and we went up another, easier slope until we reached the tall house at the end. I was paying off the cabbie when its door came open – a grey-haired woman in a pale blue frock was standing there, an apron tied around her waist.

"Mrs Flannery?" I asked.

She gave me an appraising look, then favoured me with a stiff smile.

"So, you would be Doctor Bryant. Yes, we've been expecting you."

And I was wondering who the 'we' might be when two large young men of similar appearance also stepped out into view.

"These are my sons, Donal and Finn. They don't live here, but they've come to help you with your things."

And I finally saw what she was driving at – the three large trunks containing my possessions were now piled up beside the kerb. At a signal from their dam, the men stepped forward and began to lift the first one up.

"Come in, please," Mrs Flannery told me. "I'll show you around the place."

And she led me through every room, starting with the ones at the ground level. And the plain fact was that I was properly impressed – each room was large and in a good state of repair, and well-furnished and decorated too. One detail surprised me, though. All the previous occupant's belongings were still here, books and photographs and ornaments, all clustered on the mantels and the shelves.

"Did Doctor Stokes not take these with him when he finally retired?" I enquired.

Mrs Flannery – my new housekeeper – suddenly went very still, her face tightening and a glossy sheen descending over her green eyes.

"Doctor Stokes did *not* retire," was the fact she finally imparted to me. "No, one evening he simply upped and disappeared."

For my first six years as a practitioner of medicine, I worked out of a surgery down near the docks in one of the poorest neighbourhoods of Liverpool. Such work was rewarding and yet stressful too – there was not only sickness caused by poverty and malnutrition, there was injury through brute force as an added detriment. Families lived in very cramped conditions, deprivation wore at people's self-esteem, many of the local men were too fond of their drink and so domestic violence was a common thing. I did what I could to help, but the constant stream of poor wretched women – even children sometimes – with blackened eyes and cracked skulls and broken bones drove me into quite a depressed state after the first half decade. Add to that the grimy air of Liverpool, the soot-blackened buildings all around me, the ceaseless cacophony of traffic on the streets, the bustling crowds on almost every sidewalk, and by the time that stretch of years had elapsed I was having waking dreams of living in a cleaner and a calmer and even a kinder neighbourhood, one far removed from any great metropolis.

I had always taken in the medical journals, the *Lancet* and the like, and read the articles which interested me. Now I started looking at the Employment Pages too. A surgery in Birmingham needed a new resident, but Birmingham was even larger than this place. A mission in Rhodesia required some expert help, but I had not been planning to travel quite that far. I had almost given up by the time I opened a new magazine.

Trellaree, Ireland. New General Practitioner needed for long-standing and well-respected Community Practice.

My gaze stopped there for quite a while. I had never once considered Ireland, but did it not seem to offer all the pleasant qualities that I had long been yearning for? There was a phone number at the bottom of the page. I called it, was summoned for an interview with three representatives of the relevant medical board, and was immediately offered the post, with a decent wage and with a place to live thrown in. At the age of thirty-one I had no wife, my work had left me with too little time for many friends, the flat I lived in was a rented one, and so the move abroad was simplicity itself.

Now here I was ... only to be almost instantly confronted with this deeply puzzling piece of information.

"Disappeared? But how?" I asked.

"Everyone's still trying to figure that one out."

But Mrs Flannery could see that that was hardly a sufficient explanation, so she went on to fashion me with her own theories.

"Doctor Stokes, the sweet soul that he was, was getting on in years the way that the less lucky of us do, if you get my meaning there. And the past year or so, his mood was getting darker too. Troubled and depressed is what I'm trying to say. He'd sit at the window of his study gazing out to sea for hour after hour, even long after the sun had set. My opinion is his mind was going, being eroded by old age. And one evening his senses simply must have left him and he wandered off."

She gave me time to absorb that, then added: "I can have my boys clear his stuff out, if you would like?"

I shook my head. "Maybe later." Then I asked her to continue with my tour of the big house.

The surgery was at the back. Upstairs were four large bedrooms. But at the very top was the old doctor's private office.

A grandfather clock was ticking in one corner. The flock velvet wallpaper appeared to date right back to Victorian days. A massive desk built out of walnut dominated most of the small room. Behind it was an ancient swivel chair, deeply padded with soft brown leather and with broad armrests.

And directly behind that was the room's single window, which I crossed over to and looked out from. We were almost at the very front of the town, and so my gaze directly struck a broad and sandy beach and then the glistening sea beyond.

In the late afternoon light, the water seemed alive. It seemed to throb; it seemed to pulse like fluid driven by a mighty heart. Its motion was practically hypnotic, and gazing upon it I thought I could understand why Doctor Clarence Stokes had remained staring at it for sheer hours. Charles Darwin had long ago conjectured that we came out from the sea

... perhaps there was an ancient instinct in us to one day return and that somehow explained our fascination with the thing?

But then I caught sight of a dark shape in the right-hand corner of my eye that managed to break up that reverie. I leaned slightly to the left and something else came into view, the same dark shape that had previously bothered me.

The huge orphanage, Menningdale, could be made out from this window. I could see it clearly when I leaned across. It was standing almost by the shore itself, but set above it on a plinth of jagged rock.

If it had been a fortress once, it still retained that sturdy character. Words such as 'impenetrable,' 'impermeable,' 'inviolate' floated through my mind while I gazed upon its massive bulk. It looked secluded from the world beyond, cut off from it, a region on its own, and it inspired in me a feeling quite mysterious and close to dread. But why was that ... why should the mere sight of a large edifice affect me so?

I was broken out of this next stupor by the realisation that Mrs Flannery had started peering at me curiously, perhaps suspecting I was falling prey to the same affliction which had consumed Doctor Stokes. Embarrassed, I jerked, then turned away from the absorbing scene.

"I am simply quite unused to such a pleasant panorama," I explained.

But then I noticed something else, right inside this very room, which was by itself noticeably odd.

The wall facing the desk was bare. Inspecting it closer, though, I could see that there were faint rectangular patches, and some of them fairly large, on the old flock wallpaper. And, inspecting them closer, I could make out that there was a little nail at the top of each rectangle, these having been driven most of the way into the supporting brick.

I pointed.

"Were there pictures hanging here?"

"Indeed there were. Why do you ask?"

"The rest of Stokes' ornaments are still in place. And that being the case, why remove these?"

"Doctor Stokes took them down himself, a while before he disappeared."

"Do you recall exactly when?"

Mrs Flannery's brow tensed as she hunted through her memory.

"It must have been some three months back."

"And what nature did these pictures take?"

"Paintings mostly, and a couple of small etchings. Those were of old sailing ships. The watercolours … they were ocean scenes."

"Like the view beyond this window?"

"I'd suppose."

Which left a puzzle roaming around in my head. Why sit by that window for sheer hours, gazing at the actual sea, but then have renderings of the same thing removed, as though they were unpleasant things?

It made no slightest sense that I could see. But maybe Mrs Flannery was right and Clarence Stokes' mind had been going.

A loud shout from the stairway below, voiced by one of the housekeeper's sons, brought me sharply back into the present. Mrs Flannery had become considerably more business-like.

"All your luggage is now in the master bedroom, doctor. I'll leave you to settle in. Your first surgery begins at ten tomorrow morning. And this evening's meal is at six prompt."

She nodded, turned away, was gone and did not bother me beyond that point. I should have – I suppose – gone straight down and begun the task of unpacking my stuff, but a curious mood had overtaken me. A musing mood, a rather shapeless thoughtfulness, just as if I had detected something rather odd but could not point to it or describe what it was.

Almost in a drowsy frame of mind, I returned to that same window. By this time, the sun had dropped a little lower and the waves that I was looking at were burnished with a flaming bronze, so that the whole ocean appeared like some giant vat of molten metal, its surface forever on the move … Vulcan's great cauldron, mayhap?

And then I turned my gaze once more toward the big, low, dark-walled building. Against the shimmering backdrop of the sea, it now appeared to be completely black, except the shifting glow broke up its edges, making them waver and seem to almost come apart. As though the place was not entirely real. As though it properly belonged not here but in a wholly different location.

At that point, though, I stopped and forced myself to pull away, since I had no idea why I was even thinking that.

II

I was awoken gently the next morning by the distant sound of waves breaking on sand and by pure clear sunlight streaming through my drapes, and these indeed were a balm to my senses after so many years spent in a big metropolis. By the time that I had performed my ablutions and then dressed, delicious smells were wafting up the stairs and I followed them into the house's dining room, where the previous evening Mrs Flannery had served me a quite superlative mutton stew.

A full cooked breakfast had been laid out for me, bacon and pork sausages, two fried eggs, bread and tomatoes, also fried, and a small helping of sautéed potatoes. I sat down and began tucking in, and Mrs Flannery poured me a cup of tea.

"I should point out that I prefer coffee."

"Well, there is none in the house but I can get some, doctor."

"And perhaps a glass of orange juice?"

"Now where would I be getting that? I'd have to ride the bus the whole way into Dublin."

There were patients waiting in the ante-room outside my surgery by ten o'clock. It turned out that my housekeeper doubled as my receptionist and assisted me whenever that might be required. She had no medical training it turned out, but an awful lot of common sense, which can be more useful at times.

These were mostly older patients or else juniors accompanied by their mothers. A toddler who had whooping cough. A woman in her sixties who had been stung by a bee. A retired fellow with a prolapsed disc – I did my best to push it into better shape, and Mrs Flannery gave him the address of a chiropractor in the next town along. A girl of six with a strange rash. A woman in her eighties who was going very deaf. And finally, a little boy of four who had somehow managed to swallow no less than eight halfpenny coins.

Their attitude to me – the adults at least – was uniform and universal.

They were suspicious and shy at first, obviously used to Doctor Stokes, but still respectful and polite. And when they saw I really knew my business their demeanour warmed, they loosened up. I gave the boy of four a stern lecture about only eating things that counted as real food, gave his mother a bottle of mild laxative and then sent them on their way.

"Are they the last?"

"For now. You have another surgery at five, for men who cannot get off earlier from work."

The day outside was still pleasant and bright, and so I resolved to take this opportunity to acquaint myself with my new environs. Telling Mrs Flannery I would be away for a good couple of hours, I went back to my room to get my lightest coat, then I set off.

"G'mornin, doctor."

Those were the words which greeted me the very moment that I reached the high street. And they came from the mouth of a man who I had never seen – dressed in a flat cap and a pair of dungarees – who nodded to me in an amiable way.

And that pattern continued as I went along the street, people who were perfect strangers smiling and then thusly greeting me. Trellaree was an extremely small town, and word of new arrivals got round fast, or so it seemed. The fact that I was known of without even having been encountered felt highly unusual at first, but gradually I found myself being enveloped by a sense of bonhomie. I had been here less than a whole day and yet I was already an important part of this community. I must confess my chin came up and there was now a mild spring to my step.

That faltered, however, when I left the high street and approached the shore. The beach and the sea beyond were just as picturesque as they had appeared when I had first looked upon them. But then I passed a few more houses and that big low building came in sight again.

What was it that fixated me so about the place, and not in any healthy way? I slowed to a halt and stared. As I have already previously pointed out, the thing was set upon a massive seam of jagged rock, which protruded from the ground precisely between where the town gave out and the sandy beach began – pale brown rock and rather brittle-looking, which made me wonder how stable it was. Yet the structure set atop it had endured for well over a century.

The one-time fort was entirely square-edged, its walls completely flat and with no least embellishment on them. Its roof was flat as well, except I thought I could make out a low stone parapet running around its perimeter. Its two storeys of windows, precisely and geometrically spaced, were rather small and almost square and the panes in them, in this brilliant sunlight, reflected their surroundings like mirrors so you could not catch a single glimpse of what might lie inside. To the left of the structure was a single-storeyed wing that I could not discern the purpose of. Otherwise the place was absolutely featureless.

There was only one access to it, a slightly winding unpaved path that had been carved into the rock, wide enough to accommodate a good-sized truck but with no tyre marks I could make out. Halfway up its length there was a signpost, painted white and with black lettering on it, although I could not make out the script from where I was standing.

I took a few steps closer and then stopped again. What was I even doing, since I had no slightest business here? I forced myself to turn away, staring in the opposite direction.

A couple of hundred yards along the beach, a pair of small children were flying kites. Past them, a man was throwing a stick for what looked like an Irish setter. And down at the far end of the town a stone wall, apparently twice my height, broke up the progress of the shore, presumably the outskirts of a little harbour. Maybe I should go and take a look at it, so to put this other place out of my thoughts? But I could not, and I swung back.

Something had changed in the time that I had been looking away. Something was now moving on the building's roof.

It was a child that I was looking at, most likely a boy, of indeterminate size and age but with blond hair and dressed up in a white shirt and dark shorts. He was running about on that high-up space, but then he noticed my attention on him. And he stopped and stared at me in a querulous way, his small round face a pallid circle against the blue of the sky beyond.

Young children ought not play on roofs! Here was my excuse to get considerably closer to this place. I started quickly up the path, and two-thirds of the way along I went by that signpost I had seen.

Menningdale Home for Disadvantaged Boys and Girls.

Director: Professor E.W. Zwiegler.

A German or an Austrian then? What was such a fellow doing way out here? But by this time, the blond child on the roof had moved the whole way to the edge and was leaning over to stare down at me, so I increased my pace a little.

The double front doors of the building were unlocked, and when I pushed them open I was immediately struck by a strong smell of disinfectant. The lighting inside was bright but very warmthless. Stretching out before me was a short broad corridor that terminated at some kind of foyer, all of this entirely featureless as well, the walls painted stark white and the tiles on the floor a pale grey. But I could see the corner of a desk protruding from that wider space, and so I headed toward it.

Seated behind it – with her head tucked down and scribbling idly on a pad – was a young woman barely past her teenage years. Her hair was auburn and her skin was very pale. She was not attired in any kind of uniform but was dressed in normal day clothes. And she heard my approach across the tiles. Her head came up – she smiled at me.

"Yes, sir. Can I help you?"

I explained precisely who I was and told her what had brought me here, and then watched as her brown eyes rolled up slightly in her head.

"Lord, that would be Benjy Flynn again. He's always going where he shouldn't be. I'll tell one of the staff and they will bring him down."

At which, she rose up from her desk and disappeared into a corridor beyond. And she was gone for two whole minutes, which gave me the chance to study my surroundings.

Everything that met my gaze was spotlessly clean and neatly-placed, all of it illuminated with that cool electric lighting. There was no ornamentation anywhere that I could see, no pictures on the walls, no shades around the lamps, no toys scattered anywhere, which you might expect with children. There were no sounds reaching my ears either, not a shout, a laugh, a sudden cry … that was until, in the far distance, a low repetitive murmur started up, many quiet voices merged as one and all speaking at the same pace. A group of children reciting their times-tables, perhaps?

A clack of heels announced the swift return of the young woman, and she smiled at me again.

"The problem's taken care of, doctor. Can I help you in any other way?"

That was when I saw my opportunity and grasped it.

"I was wondering if I could take a look around? I am responsible, after all, for the well-being of this town, and that has to include this place."

The smile vanished from the woman's face as she sat back down behind her desk.

"We have a nurse."

"I'm sure you do. But a nurse is not exactly the same as a fully qualified physician."

There was a phone on her desk. She picked the handset up, dialled a single number, then spoke very quietly. And less than a minute later, a new set of heels was approaching me.

Another woman hove out into view, somewhere in her late twenties this time, very smartly dressed in a lilac suit, dark-haired and not unattractive, but extremely pale-skinned too.

She smiled at me tightly and presented a slim hand.

"Doctor Bryant, yes? I heard of your arrival. I am Ariadne Fisher, and I run administration here."

When I shook her hand, her palm was noticeably cold and dry.

"I'm not dragging you away from your work, I hope?"

"No, it's not a problem. I'd be more than happy to show you around."

And she turned smartly on her high-heeled shoes, leaving me with no choice but to quickly follow her.

"I know what you are probably expecting," she informed me as we walked. "Here in Ireland, almost all the children's homes are run by nuns, dried-up so-called 'brides of Christ' with empty wombs and stony hearts. They teach their charges only from the Bible, make them work like donkeys and then feed them gruel. But you'll find nothing like that here. Professor Zwiegler is a very modern thinker."

We went through another double door, into what appeared to be some kind of dormitory. Once again there was no decoration and no mess. But the beds looked comfortable, were widely set apart, and the whole long room was quite spotlessly clean.

"Would it be possible to meet with the Professor?" I enquired.

"He's in Manchester for a conference this week, and he has left me in charge," came the response.

And Miss Fisher – I could see no wedding ring – turned abruptly on her heels again, led me back the way that we had come, then up another lengthy corridor.

"He's German?" I asked cautiously.

"By parentage, yes, and he completed his studies in Heidelberg and Munich. But he was born and grew up in the Northern Marianas."

Where? I had to confess I had never heard of such a place.

"A former German territory. A cluster of small islands in the West Pacific, tropical ones, or so I understand. So he must have had a quite idyllic childhood, and he always likes to have a clear view of the sea, which is why he set up here."

We had reached another door, a single one this time but with a broad pane of glass set into it. Miss Fisher made no move to open it, and peering inside I found out why. Ranks of desks were lined up in this smaller room, with a child sitting at each; some thirty children round the age of six, an equal mix of boys and girls, and dressed in the same uniform the boy up on the roof had been wearing. Standing at the front of the class was a densely-bearded, very thin and tall young man in a Tweed jacket and a pair of slacks. He was somewhat pale-skinned too, and he was leading the children in reciting – yes – the eights and then the nines in their times-table.

"That's Mr Fitzgerald, one of our best teachers. But let's not disturb the children, shall we? We'll move on."

There followed another lengthy walk – I had the feeling we might be trying to traverse the entire building. But finally another pair of double doors came into view. And from behind them I could hear a regular procession of heavy hollow thumps, like something being banged down on a wooden floor.

Which proved to be in the main correct. This turned out to be a sizeable gymnasium, with climbing ropes, a trampoline, medicine balls lined up against one wall. A pair of vaulting horses had been pulled out to the centre of the room and two rows of boys and girls, around the age of nine this time, were waiting in turn to leap over them. They were wearing polo shirts by now, and their navy lower garments had all been replaced with plain white shorts.

To the last they looked remarkably fit and took their jumps with real athletic zeal. Another young woman – dressed the same way they were with a whistle hanging round her neck – was keeping a close eye on them.

"How many children are there here in total?" I thought to ask.

"In the whole place? Just short of one hundred and thirty."

"In a building of this size? They have a lot of room to move around."

"One of the Professor's main ideas." And past that point, I had the feeling Ariadne Fisher was directly quoting him. "Children should not be confined. It stunts their minds and impairs their potential."

She stared at me pointedly.

"Well, are you satisfied with what you've seen?"

"Very much so. These children seem well cared for."

"I could take you to see the nurse's station, if you'd like?"

"No need. I'm sure it's fine as well."

And so we started heading back. Except we took a slightly different route, and at the turning of one corner I noticed there was a stairway leading down.

"This place has a basement level?"

"For storage only, Doctor Bryant. The children are not allowed down there."

We continued side-by-side, and finally returned to the place where we had first started off from. The auburn-haired young woman was still sitting at her desk. Miss Fisher reached calmly out to shake my hand again.

"This is a much better place than I imagined it would be," I told her. "Thank you for the trouble that you've taken."

"And," I added as an afterthought, "I'd still be interested to meet with your Professor Zwiegler at some stage."

"He's a very busy man. But he's not going anywhere and neither, I presume, are you. And so I'm sure you'll run into each other at some point."

Once outside, blinking in the daylight, I swivelled round and re-studied the building. And it still looked precisely the same, but it seemed no longer quite so ominous to my taut gaze. My sensations of foreboding had been swept away.

But they were woken again one week later.

III

My bathroom was at the front of the big house, with a small window overlooking Sinclair Avenue. And I was standing by it idly that morning, scrubbing at my teeth, when I saw a door come flying open further down the quiet road. A man and a woman came hurrying out, and apparently in an agitated state. They dashed quickly off toward the high street.

I set down the toothbrush and swilled out my mouth, then opened up the window and leant out. A constant stream of the town's citizens was going past the open junction down there, all of them in the direction of the harbour, and so something was quite obviously happening there.

I was already familiar with the harbour by this stage, a tiny little walled nook of a place with room for not much more than half a dozen little inshore fishing boats. I had visited it several times, since I had gone out for a walk each day since I had arrived here, exploring all of Trellaree and even portions of the countryside.

But I had never seen the people of this town in such an unsettled condition as they seemed to be right now. Becoming anxious myself, I went out on the landing and called down.

"Mrs Flannery, do you know what's causing such a commotion outside?"

But – judging by the sounds emerging from below – she was busy in the kitchen and she could not hear me. And so I pulled on a jacket and some shoes and headed out myself.

And when I joined the moving throng, several people glanced at me but not one of them said a word or even nodded a greeting, which was fairly unusual in itself. I had been conducting my surgery the whole of the past week and – once word had got out that I was wholly reliable and safe – my patients had discarded their suspicions and had started treating me in a more friendly way. The people at the post office and newsagent and grocery all knew my name, and always greeted me quite cheerily. I had even stopped a couple of times at a nearby tavern, the *Paddy Shaughnessy*, and ordered half a pint of Guinness – the landlady had refused all attempts at payment on my part and the other patrons, they had raised their glasses to me.

I was known in other words, a well-ensconced and well-respected part of this community (though I could still scarcely believe that it had all happened so quickly – that would never be the case in a much larger town).

But now these people barely took a glimpse of me, then turned their heads away and held their tongues. Their faces were tight and strained and there were gloomy shadows lurking in their gazes. What exactly could the matter be? All that I could do was follow along quietly as this silent, strange procession took me closer to the harbour walls.

The chugging of an engine reached my ears. Out there on the calm grey sea, a slightly larger boat than I had seen so far was coming in, and I could clearly make out it was decked in the blue-and-white colours of a Coastguard vessel. It had a tightened rope fastened to its stern, and it was towing in one of the little trawlers I had noticed those times I had lingered here before.

Quite a crowd had gathered on the dock by this stage, every eye fixed out to sea and several people crossing themselves. Then someone finally touched my elbow – when I turned, he spoke to me.

"Tis good of you to come here, Doctor Bryant, but I don't think there's much you can do to help."

It was Tommy Gibley I was looking at, a scrawny man and with a grizzled chin who was the local carpenter round here. I had given him a tetanus shot and dressed his left hand just last Friday when his saw had slipped.

He still had the bandage on – I could not help but notice it was getting rather dirty. But his expression was just as rigid and as dour as all the rest, his thin lips bloodless and that same dark shadow deep within his eyes as everybody else.

He took a rolled-up cigarette from his waistcoat pocket, popped it in his mouth but did not light it. Then he tipped his chin toward the water.

"Tis Fergal Conway's trawler you be looking at, him and his son Avery. They must a been out fishin in the night. Come dawn this morning, someone noticed their boat was adrift and simply movin with the tide, nobody apparently controlling it, which was when they called the Coastguard in."

A sudden stir went through the crowd. The local constable – Bernard Raddle, I believed the man was called – was pushing his way through in his tall helmet. And he was going down the short flight of brick steps at the precise same moment when both boats hove to.

Ropes were thrown about and moorings tied, and then one of the coastguards stepped across from his vessel to the one behind. The open deck was clearly empty, but he went inside the little cabin and he even checked the locker where the fish were stored. Then he stood up and shook his head. Apparently, both men were gone.

My throat was tight and my mind felt rather dazed by the time I asked my next question.

"Was there bad weather last night?"

Tommy shook his head. "Flat as a millpond throughout the dark hours, with barely a whisper of a breeze."

All three crewmen from the Coastguard boat had by this juncture come ashore, and the constable was conferring with them, taking notes. I looked away from them and turned my head bewilderedly, studying the crowd around me. And I started to take in the plain fact that there was not just sadness and distress written on these people's faces. There was weary resignation too. And that was when a new notion started occurring to me.

I returned my attention to Tommy once again.

"You've all been here before, now haven't you?"

"Doc?"

"This is not the first time this has happened?"

"No. Three months ago the same befell an old line-fisherman out there in his rowing boat ... Haddon Briggs, the man were called. And in the late September of last year, a trawler out of Saint-Malo in France was found drifting off these shores without its crew of five poor souls."

"And with no reason and no bodies found?"

Tommy finally lit his cigarette, then shrugged his shoulders in a philosophic way.

"The sea is a mysterious place, doc. It holds within it secrets that no man will ever know. And nothing in your whole array of potions and big scientific books will ever change that basic fact."

And with those words, he turned away from me. The constable was coming slowly back up the steps, and the crowd was finally starting to break up.

In a mere few minutes my whole pretty bubble had been burst. I had imagined I had moved to a place wholly free of hardship and real trauma. I had believed I had put the evils of the world behind me and come to a location where everything was calm and tranquil, where brutishness and cruelty were not part of the local language and the sun shone down on all with a broad smile.

Take note of this carefully: there is no such location in this capricious, demanding world. Happiness and peace come sometimes, but are temporary occurrences. There are days when we laugh and dance and sing, but then night falls and those days end. The road ahead of us might seem a pleasant one, but tragedy still follows along at our heels in the manner of some skulking dog.

Quite honestly, I felt stunned, scarcely able to believe that this new home I had taken to my heart nonetheless contained some kind of lethal secret. Eight men gone now? Disappeared without a trace? This day was another sunny one, but I was filled up with an inner cloud.

Save for myself and the Coastguard crew, the dock was almost empty now. I had been standing here completely lost in my own sombre thoughts, but now I could see that I had little choice except to go back home.

The whole idea of walking through the town again, however – of having to face those same Trellaree people but with the gentleness robbed from their faces and that shadow in their eyes – was too much for me to bear. And so I clambered down from the harbour wall and I began walking along the beach.

I seemed to be halfway into some manner of manic stupor now. Every single of my crunching footsteps on the sand sounded to my ears like the rumble of artillery. Every wave that beat upon the shoreline made a noise that echoed through my skull. There was only a mild breeze and yet it seemed to claw at me.

Had I been mistaken in coming here? I tried to tell myself that that was not the case. Very bad things happened in Liverpool as well, and not occasionally but almost every day. Trellaree was a seaside community and the ocean claimed people sometimes ... I already knew that, did I not? This was a tragedy, for sure. An enigma, most certainly. But maybe Tommy Gibley had been right and there were secrets out there on the water we were not supposed to know.

I stopped a moment, gazing out across the low and rolling waves. *What exactly are you up to, eh?* I thought. *Trying to scare a townie from the big city who's not used to your tricks? But you will not frighten me that easily.*

And with those words running through my head, I began to feel somewhat restored. I was a physician, was I not? I dealt with the unexpected all the time. I had known a healthy patient go walking down a street and suddenly be struck down by a coronary thrombosis. I had known an ardent sportsman quite abruptly have a stroke. And how was this is any wise a different thing? Terrible things happened when you least expected them.

I was finally getting back to my old self, and my house was coming into view as well. But then I glanced further along and could see busy movement on the shore.

Beneath the low dark bulk of Menningdale, little children in the same white clothing I had seen in the gymnasium were running on the beach. And standing by them were four adult figures. I stepped up closer and could make out who they were.

One was the teacher, Mr Fitzgerald, dressed the same way as before but with a straw hat perched upon his head. The second was the instructress I had seen in the gym – her skin looked very pale as well in the clear sunlight.

The third was obviously Ariadne Fisher. But the fourth was a tall figure I had never seen before.

I drew closer. They noticed my approach. The unknown figure leant toward Miss Fisher and she murmured something in his ear.

Then he detached himself from the others and he came striding briskly toward me.

IV

"Doctor Bryant, I presume?"

But then he realised what that was an allusion to, and stopped and then let out a hearty chuckle.

"Oh, excuse me, sir. I got that slightly wrong. You're no Livingstone and I'm no Stanley. Let's begin again, shall we? I'm Ernst Zwiegler, and I'm very pleased to meet you, doctor."

He stepped forward and extended a large hand.

Everything about the man was striking from the first. His age was indeterminate – he could have been in his late thirties or he could have been as old as fifty. But he stood several inches over six foot tall, lean, with not an extra ounce of fat and yet in no way scrawny or depleted. He was wearing a loose white shirt with thin grey stripes, open at the neck and with both sleeves rolled up the whole way to the elbows. And below that a pair of heavy dark blue trousers I imagined might be denim jeans, a style of clothing I had only ever seen before in cowboy movies like 'The Bandit Buster' or 'The Fighting Buckaroo.' I could not help but notice that his feet were bare.

His eyes were a piercing blue. He had a very neatly trimmed short beard and a moustache, and both those and his head of hair were so very blond that they were almost white. It was the shading of his skin that struck at me the most, though. Quite unlike his pallid subordinates, it was tanned to almost a dark walnut colour that looked natural and permanent – I remembered at that point what Miss Fisher had told me; he had grown up in tropical climes.

When our hands shook, his grip was very strong, muscles like steel hawsers shifting underneath the skin of his forearms. And when he smiled again, his teeth were very even and perfectly white.

"I've been hearing some good things about you, doctor," he told me.

His accent was definitely Teutonic, but with no slight deviation from the English way of saying things, no zed for tee-aitch, no 'zis,' no 'der.'

But then – without the slightest warning – the man stepped forward even closer, put an arm around my shoulders, clasped me tightly and turned me around.

"Come. Let's go watch the children, shall we?"

I must confess I was rather unnerved. This fellow was a perfect stranger I had only met a few seconds ago, and yet he was treating me like we were utterly familiar. But I had no wish to offend him, so I allowed myself to be led across the sand until the children from the orphanage were in clear view.

There were about eighteen of them, again a mixture of both boys and girls and all of them around the age of seven. All of them entirely healthy-looking … far better than that in fact, as fit as proverbial fiddles. Like the professor himself, they were bare footed. And the sports instructress was lining them up in groups of six and making them race across the beach toward a pair of sweaters set down further on that counted as a finish line.

Zwiegler grinned again, relaxed his grip on me, then pointed at the ground.

"Sit, man, sit. No need to be bothered by a little bit of sand."

I did as I was … asked? No, I was not quite sure that was the correct word. The man plumped down heavily beside me and produced a silver stopwatch from the breast pocket on his shirt. Another group of half a dozen children had just started running off.

He watched them very closely until they had reached their goal, clicked a button on the stopwatch, then called out to the instructress.

"No, Katherine, that is not nearly fast enough! Give them a few seconds rest, then make them go again!"

Which left me surprised a second time in quick succession. These were only little infants after all. I was unsure if I ought to raise any objection, but then I told myself I was a doctor and these children's well-being was my rightful business.

"Don't you think you're working them a little too hard, professor?"

Zwiegler's pale eyebrows came bobbing up, like he was quite unused to being challenged. But then he saw the worry in my eyes, born of a professional concern, and his entire expression loosened up and went quite mild.

"I wish I'd had you watching over me while I was growing up," he mused. "But tell me, Doctor Bryant, what exactly is the human body, even the body of a little child?"

All that I could do was frown uncomfortably, not entirely sure I understood the question.

"It is a machine that carries the brain around. And if that machine is not working properly, the brain cannot function to its full capacity. Let me ask you something else. What is the foundation our society is built upon?"

Again, I was silent – I had not expected this type of peculiar inquisition. Zwiegler waited for me, then continued on.

"The family, doctor. The family, of course. I had one. And I presume you had one, yes? Almost everyone in town has one. And yet these children," and he waved a hand, "have not. They have been robbed of that essential social foundation, and at the earliest stages of their lives. And they are unarguably greatly disadvantaged on account of that. And so to make up for that, as they progress through their lives, it is not good enough for them to be the equal of the family-folk. No, they must be *better* than the family-folk. Stronger, faster, better-educated, quicker-witted, healthier, smarter."

I felt shocked a third time in a row.

"You mean a … superior breed?" I ventured quietly.

And I watched as, once again, his eyebrows rose and then came down. His whole demeanour became very thoughtful and he clasped his hands together, propped them underneath his chin.

"Oh dear – oh no. I think that you're now getting me confused, yes, with that noisy pipsqueak in Berlin with his absurd… what is it? … National Socialist German Workers' Party. A short slight man with dark hair and a dark little moustache who nonetheless extols the virtues of blond giants. If he ever comes to power then God help us all."

He shook his head and gave his wrist a flick, dismissing that last idea as totally ridiculous.

"No, doctor, this is not eugenics and there is no master plan. I am simply trying to give these kids the best possible chance in life."

Then, without any preamble, he stood up and began striding away from me, clapping both his palms together.

"Enough running, children! In the water now!"

I had never seen a crowd of such young boys and girls obey a command so instantly. As one, they stripped their white polo shirts off. As one, they ran toward the surf. And they were plunging into the waves without hesitation, breast stroking out till they had cleared the bottom and then changing their stroke to a rapid crawl. Silvery streams of brine shot up from their arms and glittered in the sunlight. Every single child was swimming at a rate I knew that I could never match.

Fascinated, I stood up myself and joined the professor at his side.

"Quite wonderful, are they not?" he smirked without even looking round at me.

"I'm very much impressed."

"Then prepare to be further so."

Zwiegler cupped his hands around his mouth, then shouted, "Down!"

In unison, the children put their legs together, kicked them high into the air and disappeared beneath the surface of the sea. And I waited for them to come back up.

And kept on waiting. The professor was studying his stopwatch again.

I was not entirely sure, but it felt like a whole minute had passed. My heart had started thumping in my chest. Surely something had gone wrong? I began stepping forward, except Zwiegler laid a palm against my chest and stayed me.

Abruptly, there was a violent eruption. All the children's heads had come back up and they were sucking at the air. Every single one of them was safe – I felt my insides crumple with relief.

"Practically two minutes, but not quite," I could hear Zwiegler saying. "Do you know how such small children managed that?"

Yet again, I had no answer and I shook my head.

"The exercise programs I set for them greatly increase the capacity of their young lungs. And what fuel does the brain need, Doctor Bryant?"

"Oxygen," I managed to get out.

"As much of that as it can get. They are bright and sharp-witted until they go to sleep, and their attention never wavers when they are in class."

"*Mens sana in corpore sano*, then?"

"A sound mind in a sound body. Yes, doctor, precisely that. Now, if you'll excuse me, I have other business that requires attending to."

And without another single word, not even a 'goodbye,' he turned away from me and headed off toward the building, not even bothering to use the path but climbing up the jagged rocks in his bare feet.

He reached the top and disappeared from sight.

When I finally arrived home, Mrs Flannery was waiting by the front door in an overcoat and with a black hat on, her handbag dangling from her grasp. It turned out she was friends with Mrs Conway, the mother and the wife of the two men who had vanished.

"Go," I told her. "Take just as long as you need. I've run a surgery on my own before."

Once my last patient was dealt with I returned to the main house, which was absolutely silent now save for the distant rushing of the ocean.

I started going round the place, wandering idly from room to room and studying small objects, touching them. A little model of a spinning wheel. A leather-bound book filled with collected coins. A glass globe full of water and a scene from Basle, Switzerland, which snowed when you turned it upside down. These were all Doctor Stokes' things and maybe I *should* clear them out, but I had few ornaments of my own and found these trinkets somewhat pleasing.

Before I knew it, the stairs that led down to the basement level were looming ahead of me. Mrs Flannery had her room down there, and maybe I ought not intrude. But surely there was more than simply that? I had never thought to look before.

It was obvious which her door was by the strong smell of lavender emerging from within. Except there was another door, one with a black metal handle which I turned.

I found a light switch, clicked it on and saw this was some kind of storage room. There were tall, untidy stacks of files, presumably of a medical nature. There was a grey metal cabinet but it was locked and I could find no key to open it. Other random items were scattered about – a tennis racket with some broken strings, an ironing board that had rusted down its edges, a pair of heavy boots with one sole hanging off, an old fur coat wrapped up in cellophane.

Over in the corner, sitting on the lid of a quite ancient-looking gramophone player, was another stack, this time of large thick books which looked as though they might be photo albums. When I picked one up and opened it, I saw that was correct. These were almost certainly photographs of Doctor Stokes and – one presumed – his wife from earlier days. Their dress was in the style of the 1910s and they looked to be somewhere in their forties. Mrs Stokes had been a handsome woman, tall and possessed of a dignified bearing. Her husband cut a shorter and more lumpish figure with a rounded face and a snub nose, his hair unkempt and billowing wildly from his head.

I was flicking carefully through the large stiff pages when I noticed something else. In the narrow gap between the gramophone and this room's wall, there was an upright stack of jagged flattened shards, but I could not discern what they might be.

I set the album back in place, then reached down and tugged at one. The tinkling sound of broken glass was the result of that action, and I believed that I could see the silver edges of a picture frame.

So I started drawing fragments out. Part of an etching of a sailing boat. Several portions of a watercolour seascape. These were the same pictures that had once been hanging on the study wall upstairs. Doctor Stokes had not merely brought the things down from there, he had smashed them up into the bargain, as though in the grip of some furious rage.

Here was something else, then, I was struggling to understand. This behaviour made no sense. To sit for hours, even in the dark, by his window gazing at the ocean's waves … and then to turn around and destroy pictures with the self-same theme? Had the fellow's mind completely gone, or was there something else involved? Vandalism of this kind spoke not only of anger but of actual revulsion. But whatever the cause of that might be, it was perfectly un-guessable and utterly unknown.

I finally put the fragments back, clicked off the light and wandered back upstairs, my thoughts a muddle all over again.

V

Two days later, with the weather still good, I was sitting down to a light lunch prepared by Mrs Flannery when the telephone in the hallway started ringing.

"Doctor Bryant?"

It was Ariadne Fisher.

"I'm in the nurse's station, doctor, and we have a problem. One of our boys has come down with a fever, combined with a terribly sore throat. The nurse has examined him and has found swollen glands on both sides of his neck."

"Are his cheeks a little reddened?"

There was a short pause.

"Yes, they are."

"Then he might well have scarlet fever, which can turn into pneumonia if left untreated. And it's horribly infectious, too. Keep him away from the other kids and, if you and the nurse have been touching him, then you must wash your hands with strong carbolic soap. I'll be there as soon as I am able."

To the obvious disgust of Mrs Flannery, I left the lunch untouched, picked up my medical bag and went on out, not even bothering to put on a coat.

I was halfway up the path toward the orphanage when the front doors swung open wide and Miss Fisher stepped out into view. She thanked me for coming so promptly and then led me to the nurse's room, which I had no idea of the location of. Menningdale seemed precisely the same way that it had been before, clean and spacious and entirely unadorned, wide empty hallways stretching out around me and the smell of disinfectant still quite pungent on the air. At one stage, we passed another classroom. And once again, the pupils from within were chanting out in unison, not the times-table this day but the capitals of all of Europe. *Sweden – Stockholm. Denmark – Copenhagen.*

We finally reached the nurse's station, which was pretty much a rather smaller version of my own humble surgery. The nurse herself was short and rather round, done up in a pink uniform – her skin was pale as well – and introduced herself as Constance Heskin.

The child sitting on her large padded consulting chair turned out to be Benjy Flynn, the same blond boy that I had seen up on this building's roof. Viewed up close he looked rather scrawny, rather small for his eight years, far less healthy than the other kids, though he was dressed the same as them. His eyelids were drooping slightly and he peered at me with wary apprehension as I sat down on the chair beside him.

I slipped on a pair of latex gloves before commencing my examination. I took his temperature and carefully felt his neck and then asked him to open up his mouth. The back of his tongue had a faint white coating on it.

"Could you unbutton your shirt please, Benjy?"

Warily, he began doing as I had asked. He was so thin that you could clearly see his ribs, and so I could not help but wonder why he was so different from the other children. But there were traces of a delicate red rash across his chest and it was quite sandpapery to the touch.

"Scarlet fever, definitely," I said, "but only a mild case of it. Slip the shirt right off, my boy – I'd like to see your arms as well."

And he did that, but only very slowly.

There turned out to be a small round plaster on the upper part of his left arm. And below that were several rounded puncture scars. And I had not been expecting anything like this and, rather in a startled manner, I probed at them with my thumb.

"What in heaven's name are these? Inoculation marks?"

"They are from the vitamin shots the professor gives all the children," Ariadne Fisher told me.

I could scarcely believe what I was hearing, and the heat of my own mood went sharply up.

"Vitamin shots, for ones so young? All they need is a proper healthy diet! I have never *heard* such tripe!"

"Tripe is a good source of iron, and many other nutrients," came an all-too-familiar voice from directly behind me.

Professor Zwiegler was now standing in the doorway. He had on a different shirt, except the same blue jeans and open sandals on his feet.

And I might have expected him to look annoyed, but his expression was merely a bored and rather weary one.

"I respect you, doctor, honestly I do. But you are merely a GP, a medical jack-of-all-trades. Whereas I have researched extensively and have qualifications in the sciences of human metabolism, nutrition and energy transformation."

I opened my mouth to object. But he looked away from me, raised one of his hands and peered down idly at his fingernails.

"There are not merely vitamins in the shots that I administer. No, amino acids, complex minerals as well, each weighted to the precise dose, designed to strengthen both the body and the mind."

"But –"

"Remember what I said?" The tone of his voice had become a little sterner now. "They must be provided with the best possible chance in life. I see that as my duty. And so, please doctor, continue with the task in hand."

I felt deeply flustered, but there appeared to be simply no arguing with the man. I told Benjy to put his shirt back on, then took a small pad from my bag.

"I'm writing him a prescription for penicillin tablets," I told everybody from between my teeth. "Keep him isolated till the symptoms fade. But follow the instructions on the bottle and he should be on the mend in a few days."

"That's good news," Ernst Zwiegler smiled, "because next week Benjy is leaving us. An agreeable family in Westport has decided to take him in."

He turned his attention directly to the boy.

"Looking forward to that, eh, Benjamin? No more gym and no more swimming? You're sick and tired of all of that – I know perfectly well you are."

There was now movement in the corridor behind him, since the class that I had heard before was by this juncture breaking up. The pupils had noticed there was something going on – they were gathering behind the professor and were peering in with open fascination.

This close up, they appeared even better formed than they had appeared on the beach, their skin flawless, their limbs well-muscled for the age they were, not a spare ounce of fat on them ... not unlike the professor himself. Could it be that he was moulding them in his same image? Did he think he was some kind of god?

They gawked at me silently, their gazes almost round in their pale faces. Not a single one of them so much as fidgeted or stirred while they did that. But in the stark electric lighting of that white-walled hallway, I began to notice something odd.

Whatever hue their irises might be, there seemed to be a very faint but a peculiar gloss across their eyes. A slightly watery gloss, I thought, a sheen such as you might get from a strangely-tinted mirror, and it made their gazes seem a little larger than they genuinely ought to be.

But it was very pale and warmthless lighting out there in the corridor, and that often did peculiar things with colour and perception, so I quickly shook that strange impression off. I snapped my bag shut and stood up.

"Thank you so much for the good you've done," the professor said to me.

And he stepped across to shake my hand again. His grip was even tighter than before, his blue gaze boring into mine.

"Say goodbye to Doctor Bryant, children," were his next six words.

They did that thing in perfect unison, the same way they appeared to do almost everything that they were asked.

But I went away from that place deeply troubled, wholly in the grip of the strongly nagging sense that the professor regarded his young wards as little more than his personal playthings.

I was still brooding on that dark suspicion by the time that I had finished up my evening surgery. Mrs Flannery had fixed me yet another of her excellent stews and yet I ate it without tasting it, my eyes diverted from the table and my mind elsewhere.

And once the meal was done, I was left on my own again. The sky outside was darkening now. I went into the living room, started up the radio, and found myself listening to a Gershwin Evening being broadcast from the University College in Dublin. The lilting, trilling chords of a tune that had never before alighted on my ears – called *Rhapsody in Blue* – filled up the room, but they did nothing to relax my mood.

What precisely was Ernst Zwiegler all about? And what had agitated Doctor Stokes, my aged predecessor, so? There was no way to answer the first question, but as far the second matter went ...

I clicked off the radio then headed to the top of the big house.

I had not gone into the study since my first day here, but it was exactly as I had left it. The desk, the swivel chair, the ticking grandfather clock, and those bare patches on the wall. I switched off all but the desk lamp then went across to the window again.

What had Stokes been seeing out there? What had garnered his fixation so? The darkened sea was flat and calm, softly lapping at the shore, and I could make out no other movement save a very distant ship, a small light winking from its mast.

Menningdale itself was but a seamlessly dark bulk, less than half its windows lit. I peered at it, then sat down on the chair, turning it toward the glass and then switching the desk lamp off.

Weariness must have overcome me in the handful of quiet, slow minutes which followed after that. The scene ahead of me appeared to slightly blur ... and then, before I even knew it, I was jerking, waking up.

The moon had risen while I had been in a doze. Menningdale was now pitch-black, with not a single window lit. Nothing further was in view, so I could see no point in staying here and I stood up and started turning for the door.

But then my eye caught a sudden motion on the tide below.

First one bow wave and then two more appeared, about six feet distant from the shore but drifting off from it at a high speed. As though some kinds of shapes were on the move directly beneath the water's surface and speeding away at an alarming rate.

There were three hollow swirls a second after that and all three bow waves dissolved into nothingness.

I was deeply puzzled. What precisely had I just been looking at? More than likely, no more than a vagary of the ocean's strong currents. I lingered a short while longer, but I could see nothing more, and so I went away from there.

VI

For the next more than a week – whenever I could find the time – I made it my business to keep a close eye on the orphanage. I did not go up close, but simply observed it from my house's windows or else loitered on the shore a distance off. I watched the staff, and tradesmen too, coming and going on that unpaved path; I watched the windows of the whole place brighten then grow dark again. I even saw it when a small grey car drew up one morning and a couple in their thirties clambered out and Benjy Flynn was driven off.

Only one occurrence, in all that time, struck me as exceedingly odd. A group of the children were out there on the beach once more, in their white strips and running back and forth. And the same group of adults was attending them, Miss Fisher, Katherine the sports mistress, Mr Fitzgerald – again in his straw hat – and the professor himself. And the racing was progressing normally when quite suddenly Mr Fitzgerald, for no clear reason that I could make out, stumbled and fell over on the sand. And, young though he might be, he could not manage to arise from there and finally needed helping up. Was there something amiss with him? There was no way that I could tell. I made a mental note of it, but that was all that I could do.

By the following Thursday afternoon, the skies had finally begun to change. Clouds had started moving in like a flotilla of dark galleons and a hissing wind had now sprung up that churned the once-calm sea into a frenzy. By the time my evening meal was over it was getting even worse. The view from my study window was a blurred, uneven, shadow-dappled one and I could make out almost nothing, and so I gave up and went back down.

I spent a while re-ordering the notes that I had taken during surgery that week. Then I picked up one of the novels that Doctor Stokes had left behind and spent a couple of hours reading it.

I was in the bathroom – brushing my teeth before retiring to bed – when a peculiar sort of instinct took a hold of me, the same kind that had gripped me when I had first arrived in that taxicab and set my eyes on

Menningdale. I could even see it in the mirror – a sudden widening of my eyes; an abrupt shiver down my entire frame. I headed up the stairs again.

The moon was out once more, and full, but clouds were passing across it at speed so that its silvery light upon the shore was disappearing frequently, then coming back again, as though God Himself were throwing a huge switch. One moment I could see clearly and the next moment I could not.

But shapes were on the move down there, directly below the jagged rocks on which the huge orphanage stood. One of them was Professor Zwiegler – I could make out his blond hair and beard.

The other three figures clustered around him, though, were like none that I had ever previously seen. They were not slim like Fitzgerald, or shorter than their employer as were the young women that I had encountered. No, they were just as tall as him, but were considerably stockier of build. And there was something else that was more confounding.

Every time the moon shone down, I could discern the paleness of Ernst Zwiegler's shirt and even see some details of his face. Except the same was not true of the other three. Even in the direct moonlight, they remained as hulking darkened silhouettes.

An even larger cloud came sailing over. The entire beach went lightless for some twenty seconds. And when it reappeared, Ernst Zwiegler was standing there completely on his own. The three accompanying him had entirely vanished.

I almost pressed my face against the glass. Where had they all gone in such a shortened lapse of time?

The professor stopped there a while longer, gazing out to sea. But then he turned on his heels with that abruptness I had become familiar with and headed back toward the orphanage, vanishing behind the rocks. I was fully unsure what I had been looking at. Who had those three figures been?

I was still wondering that when I spotted some bow waves again, one of them at first, but then a couple more, then absolutely dozens of them, cutting up the surface of the tortured sea like there were blades slicing through it. Something was definitely on the move just beneath the surface … only what? What could it be?

The beach went abruptly dark again. So I went down to my house's kitchen and rummaged in a drawer where I knew some implements were kept. I found a little hand-held torch, and when I thumbed the switch its battery was good.

The wind yanked at me as I went along the shore and tore at my hair, and flecks of water blew up in my face. I could not make out any further bow waves by this juncture – I stared hard and all around but they were gone. I reached the spot where the four figures had been standing. It was the precise spot where the children had been engaged in their running races, and the sand was churned up by their small footprints. But then other, stranger markings showed up in my flashlight's beam.

Broad triangular indentations, maybe a foot long and still quite wet. I followed them along as they led me to the rocks and there were damp patches across those too. So, stepping carefully, I followed them up.

I was panting by the time I reached the top. But there turned out to be a small door at the rear of the huge building, a back entrance to Menningdale I had not even seen before, and the markings led to that.

This was not any pale clean corridor I had entered now. Rather, it was a part of the more functional bowels of the institute, the walls bare stone, with metal pipes running across them which creaked and hissed, and above those a cluster of thick electric wires. A second door led, I was certain, to the main part of the building. But there was also a bare concrete stairway leading down and the triangular marks, far fainter now, descended along them. So I followed slowly, trying very hard to keep the report of my footfalls to its utter minimum.

When this old fortress had been redeveloped, nobody had bothered with the basement level. The walls down here were rugged blocks of stone, fashioned into arches at some points to support the weight of the structure above. The floor was crude and rough, the few light bulbs had no shades on them, and the whole place had a musty, salty smell. The peculiar marks had all dried out by now, and I was not sure in which direction I should go.

Except a faint electric humming reached my ears, coming from behind one of the solid wooden doors that now surrounded me. And so I opened it and played my beam upon the scene within.

Two gurneys had been set up, the same kind you would find in any normal hospital. In between them was an upright silvery frame with hooks and tubes depending from it, and at the ends of those tubes there were large needles. This was transfusion equipment I was looking at, and why in heaven was it needed here?

Over by the far wall there was a large fridge, the source of the humming noise. I went across, yanked at the door, and then goggled at the strange contents within. These were the kind of plastic pouches blood was normally stored in at a medical facility. And there were dozens of the things and they were full, but when I picked one up and held it to the light the liquid inside was dark green.

Perhaps, I tried to tell myself, these were the vitamins the professor had spoken of. I could see no other explanation. Rather dazedly, I stumbled back outside and then proceeded to the next door along. This one turned out to be locked, but there was a key hanging beside it on a rusted nail, so I opened the thing up.

And was disappointed when I first did that. There seemed to be nothing in here but a pile of something shapeless over in the far corner.

But when I turned my beam on that dark mass, a human face was suddenly revealed.

An aged but rounded face, with a snub nose and with unruly hair billowing outward from its scalp.

"Doctor Stokes?"

I went dashing forward.

My predecessor was completely motionless and did not respond to my presence or my voice. He was slumped against the wall, wrapped to his neck in a thick blanket with his head tipped slightly back. His eyes were open just a crack and were reflecting my torchlight dully.

I crouched down in front of him and he still did not move. And so I put two fingers carefully to his throat. It was stone cold and I could not find a pulse.

But then I noticed something else ... some kind of peculiar growth directly beneath his Adam's apple. Something green. Almost like a small misshapen scale.

I tugged the blanket away, then went reeling back with shock.

Clarence Stokes was naked to the waist. And all over his flabby greyish torso there were patches of those growths, rows and then whole clusters of them, some of them half-peeling from his flesh. And there was even worse than that as well. His right hand had somehow become deformed, the fingers flattened out and partially fused together so that they resembled the type of flipper you might observe on a mammal of the sea.

My own palm was clasped over my mouth by now, my breath hissing through my nostrils and a strong feeling of nausea overcoming me. What had happened to cause this manner of abomination?

"He finally died this morning, I'm afraid," came a quiet, slightly apologetic voice to the back of me, one which echoed in the confines of this subterranean space. "Regrettable, but he will get a burial at sea."

I leapt up and span round, my torch beam wavering. Ernst Zwiegler was standing in the doorway, dressed the way he usually was, both of his long arms spread out, the heels of his hands resting on the doorposts. I was immediately reminded of how strong he was, and ... did he plan to keep me here, or even harm me in some way?

But the professor just kept on talking, and his voice was as smooth and calm as though we might be strolling on the beach.

"He came snooping, the same way that you did. Saw the same things that you saw, and so I could not let him leave. And seeing as he was here, I thought I'd try a few transfusions on him, hoping that he might turn into one of us."

I stiffened. What on earth was this?

"But he was far too old, alas, and too unhealthy. The result is what you see."

What sort of insanity was this? What was this arrogant madman speaking of?

"Neither did they work on Benjy Flynn. I never discovered quite why, but I was certainly relieved to see him go."

My whole frame had now tensed up. I was by this juncture seriously considering trying to make a break for freedom, but the professor was still blocking the doorway like some moveless piece of steel.

"You need to understand this fact," he said. "They almost never die. They keep on living for thousands of years."

They? Who was he speaking of?

"And they never get sick either. And if they are injured, which is rare, then they heal with remarkable speed. It is their blood responsible for that. Amazing stuff. I've studied it. An elixir flowing through their veins. Recuperative. Regenerative. Transformational, even."

My head had started spinning gently. What in all the heavens was he babbling about?

"I first met them – a pair of them – when I was only ten, on a moonlit beach upon the island where I used to live. They could have killed me on the spot – they are carnivorous predators, you see, and sometimes even ambush the crew of small ships. But I imagine they saw something in me which quite interested them. They are not without feeling, and are precisely as intelligent as human beings."

He closed his eyes for a brief moment, lost in age-old memories.

"I met with them again a good number of times past that, and not merely the first two I encountered. I learned how to communicate with them. I even learned the right method to call them out of the deep sea. And they told me about the lives they led, the wonders of their oceanic home, the certainty that comes with being nearly indestructible. And they are not only present in the West Pacific, doctor. No, they live in every ocean in the world, including the ones around these shores.

"They are a very ancient race, far more so than humankind. Most of them are staggeringly old, and these days breed very rarely. And so they agreed to assist me in my mission, to bring some younger members to their fold."

"Assist?" was the single word that I managed to stammer.

"Their blood, doctor. They have been donating it. Some of it is in my veins. You must believe me when I tell you that it feels like the most marvellous drug. As for the rest …"

He paused and turned his head slightly, since there were noises coming down the stairway to the rear of him. I paid no heed to that at first, because my alarmed mind was struggling with the truth of this. Those puncture marks that I had seen on Benjy's upper arm! Not vitamin shots at all! That was nothing but a cover story!

The noises were growing quickly louder. They were slapping sounds, a whole huge load of them, remarkably like flapping fish being emptied live from a trawler's net. But abruptly they slowed and stopped. Shapes became apparent in the gloomy passage behind the professor.

Small shapes, no higher than four feet tall, but as dark and featureless as those larger figures that I had seen on the beach. One came edging forward and it had no clothes and neither any hair. Its eyes were round and had that greenish sheen. Its skin was a faintly glossy olive-green, and with a reticulated texture to it.

Several more such faces appeared, and they stared in and hissed at me.

"The children?" I croaked. "In God's name, man, what have you *done*?"

"What I always said that I would do." And Zwiegler was smiling now. "Giving them the best possible chance in life, and what could be better than this? To live one's life devoid of any fear, any weakness, any doubt. Never getting ill or suffering from lasting harm. Never having to count the years. Never having to look up and see the Sword of Damocles that hangs over mere human beings. We will all be heading for the open ocean, where the water is extremely deep and mankind will be lost to us."

He spoke a short phrase to his charges in a guttural language I had never heard, and four of them came loping in on broad webbed feet. I cringed back at that point but they did not approach me, No, they moved across to Stokes' corpse instead and lifted it up with no apparent effort and then began carrying it out.

"*All* of you?" I murmured.

"That is what I said."

"But how about your staff?"

"Mr Fitzgerald has a tumour on his liver, practically as large as it is in fact. Miss Fisher has a congenital condition which ensures she will not survive too much past her thirtieth year. All the rest are similarly afflicted and are eager to come with. I chose them very carefully."

I could hear the body being carried up the stairs by now, and started wondering what fate had in store for me ... but perhaps Zwiegler could see that on my face.

"Oh, don't worry, my good man. One missing GP can be explained away. But two, in a place like this? It is *we* who must now disappear. Maybe I should thank you – I've procrastinated far too long, trying to get the children just as fit as they can be for the journey that lies ahead. But now has come time for us to meet our Destiny."

And with those words he swung away and started heading for the stairs himself. And in a partial shocked stupor – not even sure what I was doing now – I ventured to follow him.

He had kicked off his sandals and his feet were growing broader, making that same slapping noise as they ascended the stone steps. By the time he broke into the open air, he was removing his shirt – not unbuttoning it but ripping it physically from his body, like it were some manacle that he was happy to get rid of. His blond hair was receding back into his scalp, a bald expanse of olive-green replacing it. And that same hue was taking over his whole body as he headed down the rocks.

He was stripping off his jeans as he ran into the water. His arms and his legs had both grown thicker, the musculature more heavy than before.

Finally, chest deep, he turned around, facing me one final time. There were only swirls in the tide around him. All the others had already gone. His eyes were now perfectly circular, and so was his mouth when it opened up.

"*Mens sana in corpore sano*, doctor!" he called out, and then he spread his arms. "And *what* a body, eh? Magnificent!"

I could only watch, entirely shock-stricken, as he wheeled away again, bunched his dense shoulders and then plunged into the surf. And he was gone the way a dream is sometimes gone, leaving you to wonder whether it had ever really come into your mind at all.

The surface of the darkened ocean gradually returned to normal. It has always done that. It endures.

VII

Memories and awful dreams of what I had experienced that evening haunted me for months on end, but that was not the main event.

The disappearance of each last inhabitant – teachers, administrators, orphans, all – of the Menningdale Home for Disadvantaged Boys and Girls caused the greatest stir that anyone had ever seen, not just here in town, not only in Ireland but the entire way across the globe. Tiny, sleepy Trellaree had suddenly become world famous. Reporters flew in from every major city on the map, crowding the news conferences and even stopping people on the street. Freshly lurid headlines were exploding every day like bombs filled not with gunpowder but with words in big block capitals. The name of the town Hamelin was frequently invoked, as well as the *Marie Celeste,* although this mystery was a greatly deeper one.

Whole cadres of police detectives arrived too, under the direct command of Deputy Commissioner H.N. Cousins. Scotland Yard in London sent some experts over to advise. The newly-founded International Criminal Police Commission – later known as Interpol – also sent some of its agents. And a team of Pinkertons even showed up, all the way from the United States – nobody was quite sure who had hired those.

And the talk around town, for ages after, was exclusively of Menningdale. In the pubs, in the cafes, at the post office, the grocery store, and even in my surgery, people would propose, conjecture and project. But for myself, I listened to everyone's opinion but I simply nodded dumbly, averted my gaze whenever that was possible and held my tongue, vivid images of what had really happened welling up in my mind's eye. It was an exhausting pretence and I eventually tired of doing even that, and beyond that point I did my very best to avoid those places where too many people gathered. That became a habit I did not give up, which is perhaps one of the reasons why I never married.

Sitting through the evenings in my lonely study, recollections of all I had seen that fateful night still sprang up clearly in my thoughts and seriously pained and tortured me. God, had Ernst Zwiegler been utterly *insane*? How could he have managed such an awful thing, robbing those poor children of their normal lives, condemning them to exist only as monsters in some gloomy realm beneath the ocean deep? I could scarcely bare to look out at the sea beyond my window any more. Every time it glinted in the corner of my eye, I turned my head away.

The general hubbub out beyond my home went on for a good long while, but at the last accounting nothing was achieved. Nobody could work out where those near to one hundred and forty souls had gone. Not one sensible answer made itself apparent in investigators' minds. So the newsmen moved on to other, fresher stories; the policemen became fewer till they were reduced to just a couple of detectives, and the entire business gradually settled down. The world span on its axis as it ever does, and the pages of the calendar continued turning.

The huge building was never used again – people were afraid of going near it now. It became the domain of seabirds and then, unfortunately, rats. And then a small party of travelling folk turned up in their caravans and tried to make the place their own. The town council was having none of that. Additional police were drafted in from nearby towns, there was a forcible eviction, and then the bulldozers moved in and the whole place was demolished. All that remained once they were done were a few broken lumps of the old granite foundations. Perhaps that was this community's method of trying to put these baffling events behind it finally.

Except the years were starting to slip by. I kept up my twice-daily surgeries, giving injections and bandaging cuts and listening to people's woes. Several of my older patients gradually passed away, except that new ones were born to replace them and there were many times when I helped out with that. But I continued to have appalling dreams about that final night, and thought about it deeply when I was alone

Occasionally, it fell to me to carry out the most demanding duty that a doctor ever has the obligation to perform – the imparting to a patient of some genuinely bad news, Tommy Gibley being one of those. And every time I did that the reaction that I witnessed was the same: a sudden sitting upright in their chair and a harsh rigidity to their faces, with an awful creeping horror swelling in their eyes. And sometimes, when I saw that, I would think to myself, 'Maybe Zwiegler had some kind of point.' What would these poor people give for some of that green blood and a prolonged plunge in the ocean? *Everything they owned*, I supposed. We all know we are mortal, but we put that knowledge to the far backs of our minds until the day when it decides to leap out and confront us.

The world refused to stop for those unfortunate souls. It kept on turning underneath my feet and the calendar made a rattling noise as it was flipped. The years were going by a little faster now.

In 1932, Mrs Flannery finally retired and moved away to Galway to live with her sister and – a little card at Christmastime apart – that was the last I ever heard of her.

The following year, the short slight man with his dark hair and moustache actually *did* come to power, and we all know the horrible results of that. But Ireland was a neutral country and the War never touched Trellaree. It was more than five years, though, before peace eventually returned to our bruised and battered world.

Although it did not come for me, or not for too long anyway.

It was another pleasant summer's day in the June of 1946. I had just finished up my morning surgery when a young fellow called Danny Murdoch came hurrying in. He had been walking down the high street drinking from a small bottle of fizzy pop, had tripped on a cobblestone and fallen down and the glass had smashed and cut his palm.

I cleaned the wound with a mild antiseptic and was just about to start stitching it up ... when my own hand, which had always been as steady as a blacksmith's anvil, began to tremble gently. I tried to stop it but I found I could not do that, and my new assistant – a young nurse called Meghan McGuire – had to finish up the job for me. The trembling was over by the time that she was done.

But it came back that same evening, was accompanied this time by pains in both my wrists. And the next morning, the shaking had got worse.

My colleagues at the hospital did their best to help, but I already knew what the prognosis was. At fifty-one years of age, I was looking at a slow, degrading, maybe painful end.

Two months on, I was shaking so badly that I could not practice my profession any more. Two months after that I was walking with a stick, since the weakness had now spread down to my legs. I started taking long and slow perambulations down the shore, hoping that the exercise would help to slow this horrid process. And every time that I did that, my gaze was fixed out to sea.

What was I hoping to spot? A head appearing from the waves? And if I saw one, then what might I shout? *Take me with you? Give to me what you possess?*

But no such apparitions appeared. No, there were just wave-crests and gulls.

Now it was October and the weather had started changing for the worse, the sky grey and a stiff chilly wind blowing past my home almost continuously. Meghan had become my carer by this stage, and she fixed me lunch but then had to go out – her own mother was down with a bad case of flu and needed taking care of just as much.

"I'll be back first thing tomorrow morning."

So a long and empty afternoon and then an evening loomed ahead of me.

I listened to the radio a little while, then tried to read a book, but found it hard to concentrate. Finally, I decided to set out on another of my seaside walks, although it took a long time to prepare myself. Have you ever tried putting on a knee-length, heavy overcoat whilst having to clutch tightly to a walking stick?

At a snail's pace, I hobbled to the shore. I had already decided that I would turn right and take another look at what was left of Menningdale. And I was perfectly sure that I was doing that and so continued on for several minutes ... when suddenly I realised I was looking at the harbour wall.

I had gone completely the wrong way and had not even been aware of it. Which was when I recognised the terrible, appalling truth. It was not only my nervous system that was being eroded, no. My mind was going too!

And an overpowering horror took hold of me at that point, a vast dark terror that surged up in me and then transformed into an utter howling panic. Before I knew it, I was limping right down to the water's edge, then insensately yelling out.

"Professor! I am right here at your door! And are you even *there*?"

I filled my lungs and tried again.

"I am *here*! I'm here, professor! Please, professor! Zwiegler, *please*!"

I finally calmed down enough to see how crazily I was behaving, though I was still shivering furiously and tears were running down my face. I wiped my eyes with my free hand and stared out at the surface of the sea. Nothing could be made out anywhere upon it and the only sound around me was the hissing of the waves in the fierce breeze.

My pulse had started beating in my throat. My hands felt very numb indeed. Sheer hopelessness replaced my panic, and I gradually let go of the

walking stick and settled down upon the sand, my body slumped and my head bowed. And I was still there in the same position when the sun began to set, the cold tide slopping at my knees.

There was a final flash of amber, then the beach went dark.

Beyond which point, I thought that I could hear a soft voice from somewhere behind me.

"Doctor Bryant, I presume?"

I shook my head and just ignored it though, utterly convinced it was my damaged brain playing cruel tricks on me, re-echoing snatches of a conversation I had entered into some two decades back.

But then a pair of strong hands closed around my shoulders, lifted me back to my feet and – very gently – turned me round.

I had only seen him from a good remove all those many years ago, but now Ernst Zwiegler was as close to me as he could get, *touching* me, his massive shoulders stooped and his dark face level with mine. And – in spite of those desperate entreaties I had yelled out earlier on – this vision of a thing that had once been a man sent chills through me that struck so deep they seemed to reach the centre of my bones. Save for those unblinking eyes, his head was smooth and almost featureless, with barely any nose, no ears at all. His skin, soaked through from twenty whole years of immersion in the sea, glistened like the hide of some vast amphibian. His bulk was so great that it blotted out the beach. And did I really want to be the same as him?

Doubt gripped me for a moment but then faded off, since what real choice had the reality of mortals left me with?

When he spoke again, his voice had a slightly gurgling undertone, like there was some water in his throat.

"Are you absolutely sure of this? You must be, or I will not proceed."

All my horror of before was gone and I had started thinking clearly by this stage. But for how much longer would I even find myself still able to do that, if I let this awful sickness keep on ravaging at me? Fear and revulsion, they are powerful things, but common practicality can trump them both. So I drew in a slow breath and then nodded, and could see a sudden brightness in his green-tinged eyes.

"You have no idea of the wonders you shall see. There are whole cities down below, a civilization mightier than man's, as you shall witness very soon."

"And," he added carefully, "they have their own kind of technology."

He let go of me with his powerful left hand and lifted it into view. And I could see that there was something strapped around his wrist – a wide dark band with a thin projection jutting from its edge, something like a needle but considerably larger than the kind I used to use. As I watched, it seemed to grow organically till it was practically a foot in length.

He plunged it into my right arm, precisely where I knew an artery should be. And for the first couple of seconds there was unbearable agony.

But then his green blood started coursing through my veins, and beyond that there was no pain at all.

More heads had shown up by the time that I was wading into the cold, rushing surf – smaller ones, and so the heads of some of Zwiegler's orphans, I supposed. They bobbed among the waves and stared at me with rounded greenish eyes you never could believe had once belonged to children. But these were my people now; I had accepted that plain fact. And so I sped my pace up, hurrying to join them.

Just before I plunged below the surface, though, I halted for an instant and glanced back, taking what was likely going to be my very final look at Trellaree, Many of its windows were lit up. The town itself was plunged in silhouette and yet its form and layout were all utterly familiar; the jagged rocks, the harbour wall, the rows of quaint neat little houses and the spires of the two churches lofting above those.

And I recalled how I had felt when I had first seen all of this. That I was turning a new page. That I was starting a new life. I never could have guessed – back then – how absolutely true that was.

I live in the deep ocean now, and am fully recovered with a healthy mind. *Mens sana in corpore sano.*

THE SHADOW OUT OF LONDON

Chapter One

An Encounter at Thorburn Creek

Had I known what was awaiting me – the horrible and the brutal extent of it, the foul carnivorous nightmare that had grown up merely a few dozen miles from where I now lived out my life – then perhaps I would have remained where I was, attempting nothing, conjecturing nothing, making no plans and harbouring no ambitions. But we mere mortals cannot see into the future, however violent or grim those times ahead of us might be. We cannot guess at an approaching Evil. We can only react when it arrives at our door and lays its cold dead fingers on our sleeve.

It was still dark when I awoke. But at the window of my little cabin there still lingered that perpetual green glow that has emanated throughout these past five years from far-off London.

Sam – my border collie – roused himself as soon as he had sensed that I was up and he trotted across to lick at my bare feet. I tickled him behind the ear, then stretched my limbs and went to prepare breakfast, for both myself and the dog.

Suitably nourished, I dressed myself in my usual shabby clothes and Sam and I set off toward the nearby creek, the dank soil of the Essex Marshes squelching beneath my heavy boots. Around us there were other cabins – little more than large huts really, since the boggy ground would not support a greater weight – set widely apart and with their windows blackened. This is how humanity has existed, or rather the bare remnants of it, ever since the Hollow Plague finally drove us from the towns and cities where we used to dwell. It was drizzling a little, cloudy overhead. But dawn had started breaking on the far eastern horizon, limning it a silvery grey, and my surroundings could be made out dimly.

There was not a tree in sight, the ground around me absolutely flat. To my right the Dartford Bridge could be made out faintly, almost like a wide strand of smoke, where it arced across the Thames. And to my left and over on the Kent side of the mile-off river there were several huge and towering smoke stacks that had issued nothing for the past five years. Otherwise my environs were largely featureless, save for that green glow that issues every night from out of dozen-cursed London. I did not have the fortitude or will to stare at it directly and could scarcely believe that I had lived there once.

We came to a halt on the banks of Thorburn Creek and slowly made our way along it, myself stooping once every so often to check the contents of the traps that I had submerged the previous day. Thorburn Creek is slightly brackish, so there were not merely eels but crabs and a few flounders too. All went into a large bucket by my side and Sam sniffed at them curiously.

By the time I had completed this dreary and repetitive task, we had travelled practically a mile from my small home. Looking for it, I could scarcely make it out, but several other nearby windows were illuminated now, indicating that a few of my near neighbours had arisen. The day had grown a few shades brighter too, although the dark clouds strove to mute that fact. And since time, these days, was no longer of great essence I decided to pause before I headed back. I found a hummock dry enough to sit on, perched myself upon it and then lit my pipe.

How had my life come to this? I had once had a wife and child, a respectable job, a proper home. Except the Hollow Plague had stripped them all away. I chewed at the stem of my pipe bitterly.

And I remained caught up in sour reflective thought until a volley of furious barking from my faithful Sam broke me out of my grim reverie.

He had returned to the waterside, was standing at the direct edge of the slippery and crumbling bank. And he was letting out aggressive howls, following those up with a continuous deep growling. His hackles were raised and his whole body stiff. What had he found to disturb him so very much?

"Sam? Come over here!" I ordered him.

But my hound did not so much as cast a backward glance at me when I spoke out, and that was not at all like him. Getting curiously to my feet, I wandered over until I was standing directly to his rear and I could see what he was seeing.

Salty it might be, but the water of the Thorburn Creek is usually fairly clear, the way all flowing streams are clear now that the human race is cut down to the quick. On a bright and sunny day you can see almost to the bottom, and even on a morning such as this one's gaze should penetrate a good way through.

Except that that was no longer the case. Something jet black was obscuring it.

A massive stain beneath the surface of the creek, almost like an enormous dark shadow. But not one that behaved in the same way that any patch of inert matter ought to when immersed beneath a stream. The flow of the water did not carry it along, nor disperse it in the least. Rather, the lightless stain remained in place, standing firm against the current. It seemed to regularly expand in size and then contract, pulsing outward and then drawing in. And it did this regularly, rhythmically, in the same way that a lung might breathe.

I took those facts in with astonished eyes. But there was even more to come. The shadow appeared to detect our presence. It paused a moment and then crept slowly toward us, that strange motion making me flinch back.

A narrow strand of its dark essence reached in our direction. Then a second, third and fourth, until there were a dozen. And they looked to my appalled gaze practically like tentacles – I actually became afraid that they might break the surface and come reaching out.

But this was all too much for Sam. A good dog will not stand to see a threatening move against his master. His growling rose in pitch until it reached a feral level and he flung himself at the dark mass, his front legs going the whole way in and his jaws snapping at the obsidian presence. And my dread and confoundment were forgotten at that point, since I became afraid my best companion of these past five years might fall into the creek and drown. I lurched forward, grabbed him by his scruff and hauled him out, then pulled him away a good distance from the bank.

It took me a long while to calm him down, since any creature like a dog – once the impulse strikes him to attack – prefers to keep on going till the job is done. But finally he returned to his far more normal gentle mood and stared up into my taut face with that grateful, faithful yellow gaze particular to hounds.

Water was still dripping from his lower jaw. And some of that water was black. I rummaged in my pockets till I found a strip of rag and used that thing to wipe him clean. The black smears seemed to writhe against the cloth a moment and then vanished.

Which did not make the tiniest bit of sense. In fact, nothing I had seen since that dark shadow had appeared corresponded in the slightest way to a human's idea of logic. Very carefully, I stood back up and took a couple of forward steps till I could see the little river once again.

There was no longer any faintest trace of the blackened apparition, though. Had the current finally moved it on, or was there some other cause? I hunted for answers but my mind was blank.

And when an occurrence cannot be explained, what is there to do these days but write it off as one of the world's mysteries? Shaking my head slowly, I went back toward my home with Sam now trotting calmly at my heels. Several of my neighbours were now out of doors. And the one who lived the closest – Ewan Weller, once a barrister of note – was digging at the small patch of potatoes that he had established.

We greeted each other cordially enough, but he could obviously see that I was not my usual self, that something had unsettled me. And so I decided to tell him of the very curious incident down by the creek.

The only explanation he could see – and Weller has a sharp, perceptive mind – was that some dense pollutant of some kind had found its way into the little stream. I pointed out to him that there had *been* no pollutions in the past five years.

"But there are reservoirs of that stuff still remaining, Graves, and they've had half a decade to fester and brew. And we've had heavy rains the past few weeks. Perhaps one of them overflowed?"

It was a clever explanation but I was not sure it was correct. When I nodded, it was simply from politeness.

It was fully day by now and the cloud cover overhead had thinned out just a touch, the flat landscape around me washed in bleak colourless light. And when I turned my face in the direction of London, that green glow was finally gone.

As I said before, I used to live there back when I still had a family. We inhabited a large apartment in a mansion block just off Avenue Road, in the district known as St. John's Wood. And it was a pleasant enough way to live at first, Regents Park and its huge zoo both reachable on foot, the restaurants and theatres of the West End merely a short trip away on public transport.

And yet as one year overtook the next, the city around us ... it began to change, and not in any favourable way. The people living round us became far cruder and more selfish, strewing garbage on the streets, getting into quarrels at the slightest provocation and treating officialdom with first disdain, and then utter contempt. And as the nature of the place became more bilious and spiteful, crime started growing exponentially. Gangs started appearing even in our genteel district, daubing our walls with the hideous graffiti which they used to mark their territorial bounds. Break-ins and street robberies were frequent. Some pathetic skinny addict could be seen hunched up in almost every doorway that you passed, and as soon as the light began to fail gaunt women of ill-repute would appear on our sidewalks, plying their crepuscular wares.

It was soon too much to bear, and so we became refugees, fleeing to the charming little Essex village of Havering-atte-Bower.

And we were generally very happy there. The nature of my job was such that I could mostly work from home. But every couple of weeks or so, I was obliged to commute back into the city. Every time I went there, things were worse.

Drunkenness was all about. Drugs were being openly consumed. As soon as I got off the train – and this was in the morning too – harlots would start to importune me on the very platform of the station. And pickpockets would begin targeting me as soon as I had stepped out on the open street – I had to lash out with my elbows just to fend them off!

It became quite rapidly apparent that a lot of decent people like ourselves had done the same thing we had done; had fled the huge metropolis in search of a cleaner and a safer life. And to fill that vacuum, thugs and lowlifes had moved in, not merely from all over this small island but from all over the teeming world, drawn to London like iron filings to a magnet.

I could see no choice but to respond to this, and managed to adjust my way of working so I would not have to visit London any more. And having done that, I considered myself safe.

But that was when the Plague first struck.

In the little cottage we had bought, we were able to remain isolated so that we were quite untouched at first. But we watched in horror as the news kept coming in. And it was very bad news all over the world, except the reports coming from our old home city were the most unnerving of them all.

The rest of England was taking precautions, keeping distanced, sterilising everything and wearing gloves and masks. The denizens of London, though, seemed to have decided on a different course, not merely gainsaying precaution but then throwing every tiny scrap of caution to the wind. Massive drunken parties started up, and there were orgies in the self-same park where I had once wandered peacefully with my family. "If we are going to die then we shall go out with a blast," appeared to be the attitude that had now taken hold of many of these people. *Apres nous le deluge absolu.*

All of which was bad enough, but then events proceeded to an even darker scale. Bizarre sorts of cults grew up with grotesque names like Daughters of the Plague, who worshipped the sickness like a god, went around dressed in black robes and did their best to spread the foul disease. There was a turn to Satanism too, with black masses performed inside Westminster Abbey, all the crucifixes in there turned up on their heads, every holy image defiled and the altar fouled with sacrificial blood.

(By this stage, despite our efforts, my wife and child had both succumbed and vanished into hospital, never to be seen again. It turned out that I was immune, and there have been absolutely countless days when I have rued that simple truth).

I was still caught up in personal tragedy when the whole world heard the direst news of all. Because of all this wild reckless behaviour, a new variation of the Hollow Plague had now emerged in my home city – so fast-acting and so virulent, so merciless and violent in the way that it consumed a human body from the inside out that it was quickly termed the Screaming Death. It was consuming everyone in London, and if it went out past that town's borders it would not decimate us as the first disease had done … no, reader, it would destroy us all.

A skeleton force of our proud military still remained. An airplane was prepared, with a basic crew. And onto that craft was loaded a weapon which our government had kept entirely secret, called by the code name The Oblivion Device.

The plane went up just after dawn, flying to the heart of the sprawling, doomed metropolis. The bomb was dropped and detonated once the crew was clear. There was an almighty flash and a rumble like the world had broken clean in half.

And all that now remains of London is that sickening green nighttime glow.

It was drawing toward evening now, the end of a day largely uneventful save for its peculiar start. The light from my window was poor, so I was sitting at my desk with an oil lamp beside me and my spectacles perched on my nose, scribbling studiously in the diary that I kept. But more about that in a little while.

Did I mention at the start of this that in my previous incarnation I had been an archivist? I used to do that work on a computer, a fact that had allowed me once to carry out my job from home. But there has been no trace of electricity for five long, largely warmthless years, so such tasks must be carried out with weary but painstaking hands.

And old practices are not let go of easily. I still was in the habit of collecting and compiling all the written records I could find, venturing into nearby empty suburbs or small dormitory towns, going to a town hall or some other public office block and coming home with my arms loaded, my haul being numerous maps, reports and files, all of which I would carefully collate and store away. As a result of which the inside of my home looks like it is occupied by some gigantic pack rat, solid reams of paperwork stacked on all the shelves I built, more of them above the cupboards of my tiny kitchen, even more beneath my bed.

And by now you surely must believe that beneath the strain of all the tragedy I have experienced, my mind has – not snapped exactly – but become somewhat warped, obsessive and compulsive. Maybe that is the truth and I cannot even see it, but I have a rather different belief.

Humankind has been laid low, its civilisation utterly destroyed, its great cities turned to hollow shells, its technology silent and rusting. Except that I believe that we shall one day re-emerge, picking back up our mantle as the rulers of this world. And when that day finally comes, what shall these new masters have to remind them of what had gone before? Long after I have passed away, it is my urgent and my fervent hope that some new Prometheus shall find this place and learn of those who once carried the standard of the human race.

The same is true of my little diary, which I worked on assiduously every evening about this hour, recording every single small event that I had witnessed or else heard of during the preceding day. For surely if this new Prometheus should fully understand his history, then he must know about the few of us who managed to survive and how we lived from that time on.

A big round clock was ticking on my wall (the thing needed to be wound by hand). The flame of the oil lamp guttered, flickered. Sam was fast asleep beneath the shotgun that I have hung on my wall – all my neighbours own such weapons. And a faint and drowsy heat was drifting from the range on which I cooked my food – my stomach was complaining gently now. So I blinked some dampness from my eyes and hurried up my stiff, slightly arthritic fingers, setting down my last few observations so that I could close the diary and then eat.

I was just scribbling the final words when a growling reached my ears.

"Sam?"

My dog had awoken and was climbing to his feet. Only that his jaws were clenched and his movements were very stiff. He appeared to be as equally troubled as he had been just this morning. Had he caught some kind of threatening scent, or heard something inaudible to me? My gaze shot to my hut's front door, but a mere instant later I discerned the truth.

It was *myself* that he was snarling at! His attention was focussed wholly on me!

And then I received an even greater shock. At first I thought that it might be a product of the shadows that the oil lamp cast, but then I realized that was not the case. The eyes of my dog – once a yellow-brown – had turned pitch-black from lid to lid. Foam was gathering round his creased-up muzzle and it was dark in colour too, black droplets falling to the floor.

Engulfed in some kind of appalling rage so that his face was now screwed up into a hideous shrivelled mask, the thing that had once been my faithful dog took a threatening step toward me. I went lurching quickly back out of my seat.

"Sam, stop this!"

But he could not even seem to hear me. His body was coiled up like a spring and I could see he was going to fling himself at me. Caught up in profound shock and barely even thinking any more, I snatched up my wooden chair and held it in between us like some makeshift shield. Then I started backing off, still trying to fathom the predicament that I was in.

There was no reaching my shotgun. And the same thing went for my front door; when Sam had stepped forward he had blocked off that. But what in heaven's name had even overcome him?

His growling rose in pitch until it seemed to batter at my ears. And – hunched down low and still tensed up – he kept advancing on me one slow shuffle at a time. The only thing that I could do was back off at the self-same pace, horrified and shivering. And I kept on doing that until my back collided with a wall.

I realised the window was directly to my rear. And even a mind as frozen as my own could see what needed to be done. Still clutching the chair with my left hand, I reached behind me with my right and unfastened the simple latch. And a moment later I was hurling the chair at the snarling hound, then hauling myself up and scrabbling through.

I landed badly, on my shoulder and my neck. Rolled over in the clinging mud till I was on my hands and knees. And still in that position – in the manner of a little child, perhaps – I scrabbled away from the edges of my small cabin with the greatest speed that I could muster.

From behind me, a furious lengthy howling rose. And then there was the sharp rattle of claws making a very solid scrabbling noise. I froze, gazing back across my shoulder. And was horrified to see that Sam had managed to climb up, his head and shoulders both appearing past the sill.

His face was like a gargoyle's, should a gargoyle ever possess lupine features. And his black eyes were like mirrors that were reflecting some Stygian deep. No slightest trace remained any longer of the creature who had been my loyal, long-term companion; he was caught up in a rage that went beyond bloodlust, a violence so profound that heroes out of Greek legend would have quailed and retreated at the sight of it.

The beast that had been Sam flung himself through the twilit air at me, his dark gaze pinned upon my throat. There was no way I could evade this, so I closed my tear-filled eyes and waited for those jaws to clamp down on me.

When abruptly, there was a deafening thump. Which was followed by a ringing silence, and the awful impact I had been expecting never turned into reality.

And when my eyesight finally returned, Sam was lying on his side halfway between the cabin and my boots, a smoking hole in one side of his chest. He twitched several times but then was still. Awkwardly, I turned my head.

Ewan Weller, my closest neighbour, was now standing nearby me in the gloom, grey vapour still drifting from the barrel of the shotgun in his hands.

Chapter Two

A Theory is Presented, Then Disproved

"I heard all the commotion, Graves. Holy Lord, but what's been going on?"

By this time he was helping me back to my feet, uncaring of the fact my palms and clothes were smeared with viscous filth. Still shaking and unable to speak, I peered at him through the gathering dimness.

Ewan Weller was – I use that word advisedly – an impressive and distinguished-looking man, several inches over six feet tall and stoutly-built although with little excess fat. A good square jaw. A steady gaze. A touch of silver to his dark smooth hair. He was a learned type as well, I knew, and fluent in several languages since he had been a traveller in his earlier days. A man of the world in other words, except our world had shrunken very small.

We both moved over and we studied my dog's corpse. Sam's open eyes were still jet black and a dark viscous kind of gel was hanging from his fangs.

"Perhaps he caught the hydrophobia?" I managed to venture with a stutter.

"No, it wasn't that," came my neighbour's retort. "I saw rabies once whilst journeying through Mexico – this is not nearly the same thing."

"But ... what else could it be?"

Weller shook his head with an air of profound puzzlement, then told me I should remain where I was and walked away toward the back of his own small cabin, returning with his strong arms loaded up with firewood. And he arranged the planks across my fallen hound, taking great care to not touch the body and steering clear particularly of the open jaws. Kindling was applied and then a flame. We both backed off.

"Heavens, Graves, but you're still shaking badly. I can see it clearly in the firelight."

Weller's face had softened up with a deep sense of kindness now. He reached across and clamped one arm firmly but carefully across my shoulders. Then, with equal care and gentleness of pace, he guided me inside his own abode. I had been in here before -- it was a little larger and more pleasantly appointed than my own cramped, cluttered hut. There were a couple of small paintings on the walls, and even a framed certificate from the days when he had practised law. Some ornaments and a large Berber rug across the floor. He had tried his best to make the place a proper home. He got me seated down on one of his cloth-covered chairs, then went to a low cabinet and produced a bottle of fine cognac.

"I was saving this for some manner of special event," he informed me with a gentle grin. "But days which answer that description have not come along since the Plague hit, so calming you will have to do."

He poured us both a healthy tot, then settled down across from me.

"I think I might have some idea what this whole business is about. Please recall for me what happened at the creek?"

I took a gulp of fine brandy, choked on it a little, then related for a second time the apparitions I had seen this morning. Weller listened utterly attentively, his wide jaw stiffening noticeably up when I reached the part where Sam jumped in the stream.

"Your dog tried to bite at it?"

I could not see his point but nodded stiffly.

"And when you pulled him out, there was black liquid round his teeth?"

Weller took another sip of cognac and then settled back.

"There are certain forms of waterborne algae that are normally completely harmless. And yet – under certain preconditions – they bloom and become quite dangerously toxic. Become neurotoxins, if you want to know the proper word. And maybe Sam fell foul of that, the poison seeping up into his brain? It is just a theory, Graves, except it bears consideration."

I was listening to his words but I was not entirely sure. Was still remembering the way in which that patch of darkness had been moving, just as though it were a living thing. But I kept such doubts to myself.

"Tell you what?" my neighbour was saying. "There is little we can do right now, but come tomorrow morning we should go back to the creek and try to figure out this entire mystery."

"I'm so sorry about Sam," he added.

So the matter was resolved, or for the while at least. My shaking had subsided by the time we were agreed. And at Weller's invitation, I remained in his hut for maybe half an hour more, our conversation turning to more mundane matters. But my head was whirling as I went back home. And once my door was shut behind me, I began to rummage through my stacks of files.

During that half hour, you see, several vague memories had sprung up in my mind. And I managed to get no sleep at all for the remainder of that night.

As a consequence of which, I was horribly bleary come the following sunrise when I opened my front door to Weller's knock. He peered with amusement at my colourless drawn face, my drooping eyelids and my downturned mouth.

"Lord, Graves, but this whole business seems to be eating at you terribly."

But was I the only one who was concerned? I could not help but notice he had brought his second shotgun with him, that weapon being a pump-action one.

The weather this day seemed better than the last. A stiff although mildly-temperate breeze had swept most of the clouds away. The sun, lifting above the horizon, was farther off than it had been in previous months but very hard-looking and bright. A recollection struck at me that plain tugged at my heartstrings at that point. This had been the kind of morning when my wife and I would don our lightest winter coats, make sure that our child was warmly dressed, then go out for a long walk in the park. There was a charming little café at its edge – we always stopped there, sitting at a table in the clear fresh air, supping from mugs of hot chocolate and talking quietly, chuckling gently.

People seem to always think that grand adventures, moments of high drama, are the episodes that mark the high points in a person's life. But they are completely wrong … it is the small and finely-structured details that truly define us. (But, my reader, I digress).

Side by side and almost shoulder-to-shoulder, Weller and I strode toward the creek. We were catching glimpses of its surface before too much longer and they struck me as decidedly unusual. Thorburn Creek appeared far darker than it had been just a couple of days back. Could that simply be a trick of the dawn's strangely-angled light, or was it something worse than that?

My pace slowed down and Weller's did the same. But it was not the strange sight of the creek that was putting the brakes on us. A curious sound was now reaching our ears.

A curious humming as from some electrical device, although there were no longer any such machines, or at least none that you could even bring to life. It rose in pitch and then subsided. Rose again, far louder this time, and it seemed to move toward us. There were now peculiar flecks of darkness in the air between us and the flowing water.

They appeared to be mosquitoes of some kind, and thousands of the creatures too. I had naturally seen them many times before – how can you possibly avoid them in a marsh? But in such great profusion at this late month of the year?

I studied them with startled eyes, and realised they were far larger than any insects of their kind that I had ever previously seen. Almost as large as crane flies really, with long spindly legs drooping from their bodies and their brittle and translucent wings lashing furiously at the breeze.

My flesh tingled at the sight of these disgusting beasts, since I expected them to descend on us in a huge writhing moaning cloud and begin trying to suck our blood.

Imagine my confusion when that did not happen. No, the great swarm remained where it was, hanging between us and Thorburn Creek as though it were protecting those crumbling banks. Such behaviour appeared utterly unnatural and it unnerved me even more. Even Weller looked off-balance.

"Why don't they move in? Why simply hang there?"

The next moment, the stiff breeze had changed direction slightly, bringing something even newer to my senses.

"Can you smell that?" I asked Weller.

"Yes, my friend, I most certainly can."

Reaching our taut faces by now was an odour that was faint and yet decidedly most vile. The appalling stench of something rotting, long expired and deep into decay. And its source was definitely the creek.

Mere seconds after that, there was fresh movement on the ground beneath the huge mosquito swarm. Something that was charcoal-grey and the size of my shoe was pushing through the ankle-high marsh grasses. And when it stopped and stood up on its short hind legs, I could see it was a rat, another type of creature I had spotted many times. All species of rat live close to water.

And that being the case, I had come across them often whilst tending to the underwater traps I set … timid rodents that would scamper out of sight at the mere vibration of my tread. And yet there seemed nothing timid about this new one. Standing up in clear plain view, it stared at us men almost with impunity.

That was when my heart began to beat far faster since – exactly like my dog – the thing had jet-black eyes.

There were more arriving within half a minute, scuttling through the marsh grass from their holes along the bank. First a dozen of them. Then another score. Then around a hundred more, and some of those were frighteningly large. They bunched around the first one and then stood up too, studying us through ebon eyes with what almost seemed to be an awful kind of sentience. It struck me that they might be acting as one beast and somehow sharing the same thoughts. Weller had already grasped his shotgun in both hands.

And none too soon. One of the largest in this verminous horde suddenly dropped to all fours and came dashing toward us at the fastest speed that it could manage. But a blast from Weller's firearm threw its lifeless corpse aside.

Three more tried to follow suit, but made the pivotal mistake of coming closely grouped together. Weller's shotgun clacked and thumped and then repeated those two sounds a second time before they were finished.

Except the rest? My God, they had all dropped down onto their sharp forepaws! And – worse – they were spreading out, arranging themselves into a horn-shaped formation that brought to the attention of my startled mind the basic attack plan of the Zulu nation. Rats have *never* managed anything like that, so was an underlying and a far more devious intelligence at work in these proceedings? I had no idea.

Only I did know this, and Weller seemed to know it too. Should they all came rushing forth at once a single shotgun – even a repeating one – would never hold them off.

We began backing off as swiftly as we could, genuinely afraid that if we turned around they would be on our necks in a few seconds. I can still recall the deafening sound of my own pulse thundering in my ears, the wheezing of my sour breath in my throat, the awful fear that I might trip and fall and thus be overwhelmed.

That backward retreat seemed to last forever and those hundreds of black eyes, they remained pinned on us and followed us the entire way. The rats, however, did not follow us and remained where they were.

At long last, when we had put some good distance between us and the horde, we felt at liberty to turn around and then retire more normally. We reached the wall of my hut gasping – Weller let his shotgun drop and leaned against the timbers with both hands. As for myself, my face was drenched with sweat. My lungs felt as if they may burst apart and even my bones seemed to be trembling.

But stark terror – as can sometimes be the case – turned gradually into an anger, one which grew and swelled up in my breast until I had no choice but let it out. And I turned furiously on Weller.

"*Algae?*" I howled. "Heavens, man, but this is not anything as natural as that! No, I tell you, it is something else!"

And grabbing him by the arm, I pulled him inside my little cabin and began presenting him with all the files I had been poring over this last night.

Chapter Three

Our Plan of Action

"his," I slammed a large sheet down upon my desktop, "is a map of all the waterways in and around London, including the subterranean ones!"

"Do you really need to shout?" Weller demurred, although his manner was considerably more subdued than usual. But then he gave the chart a steady glance.

"What exactly am I supposed to be looking at?"

"This," and I jabbed with my fingertip, "is Thorburn Creek, and look how far it actually goes. We think of it as belonging to Essex, but the source whence it springs up is *here,* within one of London's inner hills. It remains below ground the whole while that it passes underneath the city, only pushing up into the light when it reaches the countryside!"

Weller took that in. "Your point being?"

Faced with a question that enquired my intelligence, the anger started fading in me and my voice took on a calmer edge.

"Can we both agree that something quite uncanny is unfolding here?"

He nodded.

"And that it is centred round the brook?"

"That's obviously the truth."

"In which case, I would propose that the source of this new evil has the same source as the stream. The city, Weller. London itself. Some new darkness has arisen there and we are seeing the effects of it."

Ewan Weller went extremely quiet and his large body seemed to lose much of its strength, so that he found himself suddenly obliged to move across and sit down on my bed. His head stayed lowered for the longest while. But finally, he forced himself to look up at me with what turned out to be noticeably rounded, glassy eyes.

"But that cannot be," was all that he could murmur. "The Oblivion Device ..."

"I know. I know."

"So ... ?"

"Think about it, Weller. I have racked my brains the entire night and cannot come up with any explanation save the one I currently propose. Something in that foul city has somehow lasted and has re-emerged."

I watched as he turned that over.

"And having re-emerged, it will do what?"

"We've already seen the evidence that it will spread. And there's no sense in pretending that will stop. Matters are already bad, but will surely get increasingly severe."

Weller rubbed at his chin with one stiffened palm, then sought to contradict me with these simple words.

"But, Graves, if there *is* still something in that city, what precisely can we do about it? The place is sealed! We can't get in!"

And at this point, reader, it falls on me to pause a moment to explain the peculiar and dreadful workings of the weapon code named The Oblivion Device.

An atomic weapon is simply a bomb, though on a hugely vaster scale than any that preceded it. Save for the radiation it emits, it works no different to a giant hand grenade. But the Device functioned in another way, and one terrible to relate.

Once it has been detonated, it emits the most enormous shock wave man has ever known, dwarfing Krakatoa in its sheer ferocity. And that shock wave goes blasting out in each direction from its central point, not simply crushing every object in its path but sweeping the resultant rubble onward in the same way that a vast bulldozer might … and not merely for hundreds of yards but for absolutely miles. Everything before it is scoured flat, houses and apartment blocks, factories and office towers, and there were millions of those things in London.

Finally, the shifting rubble slows, the leading layer of it first. The rest piles up behind it and then on it, forming a gargantuan solid structure which is then fused together by the awful heat that the Device also emits.

Put simply – since five years back – the flat and barren space that used to be London is now surrounded by a crude but giant wall, a perfect geometric circle in its shape. Hundreds of feet high, utterly unscalable and with no slightest break. No way to get past the thing, apparently.

But I was pulling out another map.

"Recognise this?"

"Of course I do, man. It's the Tube."

That being the nickname by which Londoners used to refer to their sprawling and extensive subway system. So I pointed to the line in red.

"Then you know that this one is the Central Line. And you also have to realise that its eastern branch extends a fair way out here into Essex."

Still rather groggy at the thought of all this, Weller failed to see what I was driving at, so I continued.

"Most of the Essex part is overland and of no slightest use to us. But *here*," and I rapped with my fingertips again, "is Stratford station. From this point on the subway line passes through deep tunnels all the way to Shepherds Bush, on the west side of the city. It passes right through London's very heart, but unseen and underground."

"But Stratford is part of the city," Weller was objecting now.

"Except that's not entirely accurate. Yes, it's true that the place was subsumed beneath the authority of Greater London when that entity was founded. But before that, it was a part of Essex and it lies outside the radius of the blast."

I met his startled gaze with a far firmer one.

"We *can* get in!" I told him. "But we must go down!"

⁂

"But *should* we?" was his next question.

And that had to be the most apposite enquiry of them all.

Another deep silence fell across us. There is no way to be sure what Weller was thinking but my own imagination started filling up with images that were stark, and horrific too. We had already witnessed the first ghastly consequences of this brand-new presence we had discerned in our midst. The blackened eyes of simple beasts, the violent aggression and – over and above that – the strong sense of a guiding intelligence. Yet out here in the marshes and a good long way from town, we were more than likely only at the edges of this unknown being's influence. Who knew what lay closer in? What if bugs and rats were merely the least of it and a fate considerably more horrible than poor Sam's awaited us?

Rigid apprehension held us in its palm for what seemed an immeasurable while. Then at last, Weller wet his lips and spoke.

"You're right, Graves. What we've seen so far ... it more than likely will get worse."

Quite honestly, I hated listening to those words. A part of me dearly wished he had objected, proposing another course.

"And that being the case," Weller was going on, "it seems we only have two choices. We can stop here and wait for whatever this thing is to come to us ... or we can go to it and try to deal with it."

Which was exactly where my thoughts had led me. Not that I in any way enjoyed the thought of heading into peril. No, the precise opposite was true. But I could see that the alternative was far, far worse – waiting in stark trepidation for day after day, week after week, perhaps even month after month, never knowing when an assault might come or what barbaric aspect it might take. Direct confrontation would at least avoid that slow and death-like torture. And who knew ... if we acted soon enough then might we nip this whole thing in the bud?

But then another thought occurred to me.

"What of that green glow above the place, though? And the radiation that must still exist?"

"I think I know a little of the science of this."

I watched as Weller's head rose up, his backbone straightening and his whole expression turning firm. His misgivings of before now seemed to be forgotten, or at least put aside in favour of straight action. The man, in other words, was back to his old self.

"The isotope that powered The Oblivion Device has a half-life of about three years. Getting on for double that has passed since it exploded, so there will be radiation and still deleterious, but subdued. My best guess is that we can remain above ground for round an hour without any lasting, serious affect. And," he added, "in the time that I've been scavenging –"

And we all did that.

"— I've come across a store of pills and capsules, those including iodine, which element helps protect one against radioactive rays. I have enough that we can scoff them down like candy."

And that final objection being done away with, we set to work preparing for our expedition.

I will not pretend that I set to that task with a light or optimistic heart. My flesh felt chilled even on this mild day. There was a weight deep down in the pit of my gut as if a massive canker had developed there. My head hung down like a beaten dog's and my fingers were slow to move. Every instinct in me screamed to go no further, only I could see no other course. In the entire extent of the English language there exist no words so merciless – combined – as 'no' and 'choice.'

Each of us found a backpack and we filled them up, with plastic bottles full of water and with food of the less perishable type, with a rolled-up blanket should the need arise for that, with powerful flashlights and spare batteries for them – Weller even rigged a couple of the small ones with elastic straps so that they could be fitted across our foreheads.

Then we armed ourselves, not only with shotguns but with knives as well. Weller managed to produce a large and very sharp machete, strapping its sheath to his belt.

We did not bid anyone in our community farewell, nor explain where we were going, since we thought it far better that the folk around us did not know about this threat. They had already been through quite sufficient misery, and so why burden them with more?

Weller and I paused a moment at the very outer edge of our small settlement, gazing off across the flattened countryside. As had been the promise earlier, this day was turning out to be one of those pleasant ones that sometimes grace us even as we move into the winter, the sun bereft of cloud, the breeze gentler than it had been before, the sky a shade of blue that has a pleasant solidity to it. It was difficult to believe we might be heading into awful danger on a day as unthreatening as this.

Except we genuinely were doing that and we both knew it.

But we still set off into the vast yawning chasm of the Great Unknown.

Chapter Four

In the Shadow of the Wall

The easiest, the quickest and the most accessible route had to be the old London Road, the A13, which runs across the flattened marshes as straight as an arrow until it reaches the city's edge. We made our way to it then headed west along the lifeless stretch of asphalt.

Nothing moving was in sight. We came across a few cars but they were long abandoned, in a state of ruin. And we passed by simple farmhouses and even a few littler suburban tracts, as well as a roadside inn … they were all empty too, their roofs sagging and their walls completely overgrown with vegetation. It would be a long and tiring march, devoid of entertainment, till we reached our goal. But Weller pushed on grimly and I followed suit.

We halted around one in the afternoon, sitting down beside the road and partaking in a light snack. Trees were becoming apparent round us now, the marshes starting to be left behind. One of them was full of large black crows, squawking, squabbling, and fighting for the better perches. Weller gazed at those, then turned his head toward the south.

"We must be near the river and its outlet," he mused. "And yet I can see no gulls."

What that signified we did not know, so we just stood up then pressed on. Great clusters of houses were before much longer coming into view, the dormitory communities that for decades had surrounded London.

And the top edge of the Wall came into sight a short while later, grey and murky-looking from this distance like some vast unworldly high-floating mirage.

Somewhere just past Rainham, the road took us up the gentle slope of a low hill and from its crest we realised we could see the Thames, the great river that runs through the very heart of London, then serves as the border between Kent and Essex till it discharges into the sea. It was hugely broader here as it approached its estuary and extremely deep, I knew.

It appeared to be flowing normally, but nothing moved upon its breadth. And that same surface glinted darkly in the clear sunlight, much the same way as the brook had done. And there were *still* no gulls, not a single wheeling speck ... which should not be! *Birds* had never been affected by the Plague! And so we cut across some fields to take a closer look.

As we approached, that same stench reached us that we had detected at the opening of this day, the kind of foul decaying odour that might smother your senses should you disinter a month-old grave. And the water had a thick oily appearance of the kind you would expect on some abandoned, stagnant pond. The river was progressing to the ocean in the same way that it always had, but it looked utterly devoid of life.

Or so we thought till – right out in the middle – a bulge appeared on the broad surface, caused by something moving underneath. And that bulge kept on swelling up until it was apparent something truly vast was causing it. Weller and I both tensed up, with my jaw tightening painfully. Except the direction of movement of the thing – thank the Lord – was southward and away from us.

On the far bank we could see anchored a long row of some two dozen barges, huge ones for industrial usage, built of steel that was now red with rust and maybe sixty feet in length. The bulge moved steadily toward them and then petered down and disappeared.

There was nothing to be seen or heard for the next half a minute. But then, abruptly, there came to our ears a sharp metallic rattle and the first barge in the line-up jerked against its moorings. More violent clattering came, more shaking, sending heavy ripples out across the water, and before our startled eyes the whole barge started tipping over on its end. Its anchor chain was being dragged upon by something underneath – doubtless the same something which had caused the mighty bow-wave. And as we watched the whole long iron boat lofted upright like some massive pencil placed inside a cup, then disappeared beneath the churning waves that this commotion had created.

Shortly after that, the process was repeated with the second barge. Were they somehow being devoured, or was this a destruction purely out of spite? Whatever, the culprit must have been of horrid strength and quite enormous size. Some massive, bloated kind of octopus, perhaps? Some underwater dragon, or a sibling of the fish-god Dagon? There was no way that we could tell, since whatever it was refused to show itself.

But this further confirmed the unsettling conclusion we had both already reached. Something horribly unnatural had been unleashed and we were seeing the effects of it, in worse manifestations every time.

"Those barges have stood there untouched for five years," Weller pointed out in a low muted whisper. "So whatever is taking them … it must have only arrived recently."

The fear that gripped us at that point was that the unseen assailant would tire of metal and would begin looking for some softer substance to enjoy. Spurred on by a profound and bilious dread, we headed away from the river's side.

By the time that we had got back to the road, another barge had disappeared and the fourth one was going down.

We were badly shaken but continued on, though into what we could not guess. And presently we came to the outer suburbs, once a part of Essex just as Stratford had once been. But a crumbling abandoned double-decker bus bore, in faded tones, the scarlet livery of London and the street signs had that city's postal codes. I used to know some of the people who had lived here, salt of the earth types who worked in the markets and the factories and gathered nightly in their local pubs. And I could almost hear the echo of their jovial voices singing on the air of crowded taverns, but the plain truth was they were all gone.

We went through street after narrow silent street lined with humble houses that were quite bereft of life. Around our feet there was a filthy mess of dust and lint and flaked-off paint. As we had seen earlier on, nature had moved in and was now taking control, saplings breaking up the pavement, ivy dragging down some walls. Trees were growing inside some homes, their branches poking out through shattered windows.

Which were all otherwise completely empty? Yes. All of them hollowed out like seashells. But I could not shake the feeling we were being watched.

Perhaps that new sense of dread was instilled by the presence of the Wall.

It hung above us right now and it was no longer like a mirage. You could go to the Grand Canyon and still not see an eminence so solid. Like a tsunami that had been frozen in time. Or like the palm of Shiva poised to strike. I could not help but shudder when I glanced at it.

It was so very high that – the further in that we progressed – the more it blocked the sunlight out so we were finally moving wholly in its shadow, as though we had been submerged in some moveless and unnatural twilight. But I could make out the great Wall's details far more clearly now, and it was not simply rubble I was looking at. Here, a broken section of a bed. There, the grille off the front of an automobile. There were softer patches full of faded colour that had once been clothes from people's wardrobes. There was even a little pink-rimmed wheel that might be off a small girl's bike. I almost sobbed when I saw that.

But it brought fresh thoughts into my mind. London might have turned to wickedness but not all of the people who had lived there had been so. Many innocents had perished in the blast, including countless numbers who had been only children. And so the Wall has two separate aspects. It stands firstly as a grim memorial to all those millions of lives discarded. And secondly, it stays there as a lasting testament to the cruel and bloodless ingenuity of human science, Oppenheimer and long-lost Ozymandius fused as one.

We were making our way up Stratford High Street now and approaching its huge, derelict multi-storey shopping mall, its great wide glass panes broken as the smaller windows had been. The station that was our goal was just off to the side of it, and we reached it before too much longer.

We stood quietly, ramrod straight, on the dust-strewn tiling of its entranceway, our legs aching gently because it had taken us a good few hours to reach this place. And when I glanced back, the light out in the countryside that we had travelled through was beginning to fade a touch.

"Perhaps it would be better if we waited till the morning before pressing on?"

But Weller only shook his head.

"I fail to see the point of that. There's neither day nor night where we are going."

I had to acknowledge he was right, but did that with a heavy heart. This entire expedition seemed abhorrent to me now, but would I improve matters by just turning back?

Our muted footsteps echoed round us as we ventured in. We clambered across the ticket barriers, which had been immobile for the past five years. And finally, we reached the platform and stepped down onto the track. Ahead of us, now, was the opening to the westbound tunnel, lined with brick and gaping like some reptile's mouth, its interior solidly and impenetrably black.

We donned the headlamps Weller had rigged up. Then we went onward into utter darkness.

CHAPTER FIVE

The Everlasting Dark

"Have you noticed it too?" Weller started asking me some fifty yards along. "It isn't just absence of the gulls. There ought to have been creatures living in those empty suburbs, foxes, squirrels and the like, all untouched by the Plague. But we saw nothing the entire way through. It strikes me that wild beasts possess far sharper senses than we humans do, and maybe they detected something that keeps them away."

"And even here," he continued, shining a bright flashlight down onto the floor between the tarnished metal rails, "there should at least be spiders, mice, but there is nothing, not a hint. We have encountered not a single sign of natural life since those blasted squabbling crows, and aren't they supposed to be an omen of ill-fortune?"

I had rarely heard him talk so quickly over such a stretch of time, but for a reply I could only shrug. We obviously reacted to taut apprehension differently.

He was right, though. There were not even any cobwebs, or at least not new ones, although there were large strands of something that might be a mould or else a peculiar type of moss hanging suspended from the roof.

Perhaps two hundred yards along this grimy passageway we paused, a grave solemnity overtaking us, since by our nearest calculations we were now directly underneath the Wall. And I could almost feel the weight of all those millions of dead people pressing down on us. I mouthed a silent prayer and even crossed myself, despite the fact I am not a Catholic. And then we continued on.

And I was horribly conscious, past that point, that we had actually reached the start of our objective. We were under the outskirts of London now, and that achievement spurred us on. I will not lie and say that we progressed enthusiastically, but there was now a purposefulness to our step.

We kept on scanning ahead with our flashlights, since our greatest fear was that the Oblivion blast might have caused a section of the ceiling to collapse, in which case all of our efforts thus far would be rendered null. But the tunnel ahead was fairly straight and it looked clear enough.

We had already travelled many miles, though, and had many more to go, and all of those beneath the dank enclosing earth. And as we headed on, the new resolve I had discovered gradually began to ebb. We were inside a space like none that I had ever before walked through. A place that natural light had never in its lifetime touched. A shaft that might have been forged by some blind and giant worm. The air was stale and did not stir, and the only sound was the traipsing of our feet. The world above was lost to us with all its different colours and its sounds. We may as well have been inside a tunnel on the Moon.

Claustrophobia began taking a gradual hold on me, and was starting to claw at me with real severity when at last – after the best part of an hour – we reached the next station down. Here the tunnel widened out to make room for another platform, which we scrabbled up onto, gasping with relief. This was Mile End station, underneath London's East End … far above our heads, some six years back, the sound of the Bow Bells would have frequently been heard. But all that we could hear now was our shaky, ragged breath.

Weller and I sat down on the concrete platform face-to-face, trying to calm down and truly thankful of each other's company by this stage of the trip. His features looked strangely distorted in my flashlight's beam. And he tried to smile, but the result was very stiff.

"I've never been afraid of tight spaces," said he, "till now."

"This is much harder than I thought," I was forced to concede.

"We have been travelling most of the day, and still have many miles to go. And so it might be better if we rested for a while before completing the last leg."

And I could see the logic in those words. Who knew what we might be facing up ahead or what limits it would push us to? To attempt that with weary limbs and fuddled minds ... it seemed a tactic that might lead us to disaster.

So we took more food and water from our backpacks, then unrolled the blankets we had brought. But just as I was smoothing mine out, the small flashlight I had strapped to my head swept across the platform's wall.

There were advertising posters still on it from more than five years back. Printed images and words that were an echo from a calm age that was almost lost from memory. BUY INSURANCE ... against what, the Screaming Death and The Oblivion Device? TAKE YOUR NEXT VACATION IN THAILAND ... yet it had taken us most of the day to journey less than twenty miles!

One ragged, faded missive in particular captured my attention, though. I was not even sure what product it was advertising. But it depicted a very happy family, a father and a mother, a young son and a daughter of a slightly younger age, all walking across a sunlit open field, hand-in-hand and grinning joyously.

"I've never even asked you this thing, Weller," I enquired of my companion, "but did you once have any kind of family that you could call your own?"

The man looked where I was looking and he seemed surprised at first, and almost offended. But then he stilled himself, his large frame sagging just a little and the shadowed lines of his face softening.

"Children?" he responded. "No, those turned out to be beyond my grasp. But there was once a woman I adored with all my soul."

The lustre in his eyes had dimmed and their focus had narrowed, as if he might be gazing intently at something only he could see, because it was far back in his own past.

"Did I love her because she was beautiful?" he asked. "She was, but that is no more than an accident of nature. Because she took care of my every need? She did, yet I reciprocated fully. And so … no, Graves, no. I loved her because she had a strong, courageous heart. I knew it the first time I looked at her."

And then he quickly turned away from me, wrapped himself in his own blanket and lay down and went completely still. He had not even told me what her name was, like it was a secret he would carry to the grave. Men who are distinguished always have a very private side.

But beyond that single moment, the relationship between us changed. We were no longer merely neighbours and we were no longer simply travelling companions. We had become confidantes, and therefore honest friends.

My gaze stayed on the poster for a while. I was remembering St. John's Wood and then Havering-atte-Bower. But finally I lay down myself, my tired eyelids fluttering shut.

As it turned out, though, sleep gave me no release. The nightmares that struck at me were terrible in the extreme. In them, I was locked up, alive, in some coffin or sarcophagus. Some tiny narrow lightless space beneath the soil, even more cramped than the tunnel I had been in. I screamed for help, except no one could hear. I scrabbled against the lid until my fingernails were torn and bloody. I even pounded at it with my *forehead*. All that did was render me half-blind.

Then there was a creaking all around me. The walls of my tomb were being probed at, after which the rotted wooden panels were being torn back. Skeletal hands came snaking in and began clawing at my shoulders and my throat. Then faces appeared at the gaps, with eyes that glowed a faint and sickly green.

Dead grey faces, half the skin fallen away and hanging loosely from the bare white bone. The noses and the ears were gone. Except these were the faces of my wife and daughter …

I awoke with a loud wail and a violent start, only to have that awful dreamscape reinforced by the reality that I was in. I *was* far beneath the ground. I *did seem* to be trapped down here. In my confused state, I honestly believed the whole tunnel was tightening around me, honestly believed the roof was coming down. I howled again and tried to thrash my limbs, but they were tangled in the blanket and the fact I could not move them took my terror to far greater heights.

"Graves?"

Weller was now crouching above me, but only as a featureless and blackened silhouette. Still caught in that limbo between dream and waking, I let out a thin high scream.

"*Daniel!*"

One of his large hands pressed down across my brow. The other fastened itself to my chest. And Weller held me firmly in place till my frantic seizures started to abate.

"Breathe, man, breathe, for heaven's sake. It's only your imagination."

And those words served to snap me out of that appalling trance. The cold light of reality came flooding back. It was still a few more minutes till my heartbeat slowed to normal and my lungs stopped hissing.

I sat up very slowly, mopped at my perspiring cheeks then thanked the man.

And he looked like he was going to respond. But before he could manage that, there came a sound from further up along the tunnel, in the same direction we were headed.

A very gentle slithering sound such as an eel might make when writhing on the ground. It seemed to be the case it was a good distance away and we could only hear it in the least because the walls around us magnified its pitch.

But maybe we were not entirely alone down in this dark place after all.

CHAPTER SIX

The Ragged Claws

Bethnal Green station was next, and so we were still beneath the old East End. Ahead of us lay a longer stretch of track that we knew came out at Liverpool Street ... an important terminus in its own right, for sure, but situated only at the outer edge of the financial district. And we had already determined that – if anything at all might be awaiting us – then we would most probably find it at the city's very heart. We had not nearly finished up our grim Odyssey yet.

That slithering sound that we had heard had unnerved us both slightly, though. And at first we were silent as we made our way beside the filthy, tarnished metal tracks, our senses alert for the tiniest hint of an intrusion. But as we continued, unhindered and hearing no more noises of that kind, we maybe tried to tell ourselves that we had been mistaken. It had been such a miniscule and very distant sound, and it could have been caused by nothing but a sudden rush of air someplace.

Weller took a breath in and then cleared his throat.

"What were we talking about earlier?" His voice was slightly tense, like he was partially embarrassed by the sentiments he had revealed. "It has to be a good part of the reason why we're here."

"How so?"

"Humankind has lost so much. Our way of life, our luxuries, but most of all those dearest to us. And if we survivors perish too, then even their memory is lost. We owe it to them to keep their flame burning. It's what human beings do."

"There's another way to put it, expressed by the Welshman Dylan Thomas. We should always rage against the dying of the light."

Weller nodded but did not respond, for something else was by now reaching our heightened senses. Not a sound this time but another odour. And another foul one. Our pace slowed.

At first I was afraid that it might be that same unwholesome perfume we had come across at Thorburn Creek. This seemed rather different, though. Rich and rank, meaty and aged, but somehow familiar too.

The most difficult thing was, we could not see its source because the tunnel up ahead of us bent slowly to the right, thus limiting our field of view.

Weller signalled I should stop then slipped his firearm off his shoulder. Going forward at a slow slight crouch, he reached the bend and peered around it for a while. And then he came quietly back and spoke to me in a hushed but slightly agitated tone.

"The side wall of the tunnel up ahead ... it has collapsed for at least several dozen yards. There's still room for us to get through, except it seems a sewer runs adjacent to these tracks and it has now been openly exposed."

Which information brought one word into my mind and one stark image up into my thoughts. The word was 'rats.' The image was those black-eyed ones who had massed against us on the riverbank.

But we were in a tunnel with but one way to progress, and there was no alternative.

No choice, no choice, no choice, no choice – a pounding mantra that could drive you mad. It was either face this or abandon our quest. I took my shotgun firmly in my grasp and we went forward like a pair of thieves.

The deep stench became even fouler as we rounded the soft curve. Revealed in our flashlights was a tumbled mass of brickwork lying on and in between the subway tracks and then a massive jagged depthless hole down one side of the tunnel from which the sickly airs were emanating. There was not even the opportunity to get past this place quickly, since the myriad scattered bricks made footwork very tricky. Awkwardly, we stepped between them, taking great care not to disturb them and make a sudden rattling noise. Our gazes remained fixed the entire while on that large breach in the abutting wall, watching for an abrupt scuttling motion or for even the small gleam of a dark eye.

Nothing like that in the slightest came. And if there had been vermin in that gap then surely they would have detected us, however softly we might tread? It seemed our fears had been for nought. I swallowed – it was like a stone had been lodged in my throat. And then I raised a hand to wipe my brow. Then stopped.

That slithering noise we had heard much earlier came abruptly to my ears again. I lurched back and almost yelled, but brought my gun to bear instead.

Something had emerged from the sewer, except it was not any rat. To tell the truth, I was not quite sure *what* it was! Protruding from the open hole and lying limply on the piled up bricks, it gleamed faintly in my beam of electric light.

It was translucent and gelatinous, no wider than my smallest finger. No more, really, than a strand of mucus. Maybe it had dropped down from the tunnel's ceiling, or a sudden gaseous eruption in the sewer had discharged it out?

But then my brow began to furrow as my light followed the thing along. No, but it could not have fallen from the roof, since it extended back the entire way into the gap that we were still going past. Part of it was still under the dank and reeking waters of the sewer and ... attached to some other thing, perhaps?

Suddenly, the strand of mucus moved, and not in any way that I had been expecting. It abruptly split apart along its length, and not just once but several times.

It had started lifting off the brickwork now, and it had formed itself into a shape something like the narrowest of hands – one with seven very long spindly fingers, each of which had numerous joints.

And before I could react they snatched at me, closing sharply around my left ankle.

I was still wondering how such a thing as this could even harm me when they tightened with such force I yelled in pain. I had been pulled completely off my feet next moment, was flat down on my back and being dragged toward the sewer at an incredible speed.

Weller was above me in a flash, his large machete gleaming in his hand. He swung and instantly the pain was gone, the pale translucent claw dropping away. My friend hauled me upright in one fluid motion – not the first time that he had done that.

And none too soon! Still more of those limpid tentacles were now emerging from the sewer. Dozens of them, each one opening up to seven narrow, ragged fingers.

Weller's blade swung over and again, humming, resonating, spraying hundreds of fragments of transparent mucus through the air. And for myself, since I possessed no such weapon, I let loose with my shotgun.

A filthy, frothy bubbling started up beneath the waters of the sewer, as if something below its redolent surface was emitting a fierce scream ... whether of pain or rage I could not tell.

But all quiet progress was forgotten now. We went backward as quickly as we could, oftentimes stumbling on the scattered bricks. The grasping claws managed to follow us for quite a longer distance than we thought they should, the tentacles behind them stretching out until they were almost hair-thin.

But once we were out of their reach we stopped and waited breathlessly, afraid that something even worse might loom out into view. The owner of those tentacles, perhaps? From the amount of violent churning in the sewer, it was something pretty huge.

No disfigured beast came lumbering out, though. We could hear the waters of the sewer quieten down till they were almost still.

It became apparent, however, that when I had been dragged along the floor I had left behind most of the contents of my backpack. The remainder of my food, my blanket and even some batteries.

And more translucent claws – we had damaged many but there seemed to be a quite endless supply of them – were reaching from the gap, grabbing hold of them and dragging them away into the slimy depths, several of the batteries splitting open from the sheer force of their vicious grip.

We looked on with numb gazes till they finished up the last and disappeared from whence they came.

Weller took a slow, unsteady breath.

"Well, at least you still have your gun."

He wiped his machete on a rail and then returned it to its sheath.

"And now we know why there is not a single rat."

Yet his words did not serve to even slightly comfort me. That filthy beast that we had left behind, you see – whatever its shape and size – had to be like nothing that mankind had ever previously met in the natural world, some manner of undreamt-of and obscene abomination.

And if such entities existed now, if creatures out of nightmare had escaped into our world ... then what else might be waiting for us, lurking in the gathered shadows up ahead?

Chapter Seven

That Which Should Not Be

Past Liverpool Street there was Bank station, so called because it had once been adjacent to the Bank of England on Threadneedle Street. This had been, in previous years, the gateway to the old financial district and was possibly close in enough. And so we headed up along some grimy passageways until we reached the lofty flight of moving stairs – silent now and absolutely dead – that ought to lead us up to the ground level.

But they were wholly blocked with shattered rubble, all put there by the ferocious blast of The Oblivion Device, and utterly impassable. So we retraced our steps and then continued down the tunnel.

Fortunately, the closer to the centre that the subway system got then the nearer set together were its stations, many of them less than half a mile apart. We next came to St. Paul's, named after the nearby grand cathedral. But it turned out that our way up was similarly impaired. And the same was true of Chancery Lane, beneath the old-time legal district.

And when the same sort of obstruction greeted our dismayed gazes at Holborn station too, a dark and furious mood took hold of me.

"We can't get out!" I raged, my voice echoing through the enclosed lightless space. "We've wasted all this time and effort! The Device, with its scouring motion, has sealed every exit shut!"

And I expected Weller to share in my anguish, but to my surprise he did not. A pensive look stiffened his features and he glanced back across his shoulder.

"Stick with me, man," he advised.

And without a single other word, he turned on his heel and went jogging swiftly off. I followed after him with genuine bemusement, since he seemed to know something I did not.

His route took us through subterranean passageways we had not gone through on our way up here. And when he headed down another, shorter staircase I realised he was not returning to the railway that we had been following thus far … he was being guided by the signposts to the Piccadilly Line.

We came to the westbound platform of the same and we both headed down that brand-new avenue.

Only to dismount again at Leicester Square and then go through the same procedure, weaving through a warren of footways, our boots resounding on the solid floor.

He chose the Northern Line this time and as he went along it his pace seemed to speed up even more, which precisely matched my growing, stark bewilderment.

"Where precisely are you taking us?" I cried out. "What exactly do you hope to find?"

"All we've passed so far are normal stops, with only one way in and out. But up ahead of us lies Charing Cross. Not only do two lines bisect there but there is a railway terminus set directly above. A massive place with dozens of platforms and with many points of egress and on numerous levels."

Hunting back through the oppressed depths of my memory, I could see that he was right. I had shunned London for such a stretch of time that I had almost put such details from my mind.

We finally slowed since we had reached our goal. This platform looked like any other, but we headed upward with an air of expectation.

At first, though, our hopes were dashed. The first couple of exits that we tried were sealed as tightly as the rest had been. But Weller did not give up.

"If I remember it correctly, there's a passage somewhere to our left that leads you up into the mainline station. And the exit there is wider than the rest, and so less likely to be totally obscured."

We backtracked a few dozen yards until we found the passage he was speaking of. And when we followed it along, it opened up onto a broad, ascending flights of stairs. But there was still a pile of debris at the top.

"Except it's not all rubble!" Weller pointed out.

And he went rushing up and started scrabbling at the filthy heap. I still felt dubious, but joined him in this task.

Sheets of metal plate work fell away. There were some smaller lumps of concrete we could move by hand. There was some broken wood that must have come from one of the old station's many kiosks. Finally, what stood before us was a massive swathe of board, some kind of advertising placard. And when Weller shoved at it, it moved a couple of inches but no more.

"There must be more stonework on top of it," was his conclusion. "With me, Daniel. Push, man, *push*!"

And so we set our shoulders to it like some pair of pint-sized Atlases, straining till the cords stood out in both our necks. The board yielded another inch and then two further ones. Then suddenly there was a clatter from behind the thing.

It abruptly became a whole lot lighter and we shoved it out of our way easily. But as it slammed down emptily against the floor, I and my companion both went still as if some Gorgon had just stared into our eyes and we had both been turned to stone.

We had been expecting to regain the open air, and gratefully too after so long in all those tunnels. We had been hoping to see the sky and set our feet on the Earth's top.

Instead of which, our flashlight beams rose several dozen yards. And then they hit the inside of a solid roof.

This was not *possible*!

How could it even *be*?

As slowly and as stiffly as a pair of automatons, myself and Weller climbed the rest of the way out and stared around with rigid disbelief.

We were inside a huge and largely square structure, with not just a roof but having distant walls as well. There were no features to the place, no platforms and no ticket booths, no stores and no cafes. A sparse facsimile of the station that had been here, then, as empty as a hollow shell. Except that this made not the slightest sense.

The Oblivion Device ought to have ploughed this whole wide area as flat as a desert, here where we were standing and for many miles about. Every single building was supposed to have been swept away as though on some gigantic tide.

But this was certainly not the original Charing Cross ... so had it appeared *after* the enormous blast?

In which case ... by what means, and who had put it here? And what earthly purpose did it serve? I could find no answers to these questions, or at least not one that bore the tiniest inspection from the bounds of logic. My mind was reeling and yet numb.

When I looked around at Weller his firm jaw was hanging open and his eyes had a reflective sheen as though they were attempting to reject the bizarre images reaching them. Our breath was heavy in our throats and neither of us had the strength to speak.

Then I gazed around again and noticed something else. The surfaces above and around us ... they were not brick or even concrete. This ceiling and these walls were built of some extremely pale material that reflected my flashlight's beam with the weakest of gleaming lustres. And there were peculiar upright ridges all along them too, and I had no idea what had caused those.

Who could tell how long we stood there? We were both almost in shock, but finally we managed to loosen up a touch.

Our footsteps echoed weirdly when we moved. Our gazes darted round with trepidation. But no other shadows moved. We seemed to be the only people in this place.

We were headed for where an exit ought to be that one time had opened out onto that famous London avenue, The Strand. The walls were getting closer now, and as they came into a better focus then a sudden apprehension took a hold of me. My jaw went stiff. My hands began to shake. Because that strange pale off-white colour and those upright ruts ... these seemed to be thousands of tiles, all firmly locked together and slightly convex in shape, each of them some eighteen inches tall but only a few inches wide. And I had never gazed on any structure quite like this before and I could make no sense of it.

When suddenly, it struck me forcibly what I was really looking at, and the horror which accompanied that revelation was so utterly intense I nearly yelled.

These were *not* tiles! No, they were *human bones*, many thousands of the things! Both my hands went to my mouth to suppress a prolonged wail. My head whirled fiercely and my eyesight blurred, and for a while all reason was lost to me.

Then the questions started to pour in. These were, apparently, some of the remains of all those millions who had perished when The Oblivion Device had been set off. But ought they not be in the Wall? Who had pulled them out of there? Who or what had gathered them all up and forged them into this insane construction?

I could see no way it could be done, or at least not by any human endeavour. And so what terrible, unholy necromancy was this that I was staring at?

Ewan Weller looked as thunderstruck and utterly confounded as I felt.

We were almost at the exit to the awful structure now. Beyond the opening, a silvery wash of moonlight glimmered down.

We paused at the very threshold, stiffening up expectantly, trying to prepare ourselves for whatever new tests to our sanity might come.

And in that stillness, we heard something of a like we had never even dreamed.

Out there in what ought to be the flat and blasted wastes that had been London, we could hear a distant voice.

CHAPTER EIGHT

Into The Abyss

It only lasted for a few seconds before it faded off to a profound, echoing silence. Yet – even to our tortured senses – it sounded quite remarkably strange. Nothing at all like a human voice, rather a thin and reedy babbling, the words all strung together without break and in a language we could not discern. We strained to pick out more of it but it did not return, or not immediately, at least.

But we were freshly stunned by this brand-new occurrence. That there was a building here where nothing should remain was quite incredible enough. But someone – something? – capable of speech, and in a city that we had believed to be destroyed completely? We went on as slowly as a pair of men caught up in some fantastical opium-dream.

The moon above us ... it was almost full. There were practically no clouds, and so it was bathing the entire scene around us in its warmthless and pellucid glow. And gazing upon that extraordinary scene, I felt rooted to the spot.

It was not only Charing Cross that had been recreated. No, it was the street out beyond the station – or at least in part.

There were no sidewalks and no other detailed features. But apart from that, The Strand itself had been recreated in the same way that I dimly remembered it. The same height roofs, the same shaped storefronts, marching off away from us in two parallel lines. I could even make out, to my right, the large outline of the Savoy Hotel. But just past that – where this great boulevard had used to continue on to Waterloo Bridge and then Fleet Street – the structures petered off and there was only open ground beyond.

These empty facades were made of bone as well and glistered softly in the cold moonlight. And once again the questions came. What use were they? What purpose did they serve? Some ghostly echo of the great metropolis that had once been, mayhap? Except that they were absolutely solid and we could both see the truth of that.

So what had made this happen? *Why?*

A thin high voice made itself heard again and caused us to jolt. Our shotguns were now firmly in our grasps. Yet it was not merely a brief babbling this time but a constant string of utterances, once again issued so swiftly that they might have been a single word. The sound was coming from our left. Moving quietly and keeping low, we made our way toward that unearthly noise, crossing the wide thoroughfare in order to remain behind the cover of the final building.

And The Strand let out onto an open space we had once known extremely well – the whole world had. A massive space, Trafalgar Square. And it too had been recreated.

Over at the top was the huge National Gallery, rendered in a hundred thousand bones. Near it were the edifices that had housed the High Commissions of South Africa and Canada. And there was even, most obscenely, the beloved church of St. Martin in the Fields with its vast portico and row of huge Corinthian columns ... in earlier and better days, it had been a place renowned for charity and lively arts.

No cross stood at the peak of its roof now. Instead there was some bizarre spiralled shape that might have been a serpent trying to devour its own tail.

Even worse was still to come, for out there on the square there were no longer any fountains but there was the famous Column. Except with no proud Admiral Lord Nelson at the top. Instead, there was some kind of ghastly upright demon with a vulture's wings and with sharp spikes protruding from its head. And the same was true of the two other main statues on the square, Kings George the Fourth and Charles the First being replaced with similar monstrosities, the latter mounted upon not a horse but on some sort of writhing Hydra.

All of this appalled us deeply, but was trumped by the fact we could see living creatures out there too, the source of the weird sounds that we had heard. And they were nothing like human beings. The same general shape, for sure, but far shorter than a normal man and appallingly thin, etiolated, hairless. As pale as the moonlight striking down on them, and so I thought at first they might be phantoms. Only Luna's rays did not pass through them. They were solid flesh of one kind or another.

They were dressed in white cloaks so extremely ragged I could make out flashes of the pallid skin beneath. And they were all facing away from us and right down on their hands and knees, just hundreds of the wraith-like things.

They were all angled toward the Column. And seated on its massive sloping base – lolling like some bloated Persian emperor – was the most dreadful apparition of them all.

It was hard to be certain from the way the beast was sprawled, but it appeared to be some kind of giant ape at least twenty feet in height. Surplus fur hung down in matted curtains from its shoulders and its lengthy arms. It was prodigiously overweight, great rolls of fat quivering at its belly. Its flattened and yet heavily-creased face was somewhere between a gorilla's and orangutan's, though neither creature has such massive yellowed fangs protruding from its lower jaw. Its eyes – which rarely blinked – were a bilious shade of yellow mixed with orange. And, most bizarrely, sprouting from its head there was a pair of big thick curling horns like you might find upon a ram.

It wore a thin gold crown about its brow, and in its right hand it was clutching a large silver trident, holding it in the same way that a monarch might bear a sceptre.

All was silent for a breathless moment. Then the source of the noises that we had been hearing was revealed.

One of the wraith creatures pushed itself up on its knees. It tipped its narrow head back so that it could face its hideous lord. And, spreading wide its skeletal arms, it began to yell out in a language which I could not fathom, but in what sounded like a shrill complaining tone. Was it bemoaning its strange fate and asking for reprieve? But it kept up its entreaties for some minute and a half and then went back down on all fours again.

Only for another to repeat the same procedure, its begging even more strident than we had heard before. The next one flailed its thin arms as it screeched. And the one beyond that beat at its breast and even tore at its pale garments.

I could not understand a single word they said, but managed to pick out three short syllables that were repeated over and again. Garga'heth. So maybe that was the great vile ape's name.

For its part, the hirsute beast reacted only with contempt and apathy. It shrugged its shoulders and it rolled its eyes. And it pursed its flabby mouth, pushing out foul-smelling eructations that made its blubbery thick lips quiver mockingly.

But what on earth *was* all this? This chilling, lifeless reproduction of the Square? And this ludicrous ritual, an absurd pantomime devoid of meaning? How long would this joyless comedy go on ... for hours? Days? For weeks? Forever?

Then the truth finally occurred to me. I had been wrong in my original surmise ... my 'what on earth.' But this was not *of* our earth, not in the slightest bit. No, this was something from another world. Another plane of being or perhaps even another Universe.

Yet how had it arrived here? Had it been our fault ... had mankind set the stage? Firstly with this town's steep descent into wickedness? Then with the way its people had behaved when the Plague had descended on us? And then finally with the seeding of the terrible Oblivion Device, wiping out millions of lives at a single stroke?

Had we in fact defied the laws of God and Nature, creating a vacuum into whose dark bosom had been drawn these ghastly denizens from another place? And now that they had made their home among us would they ever plan to go away?

A fifth wraith was halfway upright now, wailing as pathetically as all those who had gone before. But then it made a horrible mistake – it shuffled forward a few inches on its knees.

That seemed to break some kind of rule. Garga'heth – if that was his

name – stiffened and sat up a little, his jaw tightening and his pendulous simian brow abruptly furrowing. His eyes blazing balefully, he swung his trident around in one fleshy paw, lunged out with it and skewered the wraith-thing through its waist.

No blood showed but the wan creature still wailed piteously. Struggling, it was lofted up into the air and swung toward its simian master. Garga'heth studied it amusedly, then wrenched it off the fork with his free hand. Then leant forward and bit its head off.

Still it continued to writhe. The horned ape commenced to mumble at the torso with its teeth until there were only the legs left, joined together by a ragged strip of skin. Garga'heth held them between one finger and thumb – and yes, reader, they were still kicking – then tossed them in his open maw and swallowed them in one swift gulp.

Thus refreshed, he raised his trident in the air and grunted some short phrases that were gravel-toned and entirely unintelligible. And the instant he had finished those, there were painfully bright flashes round the huge spear's triple tips. Which hovered there a single moment and then shot away like lightning bolts that broke up into dozens of oppressively bright strands, bouncing off the walls of the surrounding buildings, flaring up into the void and even careening wildly till they hit the nearby river – even from this distance I could hear it hiss and bubble.

The full pale moon above our heads seemed to fade off to a weaker and less vivid hue. The sky above us grew darker and swirling shadows seemed to move up there. And that was when the explanation of this entire thing occurred to me.

This was not merely a deformed gargantuan ape that I was gazing numbly at. It was some kind of demon from a Hell Dimension and was letting loose its vicious and demented magic. Making changes to our world, and perhaps letting other creatures in.

And how did the surviving wraiths react to everything they had beheld these last couple of minutes? They remained completely still, although I thought I could detect a few starved-looking elbows shudder. But then a sixth creature went right up on its knees and began that horrid warbling again, like nothing of significance had even happened.

Whatever place these things had come from, why, it had to be a plane of being where hopelessness and pointlessness and also utter madness reigned.

And it seemed to be infecting me, because my thoughts were moving in my head so very slowly I could scarcely decipher them. I was absolutely rigid and was soaked in sweat. Words and action were beyond my grasp.

Not so Weller. Stealthily, he reached into his pocket and drew something out.

Four red cartridges. Except I knew his shotgun was already loaded.

"Elephant rounds," he explained in a whisper. "Not scattered shot but solid lead. Another thing I have been saving these five years, and now they have a fitting purpose."

Was he honestly suggesting we attack these beasts? The whole idea of that sent shockwaves through my frame. But my attempt to stop him was a very feeble one – all that I could manage was to try and hold his arm with fingers that were absolutely numb. He turned his face away and shook me off, carefully emptying his shotgun's chamber and then quietly loading the new ordnance.

"Weller!" I croaked in a hoarse tight voice. "No, you will bring destruction down on both of us!"

His head went from side to side.

"You saw what that ape just did. Its powers are unleashing everything we've seen so far, here and at the river and at Thorburn Creek."

"But …"

"We must at least try," he muttered, "for if we do not stop this thing then I fear that it will bring down horror not merely on us but on the entire world beyond."

Mere seconds later he was on the move, and all that I could do was watch him.

Crouching low and moving silently, Weller sprinted down the southern boundary of the square, his moonlit shadow stretching out before him as he ran. The landscape afforded him no cover but the wraiths still had their backs to him and the horned ape, caught up once again in profound lethargy, was sprawled right back with its face turned to the sky.

Weller reached the large statue of Charles the First and hunkered down behind it. He now had a direct line of fire on the horned ape, nothing getting in the way of his first shot, and yet he paused. The creature was still lolling back, its head obscured – from my friend's angle – by the glutinous protrusion of its gut. Had it been me behind that gun I would have, driven on by sheer nervousness, still taken the shot. And missed, and failed. But Weller waited.

Another wraith rose up and began winnowing. And to my tortured mind, time seemed to have slowed down to the utmost crawl, every passing second drawn out so horribly painfully it seemed this interval might never end.

This new pale figure kept up its incessant chant. Its tone was even shriller than the rest had been. And that appeared to stir something in Garga'heth, and the huge beast grunted and peered at its supplicant.

Which brought its forehead into view.

Weller leant across the statue's upper edge and fired.

Chapter Nine

The Hordes of Garga'heth

It seemed to my startled and frenzied imagination that the span of time between the shot being fired and it striking home was interminable in length. And I know for a fact that cannot possibly be true, but the terror and anxiety inflicted on me by the terrible sights I had beheld had distorted my thoughts and warped all of my senses, so that everything was magnified or else stretched out eternally. I believed that I could actually see the elephant round flying to its target. I believed that I could hear it humming through the air. When Garga'heth blinked, I thought that I could hear that too. In fact, the noise of that brief motion seemed to roll like thunder up against my ears.

The scene ahead of me froze solid and came tightly into focus for a single moment. Then a hole appeared in Garga'heth's temple.

Orange-yellow pus of the same colour as the creature's eyes started welling up beneath it. But that only happened for the briefest second. The very next instant, the wound had disappeared again.

And – my reader – I cannot explain that process any better than I have just done. The rent in skin and skull did not heal up. It did not close over. There was nothing natural about what my gaze took in. One moment the injury was there and the next moment it was not, and so I did not understand it at the time but I have had a while to think about it since.

Garga'heth and his underlings did not come from our plane of being, so they were not subject to its rules – or at least, not to any truly meaningful degree. It was a fact the lead bullet had struck its target clean and true. It was *another* fact that it had had an effect, punching a hole in that hideous brow. But these were facts of *our* world and this bizarre beast could move past them.

Garga'heth shook his head briefly like a whining gnat was bothering him. And then his darkly-rutted face screwed up into a mask of savage, primal fury, all his yellowed fangs in view. He sat up very sharply, pointing at Weller with the three points of his trident, and he roared.

Every single one of the pallid wraiths that had been on their hands and knees before the great ape straightened up, in a single movement. And as one, they turned round from the waist.

Their faces were so elongated they were practically like exclamation points. They had no eyebrows and no ears I could make out, just shallow indentations where such things should be. Their mouths were open and completely round, with not a hint of any teeth.

But most terrible of all, they had no eyes, only empty sockets that were condensed pits of shadow.

Nonetheless their gazes – if that was even the right word? – seemed to fix on Weller and remained there steadily. And I felt certain there was baleful hatred in those stares.

To give my friend his credit, he appeared to figure out that there was very little point in trying to stay hidden. Cool-headedly, his movements smooth, he raised himself fully from behind the statue, then replaced the shotgun at his shoulder and he fired a second time. And the same thing happened I had seen before. Another hole appeared ... but then was gone.

Garga'heth did not simply roar this time. His jaws split open hugely and he howled, so furiously I felt the ground shake underneath me and the bone-built structures all around me seemed to tremble on their bases.

And on that enraged signal, the wan and eyeless wraiths all sprang up to their feet and rushed toward my courageous companion.

Weller did not even try to run – perhaps he saw it would be little use. He was standing his ground now with the shotgun at his hip, pumping and then firing as quickly as he could.

Every last one of his shots struck home, huge gouges being torn in the wraiths' drab flesh. But – as before – it only lasted for one breath before a different reality asserted itself. Even those pale figures he had fired on squarely kept on coming and surrounded him.

❧

It fair breaks my heart to relate the hideous events which occurred beyond that point. My mind fogs over at the memory of them and my hand trembles as I try to set them down.

Yet that reflects the dire condition I found myself in as I watched my true friend being overwhelmed. I was fixed very solidly in place, my mouth wide open but devoid of sound, one arm stretched out, the extended palm shaking furiously but helplessly as well. I wanted desperately to give assistance to the man, to somehow intervene, but I could tell it would be absolutely useless.

And would you call me a coward now? But no, reader. A coward is a man who shies away from something difficult and dangerous, but still possible. And this was not.

There was a great swarm of the wraiths round Weller by this stage, although they were not able to close in completely. Having fired his final blast, the man had turned his shotgun around in his hands and was swinging it like he might swing a wooden club. And he connected several times … the wraiths were so fragile that the impact sent then flying, though they rapidly arose back up, like nothing had happened, and rejoined the mob.

And Ewan found that he could not defend himself from every angle; there were hundreds of the wretched beasts. One and then another landed on his back and wrapped their grasping arms around his face and throat. At which point he lost his balance, stumbling forward with the shotgun falling from his grasp. And before I even knew it, the wretched pallid things were all across him.

I think I must have moaned with grief at that point, since my brother in this adventure had disappeared from sight. All I could make out was a writhing mass of near-colourless thrashing bodies. The narrow faces I could see were all distorted with pure fury. Narrow arms and spindly fingers rose and fell and flailed. And I felt certain that my friend was gone, torn to pieces almost instantly.

Thinking back on what transpired, that would have been by far the kinder fate.

For – even caught up in their bloodlust and their rage – these awful wraiths still had the mind-set of mere underlings. Servile creatures, and so ever mindful of the needs of their gargantuan Lord. Gradually, the flailing stopped. Weller came back into view again. The shaking of my arm ceased and the world seemed to go very still.

The dignified, composed man of the past couple of days was gone. In its place? A human shape, for sure, but one I barely recognized. He appeared only semi-conscious. Glistening blood flowed freely from his mouth and nose, the latter of which appeared to be broken. And he was half-naked too, his jacket gone completely and his shirt now hanging from him as thin ragged strips of cloth. And those were stained with blood as well, from deep abrasions all across his body where the frenzied wraiths had clawed at him.

Darkened bruises were beginning to well up on the surface of his skin as well. Caught in the grip of several dozen wraiths, Weller was hauled back up to his feet – vertical, yes, but with his large head lolling to one side. And with the dim light of the watching moon shining down on his flesh luminously, he no longer looked quite real. More like some martyr out of old biblical times, depicted in oils by such as Delacroix.

A brief and reedy babbling arose, as though the wraiths were all discussing their next path of action. And, having reached a decision, they dragged their captive back across the square until he was pinned beneath the baleful gaze of Garga'heth.

Had they not been holding him upright and with his arms stretched fully out to either side, Weller would most probably have collapsed to the ground again. His many wounds were still streaming with blood and his many other injuries were showing clearly in the moonlight now.

But then – as the enormous horned ape kept on staring down at him

– the true nature of his character started to emerge. His head, which had been lolling to the right, came slowly up. And the slight backward tilt of it proved to me that he had raised his chin. Weller's back was to me and I could no longer see his face but his whole posture as he stared back at the giant beast spoke of bold defiance.

Was Garga'heth even used to a reaction such as this? From what my eyes had told me, he came from a world in which servility and begging were the norm. The ape's shoulders jerked a little and a sound quite like a tiny gasp came out from between his rubbery lips. Next instant, though, his sickly orange-yellow gaze was starting to glaze over.

And his entire face contorted with a pure and practically volcanic fury. He sat fully up – good Lord, did he ever stand? He gnashed his yellowed teeth so fiercely I could hear that too and then let out a mindless roar, his eyes doubly wide now and his trident being brandished in one mighty paw.

I felt myself go rigid when I saw that, honestly believing he would use that triple spear to skewer my friend. Except the outcome was far worse.

Garga'heth raised his free hand high up in the air, waving it in a summoning gesture. Who or what he was beckoning to I was not nearly sure at first.

But mere seconds later, the answer came. From the barren bone facsimile of the National Gallery, from both the High Commissions and, yes, even from St. Martin's Church, my question was answered in one vast appalling tide of ragged, pallid white. There were not simply the few hundred wraiths that I had seen. No, there were *thousands* of the wretched things, each of them with rounded toothless mouths and hollow sockets where their eyes should be. All of them identical as though they had been pressed from the same mould.

Their miserable shrieks filling the air, they all came piling down the broad steps of the buildings that they had been hiding in and rushed across the square, surrounding Weller with a heaving mass of writhing paleness.

And it seemed they had not arrived unprepared. Some of them had brought along – and my tortured mind wondered why – two massive planks of wood that had been somehow fixed together as a massive X. Others had brought along great coils of rope. And in the clasp of a few others ... were those lengthy nails?

Weller was lifted by a hundred pairs of bony hands until the creatures had him suspended and prone above their heads. He tried to struggle but could not resist such numbers and the crowd passed him along that way till they set him down upon the wooden X.

And to my utter horror, they commenced to crucify him there. I turned my head away, bile filling up my mouth and my jaw setting so brutally it felt as though the joint might snap.

But more – and even more appalling – was to come. These creatures from some elsewhere plane, they were not even finished with him yet.

One of them clamped the end of a big length of rope between its toothless gums and then went scrabbling up that filthy parody of Nelson's Column, going up as swiftly as a wall-lizard and taking the cord with it as it climbed. It looped a coil around the statue at the top and then threw the remainder down. And, once it had been fastened to the cross, brave Ewan Weller – still alive – was hoisted up into the air.

An abrupt silence fell across the square, the pale wraiths staring up but going very still. It soon became apparent why. Garga'heth himself was studying this awful thing that he had ordered done. His brow was hunched in thoughtfulness and one great paw was stroking at his chin. But finally he shook his head, than pointed to the gently glistening roof of St. Martin in the Fields.

The response of the wraiths was instantaneous. Dozens of them were now climbing upward and more ropes were being flung across until a spider's web of them stood out against the sky. And by such means Weller was swung across until the creatures had him fixed atop the high roof of that once-beloved sanctuary.

I could feel the fingernails of both my hands dig deeply into the wet flesh of my palms. This was nothing but a wretched, filthy blasphemy, but that fact seemed to delight Garga'heth even more. A huge triumphant grin spread out across his face. He clapped his hands together in applause, then tipped his mighty head back and released a belching laugh.

And the great horde of wraiths took the delight of their master as an instantaneous cue. When their voices started being raised again – and they all seemed to come at once – they were just as reedy as before, but lifted in merriment this time. They cried out joyously. They let out braying sounds

that might well have been their version of laughter. And they began to caper and to dance, whirling round and round each other.

It was at that point that my mind broke, shattering to fragments like some finely-wrought balloon glass squeezed tight in the fierce grasp of some stone-skinned ogre.

Chapter Ten

Along the Paths of Madness

And that being the case, I recall very little of my journey back. Brief jumbled flashes of memory return to me every so often, none of them in a sequential order and a few of them making no slightest sense at all. But how I made it through that vast and lightless warren of long subterranean tunnels and cramped foot passages, how I found my way even back to Stratford … all of that remains a quite profound enduring mystery.

What a hideous sight I must have made. A shivering, quaking escapee from Hell, my eyes so blind with madness they were like milk-coloured glass, my fingers clawing at my twitching lips, from which drool trickled down my chin. And gibbering to myself as well and letting out inhuman shrieks.

I must have again passed the foul thing in the sewer with its many claws, so how did I escape the beast? I seem to recall – though it might be false – that I howled so wildly and I writhed so furiously that the creature must have taken me for some crazed devil and so, fearing for its own safety, it let me through untouched.

Finally, and still insane, I stumbled out into the new day's light. I wept to see it – I remember that. But beyond that point there ensued a great measureless span of time in which I stumbled blindly through the eastern suburbs, entirely confused and completely lost. The more I tried to find my way out, then the more my desperation transformed into panic. And I kept on moving ever faster, careening off objects that were in my path. (I still have bruises on my hips and thighs that attest to those violent collisions, not to mention reddened grazes on my palms that seem to prove that I fell over several times).

But at long last I found my way back to the open Essex countryside. And my sanity, though only slowly, started to come back to me. I say 'slowly' since when I saw a flock of crows perched high up in a tree I raved at them and shook my fists.

The sun was starting to go down again by the time that I had reached the part of the main road where the incline rises and the river can be seen. The waters of the Thames now looked wholly black, and of the two dozen great metal barges Weller and I had previously seen, not a single one remained. A great bulge was still moving deep beneath the surface though and, my mind clearer now, I hurried quickly on.

It was nearing midnight when I arrived back at the settlement. Not a single light was on in the window of any cabin, but the full moon of the previous evening still shone down upon the flattened land and so I made my way to my home easily.

Remember, though, that I and Weller had set off from there without a word, explaining neither where we might be going to nor what our urgent business was. And so I did not wake up any of my neighbours, no. I let myself quietly in, settled down uncomfortably upon my bed. And lying there fully-clothed, I remained for several hours with my eyes wide open and unblinking, the horrors I had witnessed all still spilling through my mind.

When sleep finally came it was filled – of *course* it was – with nightmares so extraordinarily vivid that I could not tell them from reality. Garga'heth loomed right up close, his hideous features mere inches from mine, his vile breath choking my lungs, his jaws stretched hugely to devour me.

And then the beast from underneath the Thames came slopping out and it was truly vast and had a million grasping tentacles.

The wraiths were all around me, next. And beyond them, Weller was nailed to that cross and he was pleading with me to deliver him.

I was woken by fists pounding at my door.

"What's wrong, Graves?" voices asked.

Which was when I realised I had been screaming very loudly in my sleep. Several of my near neighbours came pushing in. They dragged me upright and then tried to calm me, and a pitcher of sour red wine was brought.

And once my fits and trembling had eased, they told me of the ills that had befallen our encampment.

Those huge mosquitoes I had seen near Thorburn Creek had come drifting closer in and sucked the blood of several of our people. And those poor folks were now struck down with a bizarre ailment, some kind of strange fever which rendered them delirious and made them speak of things that could not be (or so the small crowd round me thought). One victim had murmured of a giant ape, and so I recognised this ague's source.

And as evening had approached, the black-eyed rats had come as well, attacking anybody in their path. And a woman they had bitten had gone dark-eyed too, turning savagely on those same good Samaritans who had been trying to dress her wounds – there had been no choice except to load another shotgun and then put her down.

"You've been missing for a whole two days, Graves. Where exactly did you go, and where is Ewan Weller?"

But I refused to answer those earnest requests. My head stayed down and would not budge. And finally – suspecting I was merely suffering from exhaustion – my neighbours left me to myself. Dawn had still not risen as yet.

Sitting stiffly on the edge of my mattress, my thoughts turned back to everything that I had witnessed in the past couple of days. That unseen presence in the Thames. Those myriad claws back in the tunnel. The vast horned ape and all its supplicants. And as I dwelled on these horrific facts, another realisation came on me.

The Plague had taken many billions. The Oblivion Device had slaughtered millions more. But human beings come and go from this world and the deeds they do – both good and wicked ones – are merely fleeting and quite transitory. Yet I now knew that there existed a Vast Force which no disease could ever quell and no bomb could wipe out.

It is called Evil, and it never dies. And that truth chilled me to the core.

My chin lifted a little and I noticed there was no green glow limning the edges of my window, as there had been for the past half-decade.

Very slowly, I stood up and went across till I could pull aside my curtains. At which point my mind seemed to fracture for a second time.

For the green illumination above London was completely gone. In its place there was a quite impenetrable horrid utter blackness, darker even than the night. And it did not fade, not by the tiniest degree, when the sun at last began to lift.

Instead, it was spreading out.

About the Author

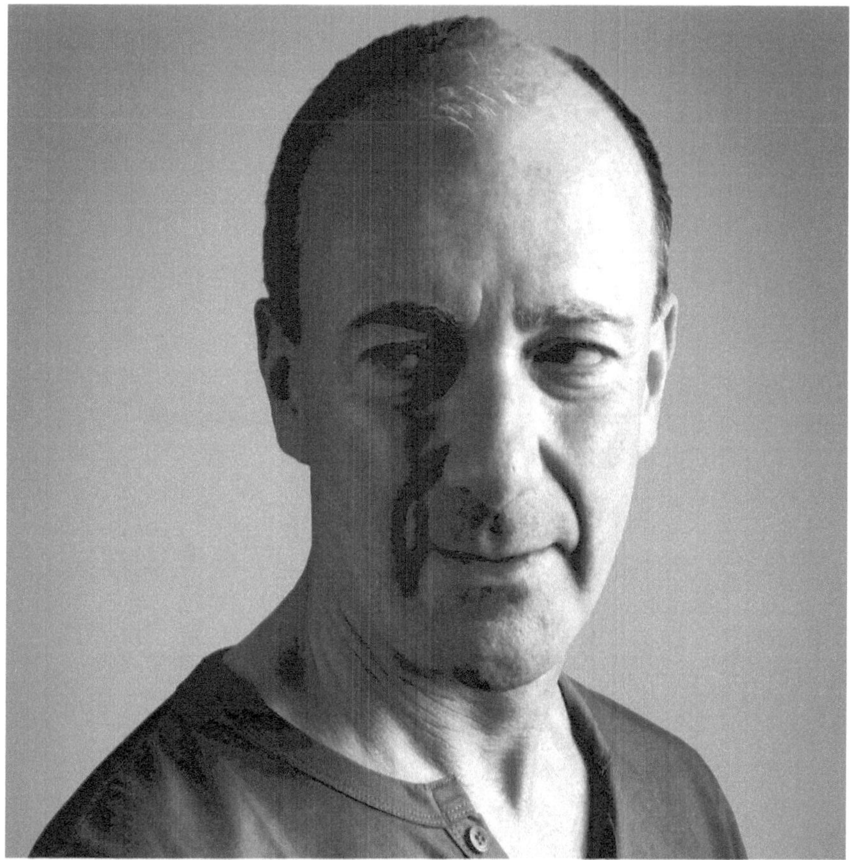

Tony Richards was born in 1956 in London, England and – though widely traveled – has lived in that city for most of his life. He sold his first short story just a few months after leaving college and has rarely looked back since. His novels have been published by Tor Books, Eos/HarperCollins, Simon & Schuster and Samhain Publishing in the States and by Pan Books, Headline and Lume in the UK and he has eight collections of short fiction to his name, many of them from Dark Regions Press. His first novel – 'The Harvest Bride' – was shortlisted for an HWA Bram Stoker Award and his book 'Going Back' was a finalist for the British Fantasy Award for Best Collection. He continues writing to this day, producing new short stories and the final novels in his supernatural Raine's Landing series.

About the Artist

Steeped in the enthralling fantasy and science-fiction illustrations of the 1960s, '70s, and '80s, artist and illustrator **K.L. Turner** brings a bit of old-school painterly style to today's methods. With more than 30 years of experience in the arts, he expertly brings an expressionistic style into his illustrations to create compelling works which captivate and draw the viewer in. His works are found in media and galleries around the world, and celebrated in pop culture. A versatile creative type, Turner is also accomplished in the mediums of photography, sculpture, and the fine arts. Choosing to live and work on the beautiful front range of the Colorado Rocky Mountains where he was born and raised, he continues to derive inspiration from nature as well as cultural influences both at home and in his travels.

www.ingramcontent.com/pod-product-compliance
Lightning Source LLC
Chambersburg PA
CBHW030320020726
47493CB00004B/1103

* 9 7 8 1 9 5 7 1 2 1 1 8 5 *